PRAISE FOR THE
UNDERCOVER DISH MYSTERIES

"A cast of fun, quirky characters. . . . Readers are sure to devour this yummy mystery."
—Sue Ann Jaffarian, national bestselling author of the Ghost of Granny Apples Mysteries and the Odelia Grey Mysteries

"Julia Buckley has not just written a fun, entertaining, and fabulous cozy, but she has introduced a truly stellar main character in Lilah."   —Open Book Society

"Buckley's latest Undercover Dish Mystery is a good entry into the series, serving up the same smart, fun, and quirky characters."   —RT Book Reviews

"Lilah is a fun, intelligent heroine that you will instantly connect with, and I enjoyed spending time with her."
—Moonlight Rendezvous

Berkley Prime Crime titles by Julia Buckley

Undercover Dish Mysteries

THE BIG CHILI
CHEDDAR OFF DEAD
PUDDING UP WITH MURDER

Writer's Apprentice Mysteries

A DARK AND STORMY MURDER
DEATH IN DARK BLUE

Pudding Up with Murder

JULIA BUCKLEY

BERKLEY PRIME CRIME
New York

BERKLEY PRIME CRIME
Published by Berkley
An imprint of Penguin Random House LLC
375 Hudson Street, New York, New York 10014

ISBN: 9780425275979

First Edition: September 2017

Printed in the United States of America
1 3 5 7 9 10 8 6 4 2

Cover art by One by Two Studio
Book design by Kristin del Rosario

This is a work of fiction. Names, characters, places, and incidents either are the product
of the author's imagination or are used fictitiously, and any resemblance to actual persons,
living or dead, business establishments, events, or locales is entirely coincidental.

The recipes contained in this book are to be followed exactly as written.
The publisher is not responsible for your specific health or allergy
needs that may require medical supervision. The publisher is not responsible
for any adverse reactions to the recipes contained in this book.

Acknowledgments

Big thanks to Kim Lionetti at Bookends, and to Bethany Blair and everyone at Berkley who worked on this book.

Thanks to those readers who are supporters of my work, notably Susie Bedell, who has read everything I've ever written, even the early stuff; Burt and Lisa Blanchard, best neighbors and friends; Karen Kenyon, my Canadian fan and friend who makes sure the books are facing OUT on store shelves; Karen Owen and Lisa Kelley, both so generous with their encouragement and promotion of my books; Lesa Holstine, who was generous with her praise of the series.

Thank you to the fellow writers who were kind enough to help in my promotional ventures: Lynn Cahoon, Terrie Farley Moran, Jeff Cohen, Miranda James, and Sue Ann Jaffarian.

Thanks to the Mystery Writers of America, especially the terrific Midwestern Chapter, to Sisters in Crime and Sisters in Crime Chicagoland, and to my own wonderful writing group, to whom I have dedicated this book.

Acknowledgments

Thanks to my family and friends, and to everyone who sent me a Facebook photo of him or herself reading one of my books.

Thanks to every single person who took the time to post an online review.

Thanks to bookstore workers and librarians everywhere.

"Spring has returned. The Earth is like a child that knows poems."

—RAINER MARIA RILKE

CHAPTER ONE

A WARM BREEZE WAFTED IN THROUGH MY CAR WINdow as I drove down Breville Road. My companion, Mick the dog, sniffed the layers of air, sorting them with his exceptional and complicated nose. "You like that smell, huh, buddy?" I asked him, reaching out with my right hand to ruffle the fur on his large brown head. "I think we've both had enough of winter."

The snow seemed mostly melted away on the streets and parkways, and on this bright and sunny Saturday, the twentieth of March, spring flowers were poking shyly out of flower beds, promising that a new season was upon us. Along with the earthy smell of spring was the delicious cinnamon-sugar aroma of my latest concoction, a rice pudding casserole of my own invention. I had become accustomed to not getting credit for some of my best dishes, dependent as I was on the regular money I earned from letting other people get the applause for my work. In fact, it was the credit they received for my dishes that made my cooking so valuable to these clients—and I had developed quite a list of them over the last couple years.

Mick and I, accustomed delivery companions, were heading to an event to which we were, for once, actually invited, although the dish we were bringing was officially going to be attributed to my friend Ellie Parker. As I squinted against the surprisingly bright sun, I reflected on the serendipitous events that had led me to Ellie—and to her son. Ellie lived in North Pine Haven in a sweet two-story home with a large and lush garden behind it. She and I had met once at a Tupperware party, and although she was old enough to be my mother, we had formed an instant bond and had continued to meet—for coffee, for book chats, for Saturday lunches. Somewhere along the line Ellie had decided that I would be perfect for her son Jay, a Pine Haven police detective, but instead of telling me that, she arranged for Jay and me to meet at her house one day. That had occurred what seemed like a year ago but had actually been in October. Jay and I did hit it off, but then we fought and separated. We had reconciled at Christmas, although we found that our schedules were surprisingly incompatible. Still, we'd had some lovely times together, my favorite of which had been a winter visit to the zoo, where we'd shared hot chocolate and learned that we both loved tapirs and outrageously expensive but weirdly delicious zoo hot dogs, and I'd had many opportunities to gaze into Parker's blue eyes at close proximity.

Then, just as things were at their most romantic, Parker was sent away to some sort of training event in New York, and he had been gone for a dismal two weeks. I had never been overly fond of texting, but I had probably sent Parker about a thousand texts in the time he had been gone. He wasn't as prolific, but he assured me that he liked mine, and would respond when he could. He texted complete sentences in his careful Parker way, so it was like getting a beautiful letter when I did hear from him.

Today I had not received anything, and my eyes flicked restlessly to my phone every few minutes, willing it to ping and tell me that Parker was thinking of me.

Mick rustled in his seat and sighed, seemingly with pure happiness. Mick loved spring because there was so much to dig out of the dirt and sniff at length. I looked at him out of the corner of my eye. We had been through a great deal together, Mick and I. "You're the best, Mick," I said.

Mick nodded. I had never trained Mick to do this as a puppy; he had taught himself this way of responding to what I said to him. His special ability to gesture this way made our relationship seem even closer—as though Mick truly understood the things I said and wanted to offer me his affirmation.

"You know, it's quite an honor for you, being invited to this party. It's because Ellie loves you so much, and I guess her neighbor is a huge dog lover. It's his birthday, and he wants to see you nod. Make sure you do it, now. Don't make liars of Ellie and me."

Mick seemed to be thinking about this. I tapped my hands on the steering wheel. I always had a song in my head; I hadn't decided if this were a blessing or a curse. In today's tune, Green Day asked me when September would end. I wondered why my brain didn't stay in season.

As we neared Ellie's house, I worried over logistics. I needed to get the casserole to her without anyone next door seeing the transfer. Her neighbor Marcus Cantwell was a retired businessman of some sort with a house twice the size of Ellie's and a rumored fortune. He had been married three times and had five children, all of whom, Ellie assured me, would be at this birthday party—his sixty-fifth. Ellie had also told me that Marcus had a gruff exterior and people misunderstood him, thinking him rude and unfriendly.

I interpreted this to mean that he *was* rude and unfriendly, but had been won over by Ellie's many charms. Ellie had spoken to Cantwell about Mick because Cantwell had four dogs of his own, and he had been "enchanted" by her stories of my dog and his ability to converse with people in his silent way.

This had earned Mick and me an invitation to the birthday party of a rich man we had never met. One of Cantwell's children had young children of her own, and Ellie had wanted to make something special that the little ones would enjoy. That's where I came in, with my new and wonderful rice pudding casserole. I'd made it with very kid-friendly ingredients, with raisins in only half of it in case some little tyke found them repulsive. My favorite child, a boy named Henry whom I had unofficially adopted as my own nephew, had taste tested the casserole and proclaimed it "pretty yummy," so I felt confident that Ellie would receive her due praise.

I pulled into Ellie's driveway, centered between two flower beds that were mostly raked earth; I saw a few tulips and crocuses, though, showing their yellow and orange noses to the world. I drove the car as close to her door as I could, then got out with Mick and retrieved the casserole, hidden inside a large, sturdy canvas tote. Mick and I ran to the door, where Ellie stood waiting.

She looked pretty, and I wondered if the thrice-divorced Cantwell had designs on the widowed Ellie. Her white hair was pulled back in an elegant twist, and her makeup, expertly applied, made her look ten years younger than she was. She wore a pair of gray slacks and a white blouse, over which she'd donned a light gray cardigan and some long silver necklaces. It looked terrific.

"Uh-oh," I said, hugging her. "I think I may have dressed down more than I should have." I had been in a hurry, so I'd grabbed a pair of khaki pants and a yellow T-shirt with appliqued roses at the neckline.

"You look beautiful—like a little buttercup," Ellie said, studying me. "Oh, what I would give for that long blond hair."

"Your hair is perfect."

A necessary and rewarding component of my friendship with Ellie was our willingness to validate each other—sometimes at great length.

Ellie smiled her thanks, eyeing my bag. "Is this my contribution to the party?"

"Yes. Rice pudding casserole, tested by Sir Henry of Weston."

"Your little friend Henry? Your friend's nephew?"

"Yes. He loved it."

"Good. There are three little ones, I'm told, and I want to be their favorite person."

"You will. Plus you're bringing Mick, and kids love him."

"Oh my, yes!" she said, stooping to pet Mick, who had been waiting for some attention. "You are a special boy, aren't you?" said Ellie affectionately. "Marcus can't wait to meet you." She turned to me. "He just loves dogs."

I narrowed my eyes. "Is that the *only* thing that Marcus loves?"

Ellie made a scoffing sound. "Don't be ridiculous. We've lived side by side for years, but we always keep our neighborly distance. Just some nice chats over the garden fence now and then."

"Huh." I slipped a hand into my pocket and ran it over my cell phone, willing it to make its familiar buzzing sound. "Have you heard from Jay?"

Ellie had been putting her nose against Mick's, but she lifted her head sharply. "No, why?" She studied me with a wise expression. "Is someone feeling twinges of love-sickness?"

"It's a little early for lovesickness," I said briskly, setting the bag down on her table. "But yes."

Ellie laughed. "Oh, I am so glad you two are finally together. I really had a vision of it ever since I met you. But I couldn't quite figure out how to best introduce you. Jay is so— Well, you know Jay."

I did know him—or at least I was getting to know him. He was wonderful: smart, handsome, hardworking, but perhaps a bit antisocial. He had made an exception for me, and now I was his girlfriend. This was still so new that sometimes Parker and I just sat and grinned at each other, glad, as Ellie was, that we had ended up together.

Ellie gave Mick one final pat and stood up. "Ugh—my knees," she said. "They're pretty creaky."

"You should sit in a chair and pet him. He'll be happy to come to you."

She shrugged and nodded. I pointed at the casserole. "There it is. Do you want to carry it in the pan or leave it in the bag?"

"The pan, I think. Looks very homemade. Oh, I do feel guilty taking credit for your work. But I also love the looks on people's faces when they eat it—and in the past, it was always my own food they were eating." Ellie's arthritis had grown painful enough to prevent her from creating anything too complicated in the kitchen.

"I know. And you pay for the right to see those looks on their faces. Enjoy it."

"Which reminds me," Ellie said. She walked across her kitchen to a cookie jar in the shape of a chubby monkey. My face grew hot looking at it, because the first time I had met Jay Parker was when I was taking money out of that jar and he had found me doing it. He had halfway suspected me of being a thief in his mother's kitchen. It was still embarrassing to contemplate the memory.

"Here you go," Ellie said, handing me a small stack of bills.

"This looks like too much," I said.

"It's not. Now tuck it away, and let's go to a party."

"I think I smell food from over there. And—is that music?"

"Oh yes. There's a live band in his backyard. I truly think his children are competing for his attention, because each one has tried to outdo the others with birthday gifts. The oldest boy paid for the band, I think, and the second-oldest boy had bagpipers here this morning. Can you imagine? Bagpipes playing 'Loch Lomond' at ten in the morning."

I giggled. "Sorry I missed that."

"And the girls came marching up the walk with huge packages and baskets and boxes. I'm not one to gossip, but I do wonder if they all want special treatment in the will. Marcus has always joked to me that he's richer than God but not as ostentatious."

"What does that mean?" I asked.

"He doesn't spend a lot. He has a big house, but not a mansion. He drives a nice car, but it's not a Mercedes. He told me he's always been a saver. Maybe his children are counting on that."

"If he's rich, then there's enough for all of them."

"You would think," said Ellie, leading me toward the back of her kitchen and the door into her yard. "We can go in through his garden," she said. "There's a little arbor tucked into his fence, and it's like a lovely, fragrant doorway to his yard."

"Okay, then."

I followed her, and the sound of music strummed on multiple guitars, to the Cantwell backyard. It was perhaps four times the size of Ellie's yard, and filled with activity. The musicians, three men with guitars and a woman with a mandolin, stood against a fence and played Beatles tunes. I had heard "I Will" from Ellie's kitchen, and now they were playing "Hey Jude." My father, a Beatles fan since way back, would have been in heaven listening to this group.

The yard was a chaos of milling bodies, running children, wandering dogs, barbecue smells, and white-smocked caterers. A photographer wandered here and there, snapping pictures of the crowd. I didn't recognize any of the servers, which meant my employer, Haven of Pine Haven, had not handled this event. A young woman with a red perm and a stiff white apron came by with a tray of punch glasses; Ellie and I each took one, thanking her, and she moved on into the crowd. I held Mick's leash with my free hand, and Ellie held the rice pudding with hers. Thus encumbered, we plowed ahead.

"Let's find Marcus before things get too crazy," Ellie said.

She led me into a spacious house dominated by dark polished wood. Here some more caterers moved surreptitiously in and out of rooms; I caught a glimpse of a large kitchen and a long, empty dining room before we entered a front room with a wall-mounted flat-screen TV that dominated the space like an electronic idol; everything else was centered around it.

The television was off, but a man in a large red armchair sat staring at it with a rather blank expression. He took occasional sips from a fancy-looking drink on a table beside him. There was no one else in the room.

"Marcus?" Ellie said. "Happy birthday!" She moved forward and touched his arm. "Thank you for inviting us to the party."

"Of course," he said in a gruff voice as though he hadn't spoken for a while. "And who is your friend?"

"This is Lilah! She brought Mick, the dog I told you about."

The man's face grew slightly animated. "How are you, boy?" he asked, talking to Mick.

Mick obligingly moved forward and thrust his skull between the man's knees. That earned a bark of laughter from Marcus Cantwell. He had a big lionlike head with a sheaf of white hair; I realized in a flash of insight that he reminded me of Andrew Jackson.

Still not acknowledging me, Cantwell scratched Mick's ears. "So you're a special dog, are you? You can understand what people say to you?"

To my relief, Mick nodded up at Cantwell, his doggy expression at its most earnest. Cantwell laughed again, and his face became human for the first time. "Excellent! What a wonderful dog. A Labrador. Terrific dog. I have a golden out there. A whole slew of dogs, big and small. Can't resist 'em. Never could," he said to Mick, massaging him with big hands. The pointer finger on his left hand was purple, as though he had hit it with a hammer. I wondered vaguely if he were a carpenter.

I tried to make eye contact with Ellie, but she was gazing fondly at Cantwell and the dog. Didn't she realize how weird this guy was?

Suddenly Ellie remembered the pan in her hands. "I

brought some rice pudding for the children, Marcus. I'm going to run it to the kitchen—I'll be back in a jiff. Lilah can tell you all about Mick."

To my great dismay, she darted out of the room. Despite the vast number of people in Cantwell's sunny yard, I was alone with the man in his echoing house, and he had yet to look me in the eye.

I scanned the room, desperate to make conversation. "What a lovely place you have here," I said. This got no response; perhaps he was deaf to clichés. "That piano in the corner looks like an antique—it's beautiful!"

"Hmm," Cantwell said. I was half tempted to tell him how rude he was, but I thought of Ellie and refrained.

"That's quite a bruise you have on your finger there," I said, gabbling out anything in my fear of silence. "My mother gets those sometimes—bursts a blood vessel. She looked it up once. It's called Achenbach's syndrome. I'll probably get it someday, too—it's hereditary." I was shocked at the ridiculous topic of conversation I had chosen, but I felt a dull obligation to keep talking.

Cantwell glanced at his finger, then shrugged. "Your dog is well trained," he said in a startling non sequitur. It wasn't even true; Mick was spoiled but innately nice.

"Thanks. He's a special boy."

"Yes," said Cantwell, staring broodingly into Mick's eyes. I wondered if he were on some sort of medication. His actions seemed weirdly delayed—even the movements of his hands in Mick's fur—and the hands shook slightly. His sleeves were rolled up to the elbows, and I noticed a jagged scar on his left arm.

"Oh my—that's quite a scar! Is it from surgery?"

"I've never had surgery," Cantwell said. "This is nothing."

A warning voice in my brain said, *Are you almost finished commenting on this man's body?*

The room was horribly silent, and I stood there like an intruder. *Talk about anything but his weird old fingers and the scary marks on his skin, Lilah.* "Uh. So you like dogs. What's, um, your favorite breed?"

Cantwell cleared his throat, then spoke to Mick's face. "Hmm. Hard to decide. I have a couple of purebreds out there and a couple of mutts. They're all special in their own way."

I peered into the hall, hoping to see Ellie or anyone else. A solitary dog came trotting toward me. It was a beautiful corgi—all golden fur and no legs to speak of. It moved right past me—did everyone in this house ignore visitors?—and ran to Cantwell, pausing to sniff Mick and be sniffed in return.

"This is Cleopatra," Cantwell said. "She's a spoiled miss."

"I understand you have quite a few children and grandchildren here today."

Cantwell could not have looked less interested. "A whole slew of them out there," he said. "Take your pick."

"Don't you want to go out and enjoy your party guests?" I asked. My tone was, perhaps, a bit judgmental.

"Soon enough," Cantwell said. He had turned to a side table and was rooting around in a drawer. He lifted out a digital camera. His eyes flicked to mine for the first time, and I raised my brows at him. "May I photograph your dog?" he asked.

It was a weird question; I felt suddenly as though I'd walked back in time and Cantwell was someone from the nineteenth century who had never been schooled in etiquette for a hundred years later.

"Yes, you may photograph him," I intoned solemnly, wishing that I could videotape Cantwell's weirdness to show to Jay. Then again, Jay had grown up in the house next door. Surely he would have encountered this strange man before. The thought was vaguely troubling, so I didn't realize at first that Cantwell was saying something to me in his mumbling voice. "I'm sorry—what?" I asked.

"I said Ellie is a good woman. I wish any one of my wives had been like her."

This was such a preposterous thing to say that I was utterly at a loss. He seemed to be expecting a response, so I answered with a non sequitur of my own. "Did anyone ever tell you that you resemble Andrew Jackson?"

Cantwell's dismayed expression brought me an unexpected feeling of satisfaction.

THE TRAITOR ELLIE eventually returned, and with a reproachful look in her direction I mumbled about needing to check something outside. I called Mick and escaped the dreary room where Cantwell stared at nothing.

We had almost made it out the back door (surely I could tell Ellie I wasn't feeling well and had to leave) when I ran into a young man—perhaps twenty or so—

who stood clutching a handful of brownies and peering into the hall.

"Hello," I said, since I couldn't pass him without acknowledging him.

"Hey," he said. "Do you want a brownie?" His face was so sweet and generous that I took one of the proffered sweets and thanked him. "No problem," he said. "I probably shouldn't eat all five of them, anyway. Isn't there some sort of disease you get from too much sugar?"

"Diabetes," I said. "But there are all sorts of healthy dishes that are sweet and can help wean you off sugar, if you have an addiction."

This amused him. "Yeah? So you can be, like, addicted to sweets?"

"Of course you can. Sugar has the same addictive effect as many drugs."

He shoved one of the brownies in his mouth and asked, with his mouth full, "Are you a doctor or something?"

"No, but I am in the food industry, and I know a lot about food preparation and the content of various ingredients."

"Okay, that's cool," he said. He was cute, with boyish good looks and messy brown hair that I thought might have been styled that way. I was betting he had no problem getting dates, although he did look a bit—high.

In a sudden panic, I asked, "Is there anything in these brownies? Drug-wise?"

His eyes widened, and he pointed at me. "You mean like weed? Hilarious!" He laughed for a while and then pantomimed smoking a joint, then laughed some more.

"No, they aren't drug brownies! My aunt Melanie made them. But what an awesome thought—Aunt Mel baking weed into her desserts." He glanced around, as though looking for someone to tell. Then he sighed with satisfaction and said, "Why did you think so? Do you think I look stoned?"

"Kind of," I said, taking a nibble of the brownie.

"I get that a lot. It's just the way my eyes are. Look at the stupid family pictures in that hallway and you'll see that I look like a stoned baby, too. It's hilarious."

"Are you Mr. Cantwell's son?"

He stuck out his brownie-free hand with automatic politeness. "Yeah, I should have said. I'm Cash. His son by his third wife, Barbara. That's my mom. She's out there with my stepdad, Burt. And who are you?"

"I'm Lilah Drake."

"Lilah. That's a cool name. So you've never met my family?"

"No. This is my first visit."

He sighed rather theatrically. "We're a complicated clan, but I can lead you through the introductions, if you want." He looked me up and down for a moment, as if just noticing that I was female. "Are you here with anyone?"

"Yes," I said.

His face fell slightly. "Well, I guess I can introduce both of you. But it would be more fun as just the two of us."

I grinned. Something about his demeanor made everything he said seem harmless and even amusing. "I bet it would. Why is your name Cash, exactly?"

"Because it's less obnoxious than Cassius, which is my real name. What sort of parents burden their kid with a name like that? A name from gosh darn *Julius Caesar*? So I was just Cash from, like, birth onward." He consumed one of the smaller brownies in one bite, his face thoughtful.

Ellie probably wouldn't have forgiven me if I left minutes after I had arrived; this guy seemed like an entertaining way to pass the time. "Where are these family pictures you spoke of?"

Cash Cantwell put a friendly arm around me and steered me back down the hall. Mick followed us, then settled on a little rug he found mid-hallway. A bit farther down we found a wall loaded down with silver-framed photographs. Cash sneered at it. "Pretty grim, isn't it? It makes you think of death, somehow."

I would have laughed except that the wall did have a dark aura, perhaps because so many of the faces were serious. Cash pointed out his four stepsiblings, his arm still slung around my shoulder, and narrated the birth order. First there was Emma, the eldest, who was married to Timothy. They had three children: Tim Junior, Carrie, and Peach. "Peach was an accident baby, but everyone loves her the best. She's, like, the only nice member of our family. You'll meet her. She's six."

I nodded, admiring Emma Cantwell's chestnut hair and regular features.

He pointed at another girl. "That's Prudence. Prue. She's an artist. She's super awesome and gets asked to paint these murals all over the U.S. She can be a super psycho, but she's still a pretty good sister. She never got married, but she's had about eight thousand boyfriends. The current one is the guy who looks like he's in a motorcycle gang—all black leather. He's pretty cool, though. His name is Demon or Damien or whatever."

"Got it. Emma, then Prue. And I doubt her boyfriend's name is Demon. Who's next?"

"Then Dad got divorced and remarried, this time with Claudia, and had Scott and Owen. Scott's the one with red hair. He's a lawyer and tends to threaten to sue people a lot. He's a major tool, but he can be all right sometimes. He hasn't been bad yet today."

"Okay."

He pointed. "And that's Scott's little brother, Owen. He looks like Scott, but without the freckles and with blond hair. Owen is between jobs, like always. But he has a degree in philosophy, which my dad says makes him suitable for no profession at all." Cash grinned at this and ate another brownie while I studied the pictures. All of the children were of above-average attractiveness, and yet Cantwell had struck me as a barely functioning human being with minimal good looks. His wives must have all been pretty and outgoing, because if Cash was anything like the others, the children had gotten all of their charm and beauty from their mothers.

"You look disbelieving. What seems so strange?" Cash asked with surprising perception.

"Oh—it's just—I only just met your dad, but—"

Cash smiled and pointed at me. He seemed to convey a lot of emotions through pointing. "You think he's totally weird." I tried to deny it, but he held up a hand. "He is; he's an old weirdo. But he wasn't always that way. There was a time when he actually left the house and went to work and interacted with people like a normal guy. But he got weirder as he got older. My mom tried to get him tested for depression or some other illness, but he was never diagnosed with anything. And now he barely leaves the house except to do his gardening or walk those stupid dogs."

"You don't like dogs?"

"They're okay. I mean, I actually like walking them and playing with them and stuff. But we all know that he loves the animals more than he loves us, so sometimes it's hard to take."

"That can't be true."

Cash pursed his lips. "He was late to Peach's christening because he took Cleopatra to get her toenails clipped. And he didn't even pretend he had a better reason. That's what he told Emma—that his dog's nails were too long."

"Wow," I said.

"Yeah. I have a weird family, no doubt about it, but what can you do? You learn to live with it. See this picture of me as a baby? Don't I look super high?"

He did. His little eyes were slit against his chubby cheeks in a look of supreme happiness. "Okay, I see your point," I admitted.

He pointed at me. "See? I've actually had teachers kick me out of class because they said I looked stoned. It's a lifelong curse, man." He was still smiling, though. Cash seemed emotionally indestructible.

"I'm surprised your lawyer stepbrother didn't threaten to sue those teachers," I joked.

Cash laughed. "He did talk about it once. You think you're kidding, but you haven't met Scott. He's one litigious dude."

"Okay, I think I have the whole family down pat. Thanks for clearing it up for me."

"Speaking of Cleopatra, I think she likes your dog." He pointed at Mick and started laughing. The little corgi had made her way into the hallway and nestled against Mick, as though he were a pillow put there for her pleasure. Mick accepted this with a docile expression.

"Your dad said she was spoiled; I guess he was right. Either that or she's just got a crush on Mick. All the lady dogs do," I joked, bending to pet the two canines. The corgi was very sweet; she closed her eyes under my ministrations and made a sound almost like purring.

"You're funny. Who are you here with, anyway?"

I pointed at Mick. "This is the guy your dad actually wanted to meet. I'm here with Ellie from next door."

"Ellie!" Cash clapped his hands, which were finally brownie-free. "She's one awesome lady. All us kids like her, and it's hard to please all of us. She was always giving us fruit from her trees, or veggies from her garden, or flowers to bring to our moms. And if we ever wanted to play over there, she was cool with it. She had three kids, too, and one of them used to babysit for me when I was little."

"Jay?" I asked, surprised.

"Yeah, that's him. He was awesome. He always brought over cool stuff, like comic books or action guys or whatever he didn't want anymore, and he'd give them to me to play with. He was already into books and girls and stuff by then. A high school kid. I really looked up to him. He was supersmart. I think he became a lawyer or something."

"He's a cop," I said. "I'm actually dating him."

Cash pointed at me in disbelief. "You're dating Jay Parker? Man, that is so cool! Is he here?"

"No, he's away at some training thing in New York."

"I'll bet he's a great boyfriend, huh?"

"Yes, he is." I studied him. "Aren't you going out with anyone?"

A slight shadow passed over his perpetually happy expression. "I like someone. She kind of threw me over, but she's out there because my mom invited her."

"And your mom is here because . . . ?"

He shrugged. "We all kind of keep it in the family. All the exes come back for the big events. I don't know if it's because of Dad's money or just because we're a weird group that sticks together even after we separate. It's nice, though. I always felt like I had tons of family, even though my teachers sometimes called it a broken home. You're not supposed to call it that, anyway."

"And who is the girl you like?"

"Her name's Lola. She's the dark-haired girl—did you see her? Her mom's Italian, which is where she got the black hair, and her dad is Irish. She's this amazingly beautiful blend of them." His face was vulnerable now. "We went to high school together. Now she goes to Columbia. She's studying music."

"Where do you go to school?"

"I'm at DePaul. But I'm thinking I won't stay. I mean, I'll finish out the year and all, but I want to ask my dad to bankroll me for a year so I can try something else. Maybe the Peace Corps or some kind of service trip or something. I'm a hands-on kind of guy."

"Then, when you came back, you could major in social work."

He brightened. "Yeah! That's what I was thinking. I like people, and I know how they tick. Right now I'm majoring in economics, and it's doing nothing for me. I can't see spending my life running some business or adding numbers in some ledger. I need to—you know—discover myself."

"That sounds smart, Cash."

"Yeah. I'm going to ask him today. I just have to get up the courage, you know? He had a spaz when Prue wanted to major in art, so I can just imagine what he would think of this."

"You have to follow your heart," I said. To myself I thought that if Cantwell was as rich as everyone hinted, it wouldn't be a big deal to let a kid spend a year overseas.

"Yeah," Cash said. He looked a bit sad, so I patted his shoulder.

"How about if you introduce me to Lola?"

He brightened. "Okay. That will give me a reason to talk to her."

"That was the idea."

"I like you," Cash said. "And your dog is pretty awesome, too. He's just been staring at us with this hilarious look on his face. Maybe he's the one who likes Cleopatra."

I looked at Mick, who wore his usual expression of perpetual devotion, and felt a pang of love. Cleopatra had almost fallen asleep against Mick's side, but as we moved down the hall, she perked up and followed Mick.

The four of us made our way into the backyard, where the delectable smell of barbecue wafted on the air. People stood in companionable clumps, talking loudly over the music and posing occasionally for the photographer.

Cash made a beeline for the dark-haired girl, who occasionally darted glances in our direction. If I knew jealousy, and I was pretty sure I did, I was seeing it on the face of the pretty Lola. Before we reached her, a loud voice yelled out, making us pause and look around. The man in black leather, Prue's boyfriend, was leaning aggressively into the face of another man. "Who is that?" I whispered to Cash.

"It's Owen, my stepbrother. He doesn't get along with Prue's boyfriend."

The yelling man seemed slightly inebriated, and Owen, red with embarrassment, was leaning away from him.

"You lied to Prue!" the leather-clad man said. "You led her on, and you lied to her! Your whole family is a bunch of liars!"

Owen said something low and drowned out by the music. The leather jacket man shoved him, and a woman stepped forward. "Cut it out, Damen, or I'm calling the police! I'm dialing them now."

"That's Emma," Cash said in a low voice. "Taking charge, as always."

The man called Damen didn't even look at Emma or acknowledge her warning. Another woman who looked like the picture of Prudence from the hallway came hurrying through the crowd, holding a plate filled with sumptuous-looking food. "Damen, stop!" she said, looking distressed.

It was too late; Damen's fist shot out and made contact with Owen's jaw. Owen recoiled, and then his fist lashed out in turn, plunging into Damen's stomach and winding him. "What the hell?" Owen yelled, his hand on his wounded face.

Suddenly a tall woman stood in between them. When Damen tried to punch again, she caught his wrist and twisted it in such a way that Damen looked almost ready to cry. "You finished?" she asked. She still held his arm in what must have been a strong grip, because he was looking like he really wanted her to let go. I decided she was my new hero when Damen pulled back his hand and, with a wounded expression, slunk away into the crowd.

CHAPTER TWO

E MMA REAPPEARED. "I JUST CALLED THE POLICE," SHE said importantly.

"I am the police," said the woman. That was when I realized that I knew her. It was Jay Parker's partner, Maria Grimaldi. I had always resented her because I feared she might end up in a romance with Parker, but now he was officially mine, and Grimaldi had just done a kick-ass job breaking up a fight between two testosterone-fueled men. I drifted toward her, guided by a budding hero worship.

"Oh," said Emma. "Should I call and cancel, or—"

Grimaldi held up a hand. "I told them I'd take the call. I heard it as I was pulling up. I'm here to get my niece," she said, pointing at Lola, the girl that Cash liked.

Emma nodded. "Okay, well—thanks. I guess Owen will let you know if he wants to press charges. Right, Owen?" She looked expectantly at her stepbrother, who was nursing his jaw with one hand.

"Nah, it's okay. We had a misunderstanding. We punched it out. Everything's fine now."

Emma snorted. "Men," she said. Then her expression changed as a tiny little girl made her way across the lawn and up to her. The little girl had wheat-colored hair and a smattering of freckles; she wore a pale green dress with a glittery flower on the bib, and on her head she wore a rhinestone tiara. It looked good and made me want a crown of my own. The little one wore a concerned expression; she said something, and Emma bent down to hear her better, then laughed. "No, sweetie, Uncle Owen is not going to die. Neither is Auntie Prue's boyfriend. It wasn't very nice of them to hit each other, was it?"

The little girl shook her head, clearly near tears, so Emma swept her up and said something into her ear, then carried her away to a food table. Cash murmured something to me and went to join his sister and make faces to amuse his niece. Maria Grimaldi had watched it all, too, but hadn't yet seen me.

"Hello, Maria," I said.

She turned; I don't know what I expected, but it wasn't the nearly joyful expression I saw on Grimaldi's face. "Lilah! What in the world are you doing here?" She gave me a spontaneous hug, which had me tongue-tied for a couple of seconds.

"Uh—I came with Marcus's neighbor Ellie. Jay's mom. She lives next door. She and I are friends."

"Oh, I remember Mrs. Parker. She was with you when that whole chili thing went down in the fall."

"Yes. Not our best memory."

"No. But it sure made you both well-known at the Pine Haven PD." She grinned at me.

"So you're related to the young lady over there?" I pointed at the dark-haired Lola, who continued to watch Cash Cantwell when she knew he wasn't looking.

"Yeah. She's my niece—can you believe it? Makes me seem old, although at least I can say she's my older sister's daughter. Sophia was only eighteen when she had Lo there. But she married her boyfriend, and they're still together. Goes to show you some young loves make it through."

"How nice," I said. Cash had caught Lola watching him, so she made a show of walking in the other direction. Cash's face fell. Gosh, guys were dumb. "She sure seems to like Cash Cantwell."

"Oh, those two. They've been on-again, off-again for two years. I will say he's a nice kid." She looked like she would say more, perhaps about the rather strange Cantwell clan, but clearly this wasn't the place. "We should meet for coffee sometime," she said, surprising me again.

"That sounds fun. Maybe you can teach me how to do whatever you did to that motorcycle gang guy."

Grimaldi laughed. "No problem. Plenty of tricks of the trade I can pass on—although I'm sure Jay has already taught you some basic self-defense moves."

"He hasn't, actually. By the time we got our dating life on track, he was off to that stupid conference."

"Aww. Someone is missing her Jay Parker." Grimaldi grinned again.

"Do you tease him like this, too?"

"Way worse. He doesn't care, though, because he's so happy. You make him happy, Lilah."

I felt a blush make its way up my neck and into my face—half pleasure and half mortification. "Good," I said, and then felt ashamed of my own lame remark.

"That little Peach is just precious. Normally I would think that name was ridiculous, but she looks just like that—a little peach." Grimaldi was just full of surprises today—breaking up guy fights, acting friendly, loving children. This was a woman I had never seen because I was too busy being jealous.

I stared at the little Peach in question; she was now laughing at the antics of her uncle Cash, and Lola had found a reason to draw closer, as well. Ellie appeared and spoke to Peach; some other children were following Ellie around as if she were the Pied Piper of Pine Haven. "And we'll have some lovely rice pudding," Ellie was saying.

"Oh!" I said. "I should go see this. Uh—Ellie was telling me how good her casserole was, and I just want to see—"

"Hey, Lilah," Grimaldi murmured near my ear. "Don't be mad, but Jay told me your secret. The whole undercover-cooking thing."

I looked at her, openmouthed, and she held up a hand. "It was when you two were fighting or broken up or whatever. He needed my opinion. He wanted to know if he had the right to be angry."

"And what did you say?"

She slung a friendly arm around my shoulder. "I told him it was a moot point because he was clearly hung up on you either way."

My face grew red again. People made fun of my propensity for blushing; I wished I could be cool and calm like the tall and elegant Grimaldi. "Well, anyway, I want to see what the kids think of the rice pudding."

Maria and I made our way inside the house, following the children and some adults to the kitchen, where Ellie had set up the rice pudding pan and some child-size dishes. "Who would like the first taste?" Ellie said. "My mother used to feed this to me when I was a child, and I always added extra cinnamon and sugar—although as you can see I baked that in for you! Oh my—it looks like some little fingers have already been in here!" Ellie said good-naturedly as she spooned the pudding into dishes and handed them to waiting children. Little Peach took hers with eager hands; I watched her taste the pudding and was pleased to see her eyes widen. Within seconds she had gone in for another bite. Score one for Lilah.

Ellie was flushed with pleasure as she fed the children, who ranged in age from about four to about twenty, because Cash Cantwell stood in line with the rest of them and accepted a bowl, grinning at me. I wondered how much sugar was coursing through his veins. Once people took their bowls of pudding, they wandered back outside;

the kitchen was stylish and looked as though it had been recently redesigned, but it was too small to accommodate lingering. When the serving dish was almost empty and the kitchen nearly deserted, Ellie gave me a subtle thumbs-up. "It was so good, someone couldn't wait to have it served!" she said.

"That was me, I'm afraid," said Marcus Cantwell, looming in the doorway of the kitchen. Apparently he had left his monastic silence to join his own party. "My mother made it for me when I was a boy, and I loved it. This is delicious, too, Ellie. You've got the touch!"

Ellie winked at me, but I barely noticed, because I saw that Cantwell's hands were shaking again, and he seemed to be walking in a rather disjointed way as he came toward us.

"Mr. Cantwell, are you all right?" I asked. I looked to Grimaldi, who had also noticed Cantwell's weird gait.

Grimaldi started to say something about how Cantwell should sit down when he pitched forward headlong and collapsed on the counter, facedown in the last of the rice pudding. Grimaldi was immediately in motion, darting forward to feel his pulse and lift his head off of the table. "He's unconscious," she said. She pointed to Cash. "Help me get him on the floor. See if he's breathing." She had her phone out already and was dialing for help. She looked at me. "Shut that kitchen door and don't let anyone in."

I did, locking in the four of us—Cash Cantwell, Ellie, Grimaldi, and me—along with the ailing Marcus Cantwell. "This cannot be happening again," I murmured.

Grimaldi flashed me a sympathetic glance, slipped her

phone in her pocket, and moved over to the Cantwells, father and son. Cash was moving furiously, pumping his hands on his father's chest. "That's good," Grimaldi said. "You keep the compressions going—you clearly know how to do it right."

We heard sirens moments later; soon there were ambulance attendants at the door; behind them stood a whole crowd of people. I could see the faces of Emma and Owen, and Prudence behind them, and for the first time I picked out Scott in the crowd. All Cantwell's children, to their credit, looked white with fear and concern. "Dad?" Emma was saying. "Is something wrong with Dad?"

Grimaldi went to the door. "Stay there for the time being," she said. "We need room in here. Please stay in the yard and let the EMTs do their job."

This did not please the children of Marcus Cantwell. Freckled Scott and chestnut-haired Emma barged to the top of the stairs, pushing their way through. Dark-haired Prue and blond Owen moved in behind them, peering over their shoulders. "Oh God—it's Dad," Scott said. "What happened?"

The EMTs were working on Cantwell now, even as they transferred him to a stretcher. "I'm not getting a pulse," one of them said. Prue moaned; her face was now even paler beneath her dark hair.

"I've got it! Pulse is thready, but it's there," said one of the white-clad men. They hustled Cantwell out to the ambulance; we moved to the window to watch. Cantwell's children followed in his wake, along with a small crowd. Tiny Peach appeared, and Emma picked her up. Another little girl sidled up to Emma and received a comforting pat on the head. Before the ambulance doors shut I could see that one of the EMTs had started chest compressions again. Cantwell's skin looked whiter than skin should look.

I turned around and saw that Ellie, Maria Grimaldi, and I were the only ones who remained in the kitchen. Ellie still held her serving spoon, to which clung sad remnants of the rice pudding casserole.

My hands were shaking. "This is way too familiar. He said he ate my food. Then he collapsed. This cannot be happening again."

Maria put a hand on my shoulder. "He could have been having a heart attack. It could have been a lot of things. Hopefully he'll get better."

Her last words hung on the air and then fell flat. We had seen Cantwell. None of us thought he was going to get better.

Ellie said, "He seemed ill long before he stole the casserole. Remember, Lilah? In the living room, when he petted Mick. His hands were shaking, and it seemed as though he was having trouble thinking clearly."

"That's true!" I agreed, remembering. "He had been sipping that drink on his side table, and—"

Maria looked interested. People like her and Parker just couldn't help it—they were always on duty, always looking for a potential crime to solve. "His drink? Has anyone else been in that room?"

Ellie shook her head. "No, I don't think so. He was sitting in there to relax, get away from the party for a moment. I didn't realize he wasn't feeling well, but that must be why—!" She looked a bit shaky herself now. She set down the spoon and wiped her hands on a napkin.

Maria nodded briskly. "Ellie. Find a plastic bag and some kind of Tupperware container. We're going to save that drink and this casserole—just in case."

My hands shook as I tapped Maria's shoulder. "If there's something wrong with the casserole—all those little kids just ate it. That little Peach—I watched her eat some."

Maria thought about it, then shook her head. "There's nothing wrong with the casserole, Lilah. Let's be logical: who had access to it besides you?"

"I gave it to Ellie. It was in a bag."

She turned to Ellie. "And was it ever out of your sight?"

She shook her head. "For maybe a minute, while I went out to tell people to come inside. And earlier I went to say hello to Marcus—Lilah was there, too—but then I returned and there was no one in here."

"Cash was in the house," I said, remembering. "He was holding a bunch of brownies, but I don't know if he got those from here in the kitchen or from the table outside."

Grimaldi nodded. "I'm saving the samples, just in case. But there's no need to panic right now. We don't know anything. Ellie, find me that plastic container." Ellie searched Cantwell's cabinets, which had clearly been maintained by one of his children, or perhaps a maid, because they were neat and surprisingly well stocked. She located a snap-top container and handed it to Maria, who left the room. When she returned with the last of Cantwell's drink in her container, she turned to me. "Could you ask his children to come back in here?"

I nodded and went outside. I scanned the crowd until I found Cash, who was talking with the photographer in low tones. I jogged over to them. "Cash, Maria Grimaldi is in your kitchen. She wants to see you and all your siblings—officially."

"What?" he said.

"Lola's aunt is a cop. She's in the kitchen, and she wants to see all of your dad's kids."

The photographer backed away slightly, sensing a private conversation. Cash pulled him back. "This is my friend Wade. He's taking pictures today, although I guess we won't want any now."

Wade nodded. "I'll probably take off, then. Unless you want me to hang around?" There was a naked curiosity in his face. Soon everyone at the party would probably wear that same expression. I wondered when I could leave.

"No, it's cool. Just send us those pics, you know. There were some really nice ones on there."

"You bet." Wade grabbed the camera bag that was slung over his shoulder and started putting his equipment away.

"Do you have a card?" I asked. "A business card, I mean."

"Sure." He pulled one out of his shirt pocket and handed it to me. He was a youngish man with a thatch of brown hair and intense dark eyes. "Are you having a party?"

"Hmm? Oh, no—it's—for something else. Thanks." I tucked his card in my purse.

Wade gave the rest of the pile to Cash. "To pass around—you know."

"Okay—thanks, man. I've got to go round up my siblings, but I'll see you later." They exchanged an odd, secretive look, and then Wade waved and walked away.

Cash held up a finger to me, a pointer meaning "Just a minute," and jogged into the crowd. I went back inside, where Maria and Ellie stood together talking in low voices. Her "samples" were nowhere to be seen.

Cantwell's adult children came barging into the kitchen, looking put out. Cash came in last, his face watchful. Maria stood before them, her face impassive.

Emma took a belligerent stance, and her pretty features twisted unattractively. "I'm sorry. Did you just summon us to the kitchen in our own father's house? And who are you, by the way?"

Maria took out her badge. "I'm Detective Maria Grimaldi of the Pine Haven Police Department."

Owen moved forward, still fingering his sore jaw. "No one wants to press charges about the fight, okay? Just let it go." He turned toward Cash. "Can you deal with sending all these people home, bud? We need to get to the hospital." He gestured to the four older children.

Cash looked irritated. "If Dad's going to die, I want to be there, too. I'm just as much his kid as you are, Owen."

Scott edged in, texting on an expensive-looking phone with a self-important expression. "Of course you're his kid, Cash—we all are. We can go together, right now. Maybe your mom can watch over things here?"

Cash nodded grudgingly. "Yeah. I'm sure she will. She and Burt can handle the crowd and clean up a little."

"I can help with that," said Ellie.

Maria Grimaldi held up a hand. "One thing before you go. There is a chance that your father may have ingested something that made him sick. I'm sure you won't mind that I took samples of the last two things he consumed, just to rule that out."

Scott's head came up; I could swear I saw his lawyer antennae rising out of his scalp. "You did what?"

Prudence talked for the first time. She was small and dark haired, pretty in a different way from the tall Emma. "You think someone poisoned our dad?"

Maria shrugged. "There was some suggestion that he looked ill while he was nursing his drink in his study back there."

"What drink?" Emma said. "Dad shouldn't be drinking. His doctor has forbidden it."

Maria turned to me. "You saw him consume it, did you not?"

All the Cantwell children looked at me, their faces surprised, as if I had just appeared in the room through magic. "Uh—it looked like a mojito or something. It had a leaf in it. I figured it was a party drink."

"A mojito? Dad doesn't drink things like that. He drinks tea and club soda and stuff," Cash said.

"Maybe it was club soda," I said.

Prudence was still looking at Maria. "Why do you think my dad is sick from this?"

"Miss Drake and Mrs. Parker saw his hands shaking. He was slurring his speech and acting strangely. Then he came into the kitchen and collapsed into the rice pudding casserole that—uh—Mrs. Parker made, but not before he said he had eaten some."

The Cantwell children, like kittens following a laser pointer, turned their heads in unison to Ellie, who held up her hands. "I certainly didn't poison my food. But there were a couple times it was unattended. The children all ate some. . . ."

Emma gasped. "Oh my God!"

Scott Cantwell's eyebrows rose and his pupils dilated. I got the impression he was shocked partly as a protective uncle, but also partly as a lawyer who smelled a class action lawsuit. In that moment I realized I didn't like him.

Prudence rolled her eyes and put her hands on her hips. "Emma, no one had time to poison Ellie's food, and we have no idea if Dad's drink made him sick, either. Right?" she asked Maria.

"That's very true," said Grimaldi. "But I'd like to have the drink and the food analyzed, just in case."

The outburst that followed was a mixture of outrage and grief and general confusion, but Prudence, who seemed the wisest of them all, held up a hand. "Listen! We need to get to the hospital and see how Dad is. I have no problem with the cops analyzing the food. If there's nothing in it, then who cares? And if there is, we need to know, right?"

She met the eyes of her siblings, one by one, and they grudgingly nodded in return. "Fine," Prue said to Grimaldi. "Go nuts. You know where we'll be." They moved out of the house en masse. I studied their faces. Emma was looking into the backyard, probably trying to check on her children; Owen looked distracted, perhaps in shock; Scott was texting again. God knew who he needed to contact at this moment. Prudence was also looking in the backyard, her expression worried. I followed her gaze and saw her black-leather-clad boyfriend, eating a hot dog on the outskirts of the group, his expression serene, as though he hadn't just punched his girlfriend's stepbrother in the face. *She wonders if he did it*, my brain said to me. I told my brain to be quiet.

Cash followed them to the door, and I touched his arm. "I hope everything is all right, Cash."

He turned, his expression polite. "It was nice meeting you," he said. He followed his siblings outside; moments later I heard a car pulling out of the driveway.

A red-haired woman and her gray-haired companion—perhaps Cash's mother and her new husband, Burt—were moving up to people in the backyard, their faces concerned, speaking in the low tones of someone at a funeral. People were clearly being asked to leave. Some party.

Maria whisked past me. "Ellie, if I can have that bag?"

Ellie handed her the bag in which I'd stowed the casserole; now it held Detective Grimaldi's evidence. "Here you go."

"Thanks. I need to talk to some people before they go. Nice seeing you, Lilah," she said, and then she, too, went out the door.

I turned to Ellie. "Not to make this about me, but how is it that people die wherever I go?"

"Not wherever you go. Just a few places," Ellie said. "And he might not have died. Don't be morbid."

"This was supposed to be a fun little party. Just some socializing, some enjoying of the party atmosphere, some showing off of Mick— Oh my gosh, where's Mick?"

I had lost track of my dog in the craziness, and now I ran to the window, craning for a glimpse of his chocolate brown fur. I spied him sitting by a bench in front of a rose arbor; three children sat in front of him, feeding him a hot dog.

"Oh no. Kids are feeding him. I need to get out there," I said.

Ellie put a hand on my arm. "Lilah. Take a deep breath. Everything is going to be all right." She had a calming influence, quiet and maternal, but I noticed that her eyes were spiked by tiny tears.

"I'm sorry about your friend. I hope he's okay," I said.

I jogged out the door, intent only on saving Mick from being force-fed all the food at the party.

CHAPTER THREE

B Y THE TIME I REACHED MICK, HE WAS BEING OF-
fered a red Popsicle by a tiny miscreant named Peach.
I sat down on the edge of the bench, next to the little girl.
Her siblings squatted in front of us, petting Mick.

"You know what?" I said, pushing her little arm gently
away from Mick's willing snout. "I think this guy has
had a bit too much today. You know, if you feed a dog
too much human food, he can get sick."

Little Peach studied me. She truly was adorable, with
wheat blond curls and round brown eyes that seemed to
fill half of her face. "Is this human food?" she asked in a
cartoony voice, holding the Popsicle.

"Yes. It's also a little cold for him. Doggies shouldn't
eat ice."

She studied her Popsicle, then me. "Are you his mom?" she asked.

"Kind of. He's my dog, and his name is Mick."

"Mick," Peach giggled. Her tiara had tumbled off her head and sat tangled in her curls.

"Let me help you, here. Your tiara went sideways."

Peach pouted her lips. "It's not a piara. It's a crown."

Her older sister stood up, looking bossy. She was the spitting image of Emma, but super short. Her chestnut hair was gathered into a neat ponytail that suggested control in the way that Peach's riot of curls suggested a relaxed attitude. "A tiara and a crown are the same thing, Peach." Then she looked at me. "Whose girlfriend are you? Are you here with Uncle Owen?"

Now Timothy Junior rose from his squatting position; he had been patting Mick and also playing some sort of video game on his phone. He looked to be about eleven, while I guessed the older sister was about nine. "That's rude, Carrie. Stop being so *blatant*."

Carrie sent him a withering look. Wow—she was going to destroy guys in the future. "Stop showing off your words from the dictionary, Timmy. We get it—you're smart." Her face creased into a sarcastic expression that I was guessing had been mimicked exactly from one of her parents—and I had a feeling I knew which one.

I held up a hand. "I think you all seem really smart. Where do you go to school?"

Tim shrugged, going for casual. "John F. Kennedy."

"Oh! I have a friend who teaches at John F. Kennedy! Do you know Miss Braidwell?"

Carrie's look turned worshipful in an instant, and she moved closer to me. "Miss Braidwell is my teacher," she breathed. Her skinny little knees were actually pressing against mine. "She's, like, the best teacher in the school," she said, tossing her ponytail in a wave of rippling red.

Tim looked torn between agreeing and wanting to be different from his sister. Hero worship won out. "She is a pretty cool teacher. I had her, too, when I was in third grade."

"Well, she happens to be my best friend," I said.

They looked at me admiringly, all pretense gone as they studied me with open mouths and curious expressions. Peach, who had been eating the Popsicle, shrugged her little shoulders. "What makes her so special?"

Carrie spared her a pitying glance. "You won't understand until you have her class, Peach. Which won't be for years."

Peach tried on her own scornful expression. It was pretty good, except that her face made it cute instead of mocking. In a few years, though, she'd be as good as Carrie. "No teacher is as good as Miss Moxie."

"Miss Moxie?" I said, half laughing. "That is a really interesting name, Peach!"

"It's not *her* teacher," said Carrie with a sniff. "It's this cartoon character in a book that she likes. It's a fox who teaches school but also solves mysteries. The first one is called *Miss Moxie Is Foxy*, and she solves the riddle of who was stealing things from the school cafeteria."

"She's a really smart teacher," Peach said, her face zealous.

"I think she sounds awesome," I said. "Can I find a Miss Moxie book at the store?"

Peach held out her little hands in a grand gesture. She was eloquent with body language. "Oh yes, you can get them at *all* the stores."

"Also at the library, which is where we get books. My mother always says, 'How did you get this room full of books when we go to the library?'" Carrie said, mocking Emma's commanding voice. "But you know, we *do* have aunts and uncles, and they always like to give us books as gifts."

"We have *lots* of aunts and uncles," Timothy agreed.

"It must be nice to have such a big family," I said. "How lucky for you. It must make every holiday fun."

"It's pretty fun," Timothy said, looking world-weary. "But there's a lot of fighting. As you probably saw today."

"Sometimes adults act like children," I said.

Timothy's face was vulnerable as he squatted down next to Mick again and played with his silky ears. "Yeah, because if I punched Carrie I would get in so much trouble! But that guy didn't get in trouble, did he?"

"No. That's certainly not fair. Do you know what they were fighting about?"

"I do," Peach said. She had finished the Popsicle and now had red-ringed lips and bright red fingers. With a sigh, Carrie produced a napkin from her pocket and began cleaning her sister. "The cowboy said that Uncle Owen was a liar and that Uncle Scott was a feister."

"By cowboy she means the guy in the leather," Tim said. His face said, *I am an adult, amused by the silly antics of a child.*

"Huh. And what is a feister?" I asked.

Tim shrugged. "He said *shyster*, but I don't know what that means."

Scott did seem like sort of a shyster, but Prue's boyfriend seemed like the last person who could complain about other people's ethics. And what, I wondered, did he think Owen had lied about?"

Carrie edged closer to me. "Does Miss Braidwell like butterscotch?"

I laughed out loud, realizing too late that it was a serious question. "Oh—uh. Sorry. I just remembered a joke your uncle Cash told me. What were you asking?"

She played with her pretty ponytail. "I wanted to make Miss Braidwell some butterscotch brownies. They're my specialty."

"Oh—do you like baking? I loved cooking and baking when I was your age."

"How old are you now?" Carrie asked.

"I'm twenty-seven."

All three children looked somber, as though I'd said I was a thousand.

I sighed. "Yes, I happen to know Miss Braidwell loves butterscotch, and she will love you for making her brownies. But I know she loves you anyway, because she told me she loves her class very much."

"She did?" Carrie breathed.

"Miss Moxie takes her class on all kinds of aventures," Peach said, bouncing in place.

"*Ad*ventures," Tim corrected, looking into Mick's eyes.

Carried bristled. "Miss Braidwell took us to the zoo

45

and to the museum all the way downtown. And we might go to the aquarium, too. We went on a superlong bus ride to see Christmas trees from around the world," she said.

"I went on that field trip when I was a kid, too. At the Museum of Science and Industry, right?"

"Yeah." Now Carrie wore the adult face. "We just go to all kinds of places like that."

I had been watching them for any signs of illness, but they all seemed fine, with good color and energy. "Did you all like that rice pudding that Mrs. Parker made?"

Peach hugged my arm, seemingly enraptured. Were all children this dramatic? "That was so good," she said. "I would like another bowl, please."

"I'm afraid it's gone," I said. "But I'm sure Mrs. Parker will make more someday soon. Then she can give it to you next time you're here."

Carrie pointed accusingly at her tiny sister. "You're not supposed to ask for seconds of sweets, Peach. Mom says."

Peach pouted, and I realized that pouting really did work sometimes. I was ready to give her whatever she wanted. "Mom said I could have some. She said so because I'm the best girl and princess."

"You're a liar, too," said Carrie with a quelling look.

Peach looked to be on the verge of tears, so I said, "Do you want to know something really funny Mick did?"

All three children switched their attention to me. "What?" asked Tim, lifting Mick's ears into alert position.

I racked my brains for a moment. "Oh, I have one. The other day he was yawning really big, and a burp came out."

The children burst into laughter. Peach actually had to hold her tiny abdomen.

When they started to calm down, I said, "But that wasn't the funny part. The funny part was that the burp scared him."

This sent them off into gales of laughter again, and they all knelt down to hug Mick, who panted and took it as his due. He noted some Popsicle drippings on Peach's arm and began to gently lick them off.

A man appeared beside us; he was of medium height, with a handsome face, sandy hair, and a slightly receding hairline. "What in the world is going on here?" he said, looking ready to be amused.

The children were still giggling, so I said, "I was just telling them funny dog stories. I'm Lilah Drake." I held out my hand, and he shook it.

"Timothy Britton. I'm in charge of this group," he said, feigning sadness. Peach ran to him and hugged his leg, and he laughed. "Just kidding, muffin," he said, swinging her up into his arms. "Is the dog funny, sweet Peachie?"

"He is funny. And this lady knows Miss Braidwell and the lady who made the rice pudding, and she is the dog's mom."

Timothy nodded gravely. "A woman of many distinctions."

"Which I should add to my résumé," I joked. "You have very nice children. They have actually been entertaining *me*."

"They get their theatricality from their mother," he said with a wink. He was charming, I realized with a jolt,

and sort of sexy. I could see how he would be a nice counterpoint to Emma's stern beauty.

Peach rested her head on his shoulder; he took off the tiara before it poked him in the eye. "I'm going to put this in my pocket, Princess. It looks like someone needs a nap."

"Not me," said Peach, but she lay listless on her father's shoulder, as though the scent of him had triggered the memory of sleep.

Timothy turned toward the other children. "Come on, you two. Say good-bye to the dog; we're going to head home."

"Can we watch a movie tonight before bed?" his son asked.

Timothy Britton stuck out the hand that wasn't holding Peach in place. "Shake on it: if you and Carrie can get ready for bed in record time, then we'll have a movie."

Tim Junior shook his hand, and he and his sister exchanged a pleased glance.

"Go say your good-byes, and I'll meet you at the car," he told them.

First, to my great surprise and pleasure, they came to shake my hand. "Thanks for letting us play with Mick," Tim said politely.

"And I'll tell Miss Braidwell I saw you," Carrie said. "Don't tell her about the brownies."

"I won't. That will be a lovely surprise. Nice to meet you, Tim and Carrie."

They ran off into the dwindling crowd. Peach had already fallen asleep on her father's shoulder. "Long day," I said, pointing and smiling.

He nodded. "She doesn't always take naps these days, but a party still wears her out."

"Any word on your father-in-law?" I asked.

He shook his head ruefully. "No. Em hasn't texted me yet, but she said she would when she knows anything. Do you have any idea what happened?"

"Just that he collapsed. Right onto the food table. If it helps to comfort your wife, you might want to mention that before he fell unconscious he was actually quite happy. He said that he'd tasted the rice pudding, and it was something he had loved eating as a boy. He was smiling."

Timothy Britton studied my face and looked thoughtful. "That's very nice, thanks. It makes me think that you don't expect him to make it."

"It's not for me to surmise."

"But he didn't look good?"

"No."

He shook his head, as if to clear it of negative thoughts. "To whom are you related in this bizarre assemblage?" He had quite a way with words, which explained his eloquent children.

"I am a friend of Ellie, the next-door neighbor. She and Marcus are friends, and he had asked her to bring me because of my dog. He wanted to meet Mick."

His laugh held a tinge of bitterness. "That's Marcus for you. Inviting a dog to his party. If he had his way, it would be just dogs. He's never been big on human interaction." Perhaps he heard how ungracious that sounded, because he said, "Although I guess there were times that he managed to be a good dad."

"You certainly are one," I said.

He looked surprised, and so gratified that I felt embarrassed. "Thank you," he said. "Lilah, is it?"

"Yes."

"And where's your husband this afternoon?" He said it absently, apparently not realizing what a rude and presumptuous question it was.

A wave of longing for the absent Jay Parker went through me. "He's in New York for a training thing," I said. "He's a cop."

"Ah," he said. His phone buzzed in his pocket, and we exchanged a fearful glance. "I don't really want to look," he said. He took it out with his free hand and scrolled with his thumb. He read a message for a minute, and his mouth became a thin, grim line.

He looked up at me. "Is she still sleeping?" he asked.

"Sound asleep."

He looked around, probably to make sure his other children were out of earshot. "Marcus is dead," he said.

"Oh, I'm so sorry."

"He never regained consciousness."

"So terrible." My eyes darted to Timothy and Carrie. They still looked fine; they were politely hugging and kissing people good-bye.

Peach looked like a sleeping angel, her face pink with happiness and the exertions of the day. None of the children at the party looked sick in any way. The rice pudding, then, had not been the problem.

And yet Marcus Cantwell was dead, and like Maria

Grimaldi, I thought that his behavior had indicated that something was not quite right in House Cantwell.

It was none of my business; I gave some quiet condolences to Tim Britton, touched Peach's soft little hand, and took my dog to the entrance to Ellie's yard. She appeared beside me. "Ellie, I would like to go. Can I talk to you in your yard?"

She put her arm around me. "I'm leaving, too. I've helped clean up, and Barbara seems to have everything in hand."

"Barbara?"

"Cash's mother. The third wife."

"Ah." Ellie, too, looked tired out, and her mascara was slightly smudged. "Let's go in your house. Do you want me to make you some tea?"

"No, no, I'm fine. But yes, let's go in." We climbed Ellie's back stairs and sat down at her kitchen table.

"Ellie, I have some news. And I want you to know you can come home with me if you want. We can—have a movie night." It had sounded really fun when the Britton children talked about it.

"Oh dear. Marcus has died?"

"Yes. Tim Britton told me. Emma's husband."

"Oh, Tim. Such a nice man. He's a professor—did you know?"

"No, but I'm not surprised. He's very well-spoken."

"English literature. At some Chicago university. I forget which one."

"Wow. Are you okay?"

"Yes. I'll be fine. As I told you, we weren't best friends; I was just fond of him. I don't know why. There was something vulnerable about Marcus. People didn't understand him, but there was much goodness there. This is quite sad. And on his birthday." She wiped at her eyes.

"You shouldn't be alone, Ell. Let me call one of your sons."

"All right," she said, surprising me. Jay had two brothers, Tom and Eric, who both lived in the area. I had met them at Christmastime, and we had become relatively friendly in a short time. I went in the next room and found their info on my cell phone. There was no answer at Tom's house, so I tried Eric. His wife, Andrea, answered.

I explained the situation in brief, and to my relief she understood at once. "Eric should go out there, sit with her for a while," she said. "Thanks for telling us, Lilah. Any word from Jay?"

"No," I said, and a wave of sadness passed over me. It wasn't just that I missed Jay Parker; Cantwell's death was a grim reminder of mortality, and I'd had plenty of those reminders lately.

I thanked Andrea and hung up. Then I returned to Ellie and sat with her until Eric arrived, about half an hour later.

He gave me a quick hug, then hugged his mother. "You'll want something to eat," Ellie said to her tall, handsome son.

Eric grinned at me. He looked a lot like Jay. "No, Ma, I will not. And if we get hungry, we can order pizza."

I waved at them both, lifted Mick's leash, and made

my way to my car. It seemed like a century since I had bounded up Ellie's driveway with my clandestine casserole.

IN THE CAR I didn't bother to turn on the radio, because Avril Lavigne's melancholy voice was in my head, singing "I Miss You." With a sigh, I pulled into my long driveway, past the giant house of my landlord, Terry Randall, and beyond it to the little caretaker's cottage that was my home. Mick's tail wagged, because he recognized our abode and seemed to be as fond of it as I was. I let him out, and he cavorted around while I fumbled for my key.

I heard a car behind me and turned to see Jay Parker emerging from a cab, which meant he was coming directly from the airport. He looked thinner; Parker tended not to eat well while he was concentrating on work. He paid the driver and then looked up and locked eyes with me. Even from the distance of twenty feet I could appreciate how very blue his eyes were, and how sexy he was when he focused them on me with that intensity that was only Parker's.

He grabbed a large bag from the car and carried it until he reached me, at which point he dropped it on the ground. "I'm back," he said with a crooked little smile.

I launched myself at him and actually achieved air, confident that Parker would catch me, which he did, laughing, while I covered him with kisses. Something about Jay Parker made me as affectionate and energetic as a puppy. "You were gone too long," I said into his neck.

"Agreed. Can we go inside? Your nosy neighbors are watching us."

Surprised, I stopped kissing him long enough to look up at Terry's kitchen window, which overlooked his backyard. He and his girlfriend, Britt, were both there, staring unabashedly at our reunion. Terry waved, grinning, and Britt gave me a thumbs-up. It was an awkward moment made more so when I waved back with an automatic gesture. "Yes, let's get inside," I said.

I led Parker into my little living room, where he flopped into a chair and pulled me onto his lap. "God, I missed you," he said, playing with my hair.

"I don't see why you needed to go on some training mission. It's not like you're in the FBI or something. You're already the best cop in Pine Haven."

He smiled. "You're pretty."

"I'll bet you forgot what I looked like. I know I couldn't picture your face anymore," I lied.

He took out his phone and clicked it on. "Luckily I have a whole gallery of Lilah photos that helped me get through each day." He started scrolling through them. Me at Christmas, in front of his family's tree, right after we had become an "official" couple. Me with Mick, playing in the snow. Me in my best black dress, sitting across from him at L'amour Parfait, where he had given me a pair of diamond earrings. I had worn them ever since. I was wearing them now.

He scrolled again, to a couples selfie that I had taken on his phone after Parker and I took a walk together after a couple weeks of dating. We looked happy. "That's a nice one," I said.

"They're all nice. I just kept thinking, how did I get such a beautiful girlfriend? I was actually asked that by a couple of people, too."

"You showed people my picture?"

"When we had downtime."

"Wow, Parker. You have it bad," I joked.

He put the phone down on my curio table and slid his arms around me. "I really do," he said, and he pulled me against him for a long, long kiss.

"Mmm," I murmured eventually against his mouth. I pulled slightly away. "I was just thinking about how much I missed you, because I saw Eric, and there is such a resemblance—"

"Eric? My brother Eric?"

I nodded.

"How did you happen to see him?"

"Oh—it's kind of a long story. Your mom invited me to Marcus Cantwell's birthday party—"

"O-*kay.*"

"I guess she told him about Mick, and his special talents."

Parker looked fondly at my dog. "I missed Mick, too."

"Anyway, I'm leading up to some bad news here, which I don't really want to tell you right now. . . ."

He sat up straight. "Is my mom okay?"

"She's fine, yes. Just sad. Which is why I called Eric to be with her, and he came out."

Parker had his alert face on now; it was unbearably sexy, but it meant that he was in another zone. "What's going on?"

I sighed. "Okay, here goes. Cantwell looked kind of weird when I met him. And I made some rice pudding casserole for your mom so she could say she made it for the children."

"Sounds like her."

"And then later Cantwell came in, saying he liked it and had eaten it as a kid, and then he collapsed right into the casserole."

"Not again," Parker said in disbelief.

"That's what I said! But it wasn't my food that made him sick, thank God, because children had already eaten it by then, and they were all fine. Maria Grimaldi was there, and—"

Parker's brows shot up. "Maria? Why?"

"Because her niece used to go out with Cash Cantwell, and she was at the party, Maria was there to pick her up, but then she started to think it was fishy, Cantwell collapsing like that, because your mom and I told her that he'd been acting weird."

"He could have just been sick."

"Yeah. But Maria had a feeling, and frankly so did I. Something was weird. And your mom had joked about the fact that his kids might all want access to his money. I guess they have it now."

"Why?"

"Oh, because—he died, Jay. At the hospital. Emma

Cantwell's husband, Tim Britton, told me when she texted him."

"Oh no. Poor Marcus. He was a good old guy."

"Really? I mean, I feel bad for everyone, but he struck me as kind of . . . weird."

"Yeah, but he was a good guy. Wow. This is bad news. So my mom took it hard?"

"Not too bad, but I didn't want to leave her alone. But I wanted to come here, really badly, so I could send you more sexy text messages."

Parker brightened. "I enjoyed all of those immensely, by the way."

"Good."

Parker's blue eyes studied mine. "So why were you with Tim Britton?"

I laughed. "You are really the jealous type, aren't you?"

"As you already know."

"I was actually with Mr. Britton's *children*, who are all delightful, and we were playing with Mick and telling jokes, and then he came up to take them home."

"That's very sweet. You're good with children. I've seen it with your little friend Henry."

"Oh, that little Peach is just adorable! Have you seen her?"

"I don't think so. I don't—I try not to ever run into Emma Cantwell-Britton."

"Why? Do you find her bitchy?"

"Yes, but I avoid her for other reasons."

"Which are? You used to be next-door neighbors,

right? And she must be right around your age. Maybe a year or two older? So what's so awkward? Are you— Wait a minute! Did you go out with her?" I stood up and put my hands on my hips.

"No, but even if I had it would have been more than a decade ago, so calm down. She went out with Tom, actually."

"Your brother Tom?"

"Yeah. They went to school together. And they were exclusive during their senior year. Anyway, once I barged into his room to borrow something—I don't know what— and Emma was in there waiting for him. With very little on. I don't think I've made eye contact with her since that moment—and at that point her eyes were all I could safely look at."

I burst into disbelieving laughter. "Her? And Tom? And she was—passionate? She seems so straitlaced and bossy."

He smiled, rueful. "Not a memory I care to reflect upon."

I sat back down on his lap. "But if Maria is right, and someone tampered with Cantwell's drink, then you might have to talk to her—to the whole family."

He shook his head. "It's Maria's case, if that's true. I would expect her to be the lead investigator. It was her hunch, and those are usually good."

I put my head on his shoulder. "You look tired. And you're probably hungry. What should I make for you?"

His hands tightened around my waist. "Nothing. This is all I want. Exactly what I was picturing on the plane—

me in your cozy little room, and you in my lap. Just—like—this." He punctuated the last three words with little kisses on my face, and I giggled. Mick strolled up, figuring he should be in on the fun, and Parker laughed.

His phone buzzed on the table, and he picked it up and looked at his text notification. Then he sat up straighter. "Hang on. I need to see this one." He read his text message, then looked up at me. "I have to go," he said.

"You're kidding me. You've been in town for about one minute, and they're already calling you in to work?"

"Not them, no." He looked concerned as he read through the text again. "It's from Maria. She's in trouble."

CHAPTER FOUR

PARKER PROMISED HE WOULD TELL ME EVERYTHING when he returned, which ended up being later that evening. I had made him some spaghetti and meatballs, since he was clearly starving, and he told me what happened in between bites. The Cantwell family, he said, had complained about the way Maria had handled things, and they wanted her off the case.

"What case?"

He wiped his mouth with a napkin and scowled. "Maria had a friend in the crime lab rush those samples. Cantwell was poisoned, all right, via his drink. Someone took the liberty of grinding up a nut and mixing it in. Cantwell had a severe nut allergy, and his whole family knew about it."

"Oh God. But wouldn't he have seen the ground nut in the drink?"

Parker shook his head. "The family said that Owen, one of the sons, had made a batch of something called a Blueberry Thai Mojito. It's a busy drink, with actual blueberries in it, along with some sort of Thai basil leaf and crushed ice. It would be hard to notice anything else floating in there. Owen had been handing them around; obviously someone took theirs into the house and offered it to Cantwell. No one saw this happen; no one has any memory of someone going into the house, because Cantwell said he needed a few minutes to nap in his chair. Then, minutes later, you and Mom arrived."

I thought about this; it had been a very narrow window of events. And yet Cantwell hadn't died immediately. "If he had a reaction to nuts, he wouldn't have been able to breathe, or talk to us. His throat would have closed—isn't that what happens?"

Parker shook his head. "Apparently it differs, depending on the person, the nature of the allergy, the type of nut. I don't know. The lab guy said that a nut allergy response can look similar to a heart attack. It can cause weakness, then cardiac arrest."

"The poor man."

"Yes." Parker's eyes narrowed, and his jaw tightened. For whatever reason, he had liked Marcus Cantwell, and this case was going to be a personal crusade.

"What exactly bothered them about what Maria did? If it weren't for her, they wouldn't know their father was murdered."

He wound some more spaghetti onto his fork. "Apparently there's some discord within the family over this. But a certain individual is threatening to sue the department—"

I curled my lip. "Oh, let me guess who. Scott Cantwell?"

"How did you know?" Parker lowered his fork, surprised.

"Because I talked with Cash Cantwell at the party. He's the only friendly family member, as far as I could tell, and he filled me in on the whole clan with surprising, uh, frankness. He said his brother was overly litigious."

"Hmm. Well, he's probably just full of hot air, but our chief doesn't want any bad press for the PHPD, so Maria is being put on something else."

"She must be angry about that."

"She is. She also thinks this makes Scott Cantwell suspect number one."

"Do you think they'll be cooperative about an investigation?"

"They have to be." He scowled again. "They will be as forthcoming as I need them to be."

"Wow." I looked at Mick. "Who's going to take care of his dogs? Everyone said he loved them more than his family. I don't think that was true, but it was clear he saw the dogs as part of his family."

Parker shrugged. "I would imagine Cash is going to remain in the house; he was the only one currently living there. I suppose they're his responsibility right now."

"He likes the dogs. He told me he walks them and plays with them. He'll be the best person to adopt them, I think. Plus this way the dogs don't have to be relocated."

Parker looked thoughtful. "You two bonded over dogs, huh?"

"And other stuff. Cash is just a friendly person, so he was easy to talk to."

"I know all of the Cantwell kids. Prudence was one year ahead of me in high school, and Scott was a couple years behind. Emma, as you know, was in my brother's class. That will either help in getting them to open up to me, or potentially hinder things." A thought occurred to him, and he touched my hand. "At Christmastime, it was actually really helpful that you could offer me bits of information that you got on the side—things people revealed because they weren't talking to a cop. I might have to ask you to do that for me again."

"Are you deputizing me?" I joked, standing to clear the table.

"Not exactly. But you're observant, Lilah, and you have good instincts. I might need to rely on those. You were at the party. You were there in the crucial moments before Cantwell's death. And Cash likes you. All of those things could come in handy."

"Huh. Cash really likes you, too. He talked about you a lot—what a cool older kid you were, and how you shared your old toys with him. I can't picture you as a kid, Parker."

"I never was one." He ate his final bite, then stood up and carried his plate to the sink.

He rolled up his sleeves and started to wash some dishes; I grabbed a towel and dried them, conscious of tall Jay Parker standing at my side, the hardness of his arm occasionally brushing mine.

Finally the dishes were done, and I hung the towel over the drying rack. Parker knew I had an early delivery, so he insisted on calling a cab to take him home; he left the room briefly to make the call, then came back in and leaned on the counter. "You have a great little house. Very snug. Thanks for feeding me; I seem to always be thanking you for that."

"You're welcome." I lifted one of his hands and studied it. "You're probably pretty tired out, huh—from traveling, and your long training thing, and then this thing with Maria."

"I am pretty wiped out, I admit. I'll go home and grab about ten hours of sleep so I can concentrate on my interviews tomorrow." He leaned down to look into my face. "Someday soon I would like to hang around. Maybe not go home at all. But we said we'd wait until the time was right."

"Yeah, sure," I said, not looking at him.

He hugged me against him. "Do you know I watched you on TV in New York?"

"What? How? *Cooking with Angelo* is a local show."

"It must be syndicated—or maybe New York is a test market, or something. I saw it on the cable channel in my room. I watched it both Fridays when you were on, and it made me homesick. You're so good on the show, I could even put up with him leering at you the whole time."

I laughed. "Don't be silly. Even you have to admit that Angelo is a real professional. He's good at what he does. Wow, I wonder if he knew it was playing in New York? If he did, he didn't tell me!"

"Maybe he didn't want to make you nervous."

"I do get nervous. But I'm getting better."

"You are great. And that last thing you made—that Chinese-inspired casserole—that looked really good!"

"I'll make it for you. It's easy."

He glanced at his watch. "Do you have a lot of work this week?"

"I have about three clients lined up in the near future, plus my catering gig, which is about six hours a day, at present. I get one weekday off because I also work Saturday. I had to take today off specially to go to this event with Ellie. I have tomorrow off from Haven, but I have an early delivery, so I'll spend the morning doing some cooking and freezing to be ready for the week."

"Ah." He studied my face for a while, tracing my eyebrows with his pointer fingers.

I enjoyed my perusal of his blue eyes, his strong face. "I did miss you a lot, Jay."

"Good. I promise I'll stay put. We'll make lots of time for each other now, right?"

I pouted slightly. "Sure. Because when you're investigating a murder, you're always super available."

He looked sad. "Marcus Cantwell was always good to me. After my father died, when I was sixteen, he used to invite me to sit on his porch with him and look at stars. His kids were always off somewhere—or maybe he purposely did it when they weren't around so that I'd have his full attention. He taught me things about the planets and galaxies, and he let me look through his expensive telescope. Sometimes he let me sip his beer or take a puff off his cigar." He held up a hand when I protested. "He wasn't trying to corrupt me; he was just letting me escape from my troubles for a while, and treating me like a man. It did me a lot of good. He came to my high school graduation; he even gave me a present. Well, a card full of money. But that is a present. And you know what he wrote inside? *I'm proud of you*."

"You're kidding me!"

"No, I'm not. So you can see why I have trouble believing these tales of his neglected children or him loving his dogs more. That wasn't the Marcus Cantwell I knew."

"Cash said his Dad was a good guy. He said he used to be way more normal but that he'd gotten kind of eccentric in his old age."

"We'll see about that," Jay said. He peered out my living room window. "Look, my cab is here." He kissed me on the top of my head, then took my hand and started walking toward the door, dragging me behind him.

He opened the door and said, "It's good to be back."

I kissed him good night, and he went out into the spring darkness.

I felt Mick staring at me, and I looked back at him. "Well, I guess we're on our own, right? Do you feel like watching a movie and making some popcorn? The Britton kids made that sound really appealing."

Mick nodded.

Soon I was bundled on my couch with my dog and some popcorn. Mick didn't like this particular human food, so there was no danger of him shoving his snout into the bowl. We watched *Six Days, Seven Nights*, which happened to be playing on the movie channel, and I admired the rugged attractiveness of Harrison Ford and the elegant beauty of Anne Heche. I thought that Jay Parker would be almost as effective as one's companion on a tropical island besieged by pirates, although I doubted he knew how to fix an airplane. And it wasn't Ford but Parker I dreamed about that night. He was wielding his gun, attempting to save me from some unknown menace, and I was about to take a sip of a blueberry mojito, when I turned to see who had offered it to me. "Of course it was you," I said, and then I woke up, but by then the face of the person I'd recognized had faded away.

CHAPTER FIVE

THE NEXT MORNING I SANG ALONG WITH "BUDA-pest" on my iPod while I stirred the ingredients for a dessert casserole that I was making for my landlord Terry's girlfriend, Britt. She and Terry were always throwing what I jokingly called "high society" parties, and I'd convinced her to occasionally send some work my way. This time she was having a Sunday afternoon reception, and she wanted something that would go well with coffee.

The casserole, which I had invented for a client a few months earlier, was a sort of deep-dish coffee cake made with pastry dough, cinnamon butter, raspberry jam, al-monds, and a special sugar glaze. I arranged the ingre-dients in a square glass dish and slid the whole thing in the oven, observed closely by Mick, who shoved his soft brown snout against my arm to get a whiff of things. "Move back, nosy," I said.

Mick's legs moved about a centimeter backward, and I laughed. I pushed past him and opened my kitchen door so Mick could go out into the yard, and the phone rang. I picked it up, still watching Mick through the window; he was chasing a squirrel. "Hello?"

"Lilah! I'm so glad you're home," said the voice of my best friend, Jenny Braidwell.

"Hey, Jenn. I feel like I haven't talked to you in weeks."

"You haven't."

"Well, as I recall, you've been pretty busy with your wonderful boyfriend."

Her voice was remorseful. "And I know yours has been away. I should have come over more often."

"True. But I know how absorbing a new romance can be. How's that going?"

Jenny giggled into the phone. "Lilah—I'm engaged!"

"What? When did this happen?"

"Last night. He took me to Cardelini's—sorry; he doesn't know your whole history with Angelo—and he proposed right after dinner. It was very romantic. They even had a band playing, and we danced."

"Oh, Jenn. I'm so happy for you! Really. We have to throw you a big engagement party."

"No, you don't. But it would be nice to get together and celebrate—me and Ross, you and Jay."

"Of course. Let's do that really soon. Jay has a new case, which as you know will take up a lot of his time, but we'll find a night sometime soon when he can steal away." I watched Mick as he rolled around in the spring grass. "This is just great. I knew the minute I saw you two together that it was meant to be. He couldn't take his eyes off you."

"I felt the same way about you and Jay. How's that going, anyway?"

Mick was sniffing something now. "It's great. I mean, sort of. He only just got back from his training thing yesterday afternoon, and now he's back at work. Which is fine. We all have work to do. It's just . . ."

"What? Do you not like him as much as you used to?"

"Oh no. I like him more and more. I am passing rapidly from liking into infatuation. Or addiction, maybe."

"How about love?"

"It's too early to say love, isn't it? I just—I halfway expected that when he got back, we would fall into a passionate stage because we'd been apart so long."

"And he's not passionate?"

"He is, but it's—comfortable. Which is good. I've always felt comfortable with him. But I hate to think that we somehow skipped over that stage where we can't keep our hands off each other and have already settled down into a sort of predictable, old-person kind of romance, where I just make my rice pudding casseroles and he does his police work and then we sit in my house and watch TV or something. I look at Cam and Serafina, and they're just constantly all over each other. But of course Jay is not like Serafina. She's all about touching, and he's very quiet and self-contained. That's fine. We'll just be the boring couple."

Jenny *tsk*ed into the phone. "It's not like that at all. I'll bet he dragged you into your bedroom the minute he got home."

Mick was at the door, and I let him in. "No. I mean, we haven't reached that stage yet."

"Really?"

"We decided we'd take things slowly, get to know each other. Which we started to do, and then he got called away. And now we're back to the slow thing. Which is fine. It's *fine*."

"How about Friday for our dinner? We can eat at my place. I'll make something special; my cooking is getting better, I swear, and Ross is a terrific chef."

"I'll ask Jay and get back to you. Is that okay?"

"Sure."

"I'm really happy for you, Jenn."

"Oh, and, Lilah? You will be my maid of honor, right?"

"Now you're going to make me cry. And yes, the answer is YES! I'd be honored."

"Then my work here is done."

"Will my dear baby Henry be the ring boy?"

"He will. He's already made some demands, the little punk. Luckily it's a pretty standard request: he wants to wear a black suit with a white shirt and a black bow tie, because that's what Bruce Wayne wears."

"Well, of course!"

"So my sister and I have to try to find just the right tux for Hen, who will be by far the most demanding man in the wedding party."

"Wait a minute—will your sisters be mad that I'm maid of honor?"

"Nah. I wasn't Tina's or Carrie's, either, but I was in the wedding parties. And Deb has assured me she's going to elope when she gets married. They'll all be in my wedding party. They get it. And they all love you."

"All right, great. Listen, I have to make a raspberry glaze and deliver a casserole. I'll ask Jay about Friday and get back to you, okay?"

"Okay. Love you, maid of honor!"

"Love you, too. And congratulations, Mrs. Ross."

She was laughing as she hung up the phone. Feeling inspired, and still holding my cell, I clicked on Jay Parker's name and sent him a text that said, Thinking of you. I wasn't going to bog Parker down with some long, involved message while he was at work. This seemed like the perfect length for him to scan quickly while he was in the midst of whatever his investigation required.

Suddenly I remembered the first time I saw him in his police role, investigating a death that had occurred in a church basement. He had looked tall and professional and surprisingly handsome. His blue eyes had had the same hypnotic effect on me then as they did now.

I put my phone down and went to the counter, where I stirred together some confectioners' sugar, warm water, softened butter, and raspberry extract. When it reached the proper consistency, I pushed it aside and checked on my casserole, which looked golden brown and smelled great.

I pulled it out and left it to cool. Then I jogged to my room to put on something nicer than sweats in order to deliver my finished product to Britt. I donned a pair of black pants, a red blouse, and a silver chain necklace, along with the earrings Parker had given me. I brushed my hair, slipped into some low black heels, and jogged back downstairs to drizzle glaze over the casserole. "Oh, Mick, she is going to love this," I said to my dog, who had nestled into his basket to contemplate his spring dreams.

He nodded gently.

"I'm going to run down the driveway. Don't be mad now, okay? I'll be back in a few minutes."

Mick seemed okay with the plan. I put a lid on the casserole, grabbed my key, locked my dog safely in the house, and started marching down the long driveway to Britt and Terry's place.

Their house, an elegant brick-and-concrete affair in light gray, was surrounded by blossoming cherry trees, pale pink and fragrant, and I breathed in deeply as I rounded the corner. Spring brought a desire to live anew through the intoxicating scents that floated on the air.

I climbed the stone steps and knocked at their big door. Britt appeared a moment later, leaning out to whisper to me. "Listen, I have a visitor, so come in but leave the casserole on the side table there, okay?"

"I can just go," I whispered back.

"Don't be silly. Come on in and I'll introduce you. I just don't want to out your secret business."

"Okay." I walked into the big hall, waving at my electronic friend, the Wurlitzer jukebox, which held pride of place in Terry's foyer. I set the casserole on a side table and walked with Britt into the kitchen, where I was shocked to see Prudence Cantwell hunched over the kitchen island on one of Britt's kitchen stools, poking moodily at a plate filled with cheese and crackers.

She looked up as we entered, and her eyebrows rose. "I know you," she said. "You were there yesterday, at my dad's."

Britt looked surprised. "What? Lilah, you knew Marcus Cantwell?"

"I only met him yesterday. I went to his place with Ellie Parker, who is his next-door neighbor. She's Jay's mom and my friend," I said to Britt. Then I turned to Prudence. "I'm sorry for your loss."

Her eyes were wide and wet with tears, but she shook her head. "No, no, I'm not going to indulge in this right now. The wake and funeral will be bad enough." She took a sip of a soft drink that Britt had given her, then directed a gaze at me. "You were there, though—you were one of the last people with my dad. That's so weird to think of, that he was basically with strangers when he died. No offense," she said weakly.

"None taken." Britt gestured to a chair, so I sat down. "I want you to know that your father was very happy in that last moment. He didn't seem to know he was in danger. He was telling Ellie how much he loved rice pudding as a kid. That he had stolen some out of her dish, just like a little boy. And that's what his smile looked like—a mischievous boy."

Prudence let out a watery laugh. "Oh, he was like that sometimes. Thanks for that. What was your name?"

Julia Buckley

Britt stepped forward and put her hands on my shoulders. "This is our neighbor and good friend Lilah Drake. Lilah, I take it you already met Prue?"

"Not officially," I said. "It was all rather confused yesterday, but yes, sort of." We shook hands across the table. "How do you two know each other?" I asked.

Britt poured me some lemonade from a pitcher that sat on the kitchen island. "Oh, in a lot of ways the art world is very small. Prue and I have known each other for years. First we would see each other at the same galleries, and then we started meeting up for coffee, things like that. Now Prudence Cantwell paintings are sold at my gallery, and I can't keep them in stock."

"Oh. That's great. I need to visit your gallery again, Britt. I think I've only been there once." I had never been back because the prices of the paintings were out of my financial range and would be for my entire lifetime; still, it would be good to support Britt now and again with my presence.

"I'll let you know next time we're having an evening event," Britt said, tucking her silky hair behind her ears.

Prudence sighed and started to gather her things. "Well, I've taken up enough of your time with my sad stories. I should go see what the siblings are doing."

Britt held up a hand. "Stay where you are. You came here to escape your lunatic brother and your obnoxious boyfriend, and here you shall stay."

Prudence dropped the purse she had picked up and slumped back on the counter. "If you don't mind, I'll stay another half hour. Maybe by then Scott will have gone away somewhere to harass other people."

"Was it your brother's idea to complain about Detective Grimaldi?" I asked.

Prudence looked surprised. "Oh, you heard about that?" She sighed. "None of us was too thrilled with her at the time, but I mean, we had just seen my dad taken away in an ambulance. And here was this cop . . . and then we found out she was right to be suspicious, and that someone had actually poisoned Dad. Did you know that?"

I nodded. Her eyes grew wet again. "It's just unbelievable, really. And yes, Scott is the one who made trouble, although now Owen and I wish we had intervened. At least Owen is speaking to me again. After what Damen did, I was afraid he wouldn't."

"Every family has its dysfunction," Britt said, and I realized I knew nothing about her family, or Terry's. They were just Britt and Terry to me.

"I suppose," Prue murmured. Then she looked at me. Her eyes were dark, like her hair; she was quite arresting, even with a tear-smudged face. "How do you know that cop, anyway?"

"She's actually the partner of the guy I'm dating. He used to be your next-door neighbor—Jay Parker."

Prudence smiled, and her face lit up. "Jay? Oh my gosh, we practically grew up together. What a nice bunch of guys all those Parker kids were. Although they were so destructive. Always breaking things—windows, furniture, cars. I don't know how their mom put up with it.

Those three were just constantly wrestling and punching one another, but usually good-naturedly. Emma was always so prim about it. She said they were like a bunch of zoo animals."

"Didn't your sister date one of them?" I asked. Prudence and Britt raised their eyebrows at me, and I shrugged. "I thought I heard Jay say something about it."

"Oh yeah, she dated Tom Parker for her whole senior year. She was really in love, actually. Wow, that seems like so long ago."

"She seems to have found the perfect husband," I said.

"Yeah—too perfect for her, in a way."

"What do you mean?" Britt asked.

"Just that Em takes him for granted. He's this total package of a guy: handsome, smart, funny. A great provider. A genius, basically. Great with the kids. And yet Em always manages to gripe about him to me. I'm always afraid he's going to get tired of her nagging and marry some young coed."

Britt shrugged her slim shoulders. "Emma is a great catch, too. She's just less passionate than you are, Prue. You're the artist, and Em's the organizer. She likes things to be just so."

And yet Parker had told me that Emma had been quite passionate about Tom, back when they were both teenagers. "She has lovely children," I said. "I had the pleasure of talking to them yesterday. They were petting my dog."

"You brought your dog, huh? I'll bet Dad wanted that." Prue looked close to tears again.

"Yes. He did request it. He got a kick out of meeting Mick—that's my Lab."

"Good. Good. I'm glad he had a nice last day, and that he didn't see much of the drama that was going on in the backyard."

Britt broke a cracker in half and looked at it. "What drama, aside from Damen punching Owen?"

Prue sniffed at that. "Do you know Damen has been texting me all day? Making his stupid apologies?"

"He's not a bad guy, all things considered," Britt said. "He was really supportive at your gallery opening. So attentive and loving, and always willing to hold your purse when you were talking with buyers."

Prue's face softened slightly. "Most of the time he's great. Maybe the best guy I ever dated. But he has this temper that comes out at weird times, and then he ends up punching my brother at a family *birthday* party— what's that all about?"

"Didn't he tell you?" Britt asked. She looked calm and detached, but I could sense that she was actually quite curious.

"He said it was nothing—just a momentary burst of anger."

I held up a finger. "Peach happened to mention something to me yesterday, just in passing."

Both women, once again, looked surprised. "My little Peachie? Oh, the ears on that kid," Prudence said, smiling. Then her smile wavered. "What did she say?"

"That the man in leather had called your brother Owen

a liar and your brother Scott a shyster. Although Peach said feister."

Britt giggled, but Prue's eyes grew wide. "Oh my God," she said. "That bastard! I don't believe Damen. I said something to him in confidence, and now he's started a family fight over it!"

Neither Britt nor I said anything, since this seemed like a private matter, but Prudence clearly wanted to unload some stress. "I was talking with Damen the other night when we were—you know, in bed together, and sort of daydreaming about the future."

I did not know, but Britt nodded.

"And we were saying we'd open a gallery somewhere, maybe in Colorado, because we've both lived there and we really like it. I said I didn't know where we'd get the kind of capital we need, even though my paintings have given me a little nest egg. Damen said why not ask Dad for a loan. I told him we kids try not to talk money with Dad; it's tacky, and we all agreed at one point that we could all wait for whatever legacies might be coming our way. We're comfortable with our own careers—financially."

"Of course you are," said Britt, pushing a plate of brownies toward Prue. The brownies looked store-bought, and I frowned at them.

"So Damen said, 'What about the slush fund?' That's a fund that Dad created once, when we were kids, and he said if one of us had a need or an emergency, we could apply to him for some money out of the slush fund, but that we had to earn it back with chores and kind acts and stuff. It was more of a teaching tool, really. But the fund really existed. Owen used it to get a cheap used car—that thing was a clunker, but he loved it. Emma tapped into it to take dance lessons at this exclusive studio, and Scotty used it to buy a couple really nice suits that he could interview in. And I got my first truly good art supplies out of that fund."

"So why not ask for money as an adult?" Britt asked.

"Because at one point Scott convinced my dad that he should put that money into some sort of untouchable account that would draw interest. But—I guess I was just being snarky—I told Damen that I thought Scott did it just so that none of us could petition for Dad's money. Even though that was the whole point of the slush fund. It was the money we *could* touch."

"Do you still think that was Scott's motive?" Britt asked.

"Sort of," Prue said, and she sighed. "Scotty was always kind of a greedy little boy. I don't know what drove him. Maybe he felt neglected by Dad. We all did, once in a while, although Dad would find weird ways to make it up to us. He wasn't your average guy, but we loved him." Her eyes grew wet again, and she dabbed at them with a napkin. Then she took one of Britt's brownies.

"So why does that make Owen a liar?" I asked. I had no right to question Prudence, but in her current state she didn't seem to notice who asked the questions.

"Initially Owen told us the slush fund was still available. We were kind of feeling him out one time, to see if that money was still there for us kids. And he and Scott know the most about Dad's finances, because they were always giving him investment advice. Which Em and I thought was a way to just have more control and access. As you can see, we're not the most loving siblings. Except when we are. It's all so confusing."

"Of course," Britt soothed.

"But then it turned out Owen was lying and just covering for Scott, because he knew that Scott had advised that the slush fund be moved out of our reach. They're both pains in the ass, but Owen is generally easier to take, which is why he had become Scott's ambassador to the other siblings. He's always smoothing the way for that red-haired shit." She sent me an apologetic look. "Sorry. I guess this isn't the time to be bashing my siblings."

I said, "I have a sibling. We bash each other sometimes." Then, because I was curious: "Did you all live in the house together, growing up?"

"No, not always. When my mom and dad divorced, Em and I went with my mom, and we usually lived with her during the week. But we'd be with Dad and the new family on weekends, and sometimes for vacations. So there were times that we were all together for weeks. Looking back, it just feels like we spent our whole childhoods together. Of course Em and I were the oldest, so the boys were sort of like our little protégés. They were sweet when they were little. We still think of Cash as our little boy."

I thought of little Henry, my pseudo-nephew. He would probably always feel six years old to me, at least in terms of my affection. "You seem like a great sister," I said.

"Thanks." Prue looked down at her hands. They were graceful, with long, slender fingers. "So you had already heard about the whole foul play thing and my dad?"

"Parker told me, but only because he was explaining why he had to replace Maria."

She didn't seem to care that I had been told the news. "It's going to be in the paper anyway; the whole sordid story will be revealed for public consumption. So you actually saw my dad drink his—deadly brew. Right?"

Her eyes were dry now, but sad, and she seemed to dread my answer and long for it at the same time.

I hesitated. "Yes. Just a sip or two. He didn't seem that conscious of it—more like an automatic gesture. I can't imagine . . . I mean, I've actually met people who have done terrible things, but it's still hard to picture it. That someone would take the time to hide a nut in that drink. To grind it up with murderous intentions."

Prudence shook her head. "It was good camouflage. We were all having those drinks. They were pretty good. Owen always likes to experiment, because he fancies himself some kind of trendy bartender, and those mojitos were popular. We kids talked later, and no one saw anyone take one in to Dad. But of course in retrospect, you realize you might have just been looking at the wrong thing. Like maybe while we focused on party things in the yard, someone was slipping right past our noses and moving right up the stairs to my dad." She gave a watery sigh.

"I'm really sorry for what happened. And I know Ellie is, too. She considered your dad a good friend."

Prue offered a little smile. "It's funny, because my dad has been married so many times, but I sometimes thought he had a crush on Ellie Parker. She's such a great lady, and pretty. Just classy, I guess is the word."

"I agree."

Now Prue got up, reluctantly, and lifted her purse. "Okay, I really have to go. Britt, thanks so much for listening. I know you have people coming, and yet you offered me your time. You're the best." She embraced Britt and gave her a kiss on the cheek. With their dark hair and stylish clothing, they both looked as if they had met at some expensive gallery instead of in Britt's home.

Prudence Cantwell turned to me. "Lilah, it was nice meeting you for real this time. Thanks for the nice things you said."

"Of course."

As Britt walked Prudence to the door, I heard Britt say, "And I'll drop by to see that latest painting. I want to hang it in my main room."

They said some more good-byes, and then the door closed. A moment later Britt walked in with my casserole. "Lord, this smells good. You are the best, Lilah."

"Thanks."

Britt gave me a casual half hug and then tucked the dish on the back of her counter. "I'll put things out in an hour or so."

"I'll get out of your hair, then."

"Not so fast. I saw that lovely reunion with Jay yesterday. Is it good to have him back?"

"Yes, it is."

"You know, Terry and I really don't know him all that well. We need you to bring him over so we can ply him with questions. Clearly he makes you happy."

I picked up one of her store-bought brownies and sniffed it. "I could make these for you, Britt," I said disapprovingly.

She feigned a guilty expression, and I laughed. "You know, you're the second person today who's said she wants to get together with Parker and me. My friend Jenny just called to tell me she's engaged, and she wants us to have dinner, the two couples."

Something flashed across Britt's face, and she turned away, pretending to fuss with things on the counter. "Oh, isn't that nice. Have I ever met your friend Jenny?"

"I don't think so. I'll drag her to your next party. Are you okay?"

"Sure. Life is beautiful."

I stood up and went to her, physically turning her back to face me. "Are things okay with you and Terry?"

"Of course. I love Terry."

Something was wrong, but it was also clear she didn't want to talk about it. I patted one of her manicured hands. "I'm just down the driveway if you ever need an ear."

"Thanks, Lilah. Sometime soon I'll take you up on that."

"Okay. I'm going to leave before Mick starts feeling neglected. Can I possibly snip a few of your gorgeous cherry blossoms to put in vases?"

"Of course! Aren't they amazing? I can smell them from my open bedroom window at night. Aromatherapy for my dreams. Let me get some clippers and I'll come with you."

We went outside together, and Britt snipped huge

sheaves of flowers for me in her generous Britt way. She loved to share with people; I wondered if that was what made Terry notice her at the very start. I had no idea how they first met. I would ask Britt soon, I thought, as I waved and marched toward my own house.

I unlocked my door with some difficulty and spent the next few moments filling vases, arranging flowers, and finding just the right spot for cherry blossom displays all over my little house. Mick looked up from his basket, mildly curious, but didn't bother to get out.

I pondered what Prudence Cantwell had said about her father, her siblings, Ellie Parker, her boyfriend. Today had been a day for talk of boyfriends, in fact: Jenny's Ross, Prue's Damen, Britt's Terry, my Jay. Was it spring that made it seem that love was in the air?

And, I realized in a sudden burst of knowledge, hadn't it been talk of marriage that had made Britt suddenly seem so sad?

CHAPTER SIX

O N MONDAY MORNING I GOT TO WORK AT HAVEN
bright and early. I had come to love this little catering company, still called "one of the best in Chicagoland"
by the critics who mattered. Esther and Jim Reynolds had
hired me on at a difficult time in my life, and Haven had
been true to its name for me. I got along well with my
bosses and the various culinary students who came in
and out doing apprenticeships. I had grown fond of the
duo called Gabby and Nicole, both dark haired and wide-
eyed and good at their jobs (and at gossiping when Jim
and Esther weren't around), but Nicole had gotten a job
at Fair Lady, a new restaurant in the city, and now Gabby
was paired with Will, a recruit from the Pine Haven Culinary Institute, and the two of them were endlessly en-

tertaining, since they had started arguing on day one, and the sexual tension between them was clear to everyone but them.

I walked through the door and past the big white counter to the working kitchen and its stainless steel countertops. Today we were prepping for an afternoon wedding shower. A Mrs. Remington was throwing the affair for her daughter, and she envisioned a grand dessert table, so we were planning to be elbow deep in sugary concoctions.

Esther was on the phone; she waved to me and rolled her eyes. I began to get out ingredients for my first assignment: a chocolate cotillon. This many-layered chocolate cake was a French Christmas tradition, but Mrs. Remington had requested it specially for her party. I had assured Esther that I had made one before, although it had been a while.

Gabby and Will were at another table, both of them looking weary and, in Will's case, slightly hungover. I wasn't old, but these two were at least five years younger than I was, and their partying lifestyle made me feel ancient. Despite their bickering, they worked well together, and with impressive rapidity, which was why Esther and Jim were willing to put up with their drama. They were working on making a cupcake tray; Gabby was starting on apple cinnamon cakes with cream cheese, and Will was making Black Forest cupcakes with dark cream frosting and cherry shavings. While she stirred batter, she criticized him. "You could at least refrain from getting drunk the night before a big event," she said.

Will scratched his cheekbone with the back of one hand. He had tied back his longish blond hair so that nothing would get into his frosting, which he was making in a blender. "I wasn't drunk—just having fun. You should try it sometime," he said. "It might make you less uptight."

Gabby's voice shot into another register. "I am *not* uptight," she screeched. "I am professional, which is more than I can say for you!" She cracked an egg into her batter, and Will grinned at me.

"Hi, Lilah," he said. "How's life?"

"It's fine," I said, selecting some eggs from a carton. "I'm glad we're getting an early start on this."

Esther finished her phone call and sighed. "Oh, that woman! She could not be more demanding. I feel like charging her extra."

I shrugged. "You should, if she's making last-minute demands."

"No, she's just anxious, so she keeps calling me to double-check food and deadlines and setup. That's fine up to a point, but she's actually taking me away from work that I'm doing for her!"

I began to separate my eggs, holding the yolk in one side of the shell while I let the whites dribble out into my glass bowl. I saved the yolks in a separate container. When I had three whites I added a tablespoon of lemon juice and began beating them with some applied muscle.

Esther started mixing dry ingredients for a pastry crust, and she sent me a wise look. "Did Jay get back? You look a bit less lovelorn today."

I snorted my indignation and checked my egg white mixture for stiffness. It made nice peaks; I started adding in some sugar. "He is back, thank you."

"That's good. Are you happy?" She was cutting some softened butter into her flour mixture.

I turned away to preheat one of the ovens, then turned back. "Of course." I noticed that Will and Gabby had stopped their quiet arguing to look at me. Both had met Jay Parker just once, when he picked me up at Haven on a cold day in January because my car wouldn't start. They had been a bit starstruck ever since; Parker had come straight from work and still looked coplike and official, and Will had spied the gun under my boyfriend's suit jacket when the latter had hugged me.

"He's so hot," Gabby said. "I would go out with that guy in a second. You're lucky, Lilah. You don't find guys like him very often."

I saw a flash of annoyance on Will's face. He added some vanilla extract to his frosting with a moody flick of the bottle. "You do if you look in the right places," he said.

"Oh, and I suppose you know of an island of noble men somewhere," Gabby said, without any particular regard for logic. Her dark eyes flashed at Will.

He smirked at this, then looked at me. "So what's his title now? Did he get, like, promoted at this training thing?"

"I don't think so. I'll have to ask him. He's not very forthcoming about cop stuff. He likes to keep work at work."

"I can relate to that," said Will with feeling. For some

reason this seemed to hurt Gabby's feelings. She turned away from Will with a swoosh of her long brown ponytail and gave elaborate attention to the slicing of an apple.

Esther smiled down at her dough. "You'll have to ask Jay to stop by sometime to say hello. Jim and I haven't seen him in quite a while."

As if hearing his name, Esther's husband, Jim, walked in, looking serene as ever and holding a tray of fruit that he needed to peel and slice for Esther's pastries. "Hey, everyone," he said. "Happy spring."

"Hey, Jim." I turned back to Esther. "Jay is investigating another murder. And once again, I happened to be around when it occurred."

The whole room went silent, and four pairs of eyes focused on me with the special intensity that people reserve for crime. Esther's hands went still. "How is that even possible?"

I sighed and explained it to them. Ellie's invitation, meeting Cantwell with Mick, thinking Cantwell was odd, noting that he was drinking something. "I—Ellie had made a rice pudding casserole, and Cantwell fell right into it, unconscious."

"Oh my," Esther said. "That must have been dreadful. Are you all right, Lilah?"

"Yes. Cantwell has five children, and they're all pretty miserable. Although I assume they will all be much wealthier soon. He was rumored to be quite well-off."

Will pushed his blender aside. "Why do I know that name? It sounds familiar. Do you mean someone killed this old dude for his money?"

I shrugged. "I don't know; that's for Jay to find out. I'm still having trouble getting past the idea that someone killed him."

He pulled out some muffin tin liners and began to tuck them into a pan. "But it's so cool that your man is always on the job, finding these killers. That's got to be a turn-on." He said it with enthusiasm, as though he was talking about some adventure movie he'd seen.

My face grew hot as I folded the yolks in with my stiffened egg whites. "Anyway, Jay's going to be busy, as always." I kept my eyes on my work.

Esther's voice was comforting and maternal when she said, "He'll find time for you, Lilah. You two have such an elaborate history, don't you? I can tell how devoted he is."

Will snapped his fingers. "I know! I went to high school with a kid named Cantwell. Cash Cantwell."

Now I was looking at Will. "That's his youngest son."

He sighed with what seemed to be real sympathy. "Oh wow. Cash was a good kid. Always smiling and friendly to everyone."

"Yes, I got that impression of him, too. He seems irrepressible."

"Big word," Will said.

Gabby had been trying to give Will the silent treatment, but now she leaned in. "Did you hang out with him in high school?"

Will shrugged. "Not really. We had a couple classes together, so we would—just kind of tell jokes and stuff. I should have kept in touch with him, actually. He always made me laugh. I think he wrote something funny in my yearbook."

We were all quiet for a while as we focused on our tasks. I measured some sugar and cocoa, then poured it into a sieve. I shook the sieve with my left hand while I folded in the cocoa mixture with my right. When I finished, I cleaned the sieve, grabbed a baking tray, and lined it with baker's parchment. I spread my chocolate mixture on it, then slid the whole thing carefully into the preheated oven, setting a timer for twelve minutes.

Esther and Jim were watching me and pretending not to as their hands worked efficiently. Esther finished her pastry dough and put it into a second oven; there were four in the Haven kitchen. As I worked, I drifted into thoughts of my own, and my brain was not interested in contemplating the murder of Marcus Cantwell. I was thinking instead of Jay Parker and the pictures he had showed me on his phone. He had enjoyed looking at them, he told me, while he was in New York. An idea occurred to me, and I smiled as I sought bottles of cognac and espresso among the many bottles in Haven's cabinet. I would be mixing them with chocolate in Esther's new bain-marie.

Jim was studying the bottles in my hand. "That cognac looks low, Lilah. When you're finished, write it on the shopping list, okay?"

"Sure." I had remembered that the photographer at the Cantwell party had given me his card. I had felt rather sorry for him at the time, since what could have been a great networking opportunity had ended with him having to leave early. What if I hired him to take some pictures of me—romantic pictures—that I could give to Parker as a gift?

I liked the idea. Jim, slicing pears into thin, delicate strips, smiled at me. "Your face just brightened, like the sun came out from behind a cloud."

"You guys need to stop watching me like I'm a television. Watch them." I pointed at Will and Gabby, who were arguing again. Will leaned in toward her, his face close to hers while he told her how wrong she was about something. She pointed back at him, touching his arm with her other hand for emphasis. We had already endured a month of this, and still they seemed blind to their mutual attraction. Someday soon I was just going to tell them.

I unwrapped bars of dark, bittersweet, and milk chocolate and began chopping them into rough pieces. I remembered something Parker had told me, just after Christmas, when I made him a special chocolate dessert to bring to work. "You're like a sugar goddess," he had joked as he stood beside me. "Or just a goddess," he'd added, kissing my neck. Parker had become more elaborate with his romantic dialogue in the months since we'd met. Surely that was a good sign?

By the time we left for our event four hours later, laden with delicious and sweet-smelling concoctions, I had already left a message for the photographer, Wade Glenning, asking him to call me back about an appointment. I trusted that he would be a good choice, since the Cantwells had hired him, but more importantly because Cash had vouched for him, and that was a tribute to the undeniable charisma of Cassius Cantwell.

*   *   *

ON MY WAY home from work I stopped at our local bookstore, the Book Tree. It was an amazing place with a handcrafted oak tree in the center of the store, with actual shelves built into its faux wood trunk. Myriad paper leaves glimmered under the ceiling lights on carefully constructed branches. I knew that Parker would be busy for long periods of time until he found his poisoner, so I figured some reading would be a good distraction.

I was hovering between the mystery and the romance sections, trying to decide what I was in the mood for, when I heard a familiar voice. I moved down the aisle until I reached the children's section, a beautiful area underneath one of the branches of the tree, where the leaves dangled downward for children to touch with their curious fingers and the walls were painted with a whole forest of oaks, and little wooden benches were made to look like roots growing out of the ground. On one of these benches sat Cash Cantwell with Peach on his lap. Today Peach wore tiny blue jeans and a blue T-shirt with a picture of a kitten on it. Cash wore jeans and a T-shirt, as well, but his shirt said *Led Zeppelin*.

"Hello," I said.

Peach waved, her face bright with the drama of our unexpected meeting. "I know you," she called in her tiny voice.

Cash pointed at me. "Hey. Lilah, right?"

"Yes. How are you doing, Cash? I was so sorry to hear about your dad."

"I'm doing okay. I'm spending some time with my little friend Peach while Emma makes some arrangements. She's good at that kind of thing, so taking Peach off her hands was the least I could do. The other two will get picked up by their dad when school is out." He looked at his watch. "Which is right around now. But Peach had a half day, so Uncle Cash came to get her, and she said she wanted to get a new Miss Moxie."

"Uncle Cash said I can have one to keep, not just a li-berry version," Peach said proudly.

"That's great. I think I might like to get a Miss Moxie book, too."

"You should," Peach said. Her tiny face was suddenly quite dignified. "They're very good books."

Cash grinned at her. He looked the same, except for some redness around his eyes, as though he hadn't slept well. "Go pick out another one, if you want, but we have to go soon, Queen Peach."

Peach giggled and jumped down, running off to the forestland of books to make her final choice.

Cash stood up, still holding the book they had been reading. On the front I saw a cartoon fox in a blue dress, holding a magnifying glass. The book was called *Miss Moxie and the Missing Moose.*

"I hope this is a good distraction for you," I said.

"It is, actually. Peach is a day-brightener." He looked thoughtful, and for once he wasn't smiling. "I was reading over *Julius Caesar* last night, thinking back on why my dad wanted to name me Cassius at all. He told me once that Cassius betrayed Caesar, but he did it for a cause he believed in. And he was brave; he went out into a storm and bared his chest, daring the lightning to hit him. That was what my dad remembered about his character."

"It's a great name. I guess our names are the first and last gifts our parents give us."

Cash studied my face. "That's pretty profound. You know what I forgot? That Cassius died on his birthday. He took his own life, but he realized before he did it that it was the day he was born. My dad ended up dying on his birthday, too. Funny how life is."

I was speechless for a moment in the face of Cash's grief. Then I said, "Cash, Jay is really upset about this. He's not going to rest until he finds out who did this to your dad."

Cash nodded. "Jay is great. He called me this morning and said he'll be stopping by soon. I guess he started the day at Scott's house." He grinned at me. "I think Scott is a suspect."

"Do you suspect him?"

"Nah. He's my brother. He's kind of an asshole, but he wouldn't kill our dad. He loved Dad, like we all did. But he was a jerk on that last day, so I'm kind of glad Jay is going to give him the business. He deserves that. Let him be interrogated for a change. He's always interrogating people himself."

Peach returned, holding a little pile of books, and Cash tried not to laugh. "I said *one*, Peach."

"These is all connected," Peach said, shrugging her tiny shoulders.

Cash took the pile and flicked through them. "Are you sure you don't have any of these at home?"

She shook her head. "No. I only have ten."

"How many *are* there?" I asked, shocked.

Cash gave me a shrewd look. "This writer, Emily Payne, has got to be rich. I think she's on number sixty-five. You would think Miss Moxie would be a hundred years old, but she's still the same age, solving a mystery about every five seconds."

Peach nodded, pleased.

Her uncle Cash sighed. "I guess it's never a waste of money if you're spending it on books, right? Especially books for a smart little girl who's going to be president."

Peach giggled. "I will be, but also a princess."

"You'll be the first princess president," said Cash, his face serious, and I fell a little bit in love with him.

He kissed Peach on the top of her wheat-colored hair and then looked at his watch. "We'd better go. Emma will be getting home, and I want to find out all the funeral stuff."

"Of course," I said. "Take care, Cash."

"You, too. I'm sure I'll see you around, since you know the Parkers."

"Good-bye, Peach," I said, shaking her little hand. "Enjoy the Miss Moxie books."

She nodded and waved, and she and Cash made their way to the checkout counter, which sat under the "shade" of a large branch of the tree.

I went to the wall and found the *P* section. Emily Payne's Miss Moxie books dominated two shelves. I took out the first thin paperback, which was called, as Peach's sister had told me, *Miss Moxie Is Foxy*; on a whim I also grabbed *Miss Moxie Solves the Case, Miss Moxie the Spy,* and *Miss Moxie Says Sorry.* The books were worth the price for the art alone; an illustrator named Claudia Stiles had created a lovely world for Miss Moxie, and even a quick flip through the pages showed gorgeous color and detailed characterizations that made Miss Moxie's neighborhood look like a place a child might want to visit.

Armed with this reading material, I went back to the mystery section and grabbed the latest Julia Spencer-Fleming, and then visited the romance section for a Nora Roberts. This would be plenty of distraction while Parker trod the mean streets of Pine Haven, seeking yet another murderer.

My phone pinged with a text message; it was from Britt, who told me that she had a gallery showing on Saturday and Prudence Cantwell's painting would be featured. Could Jay and I attend? I wrote back, telling her I would have to ask Jay. Then I stowed the phone back in my purse.

The clerk at the checkout was a perky teenager with a wealth of red curls and a universe of freckles on her face. She was beautiful. "Oh, you clearly have a Miss Moxie fan in your family," she said, scanning my books.

"No, but a little friend of mine recommended them. You must have just rung her up a moment ago."

"Oh, Miss Peach? We know her; she comes in here for story time the first Saturday of every month. She's a delight."

"She is. And she's really sold me on these books. I thought I might read them to another little friend of mine." In that instant I had a vision of Peach meeting Henry; I wondered if they would get along. Someday they would both be adults; they could potentially even marry each other. This thought made me smile, as did the image of a grown-up Peach wearing a tiara to her wedding, and Henry insisting on a Batman tux.

This brought me to another thought. "Oh my gosh, I just remembered something—do you have any books about how to be a good maid of honor? Does that sort of thing exist?"

The chestnut-haired girl stared at me for a moment, her finger on her lips, in thoughtful mode. "You know what? I'm pretty sure we do have stuff like that in the wedding section. Let me show you. Hank, would you cover the register?"

Hank, a scruffy-looking thirtysomething with a gold miner's beard, shuffled to the counter.

"Just put that pile of books aside," she said. "I already rang them up."

Then she led me to another corner of the store and a shelf full of books about perfect weddings, location weddings, DIY weddings, wedding photography, wedding catering (that one looked interesting, but it was too expensive), and, amazingly, guides for the maid of honor or best man. There were three different planning books; I ended up choosing the one called *Make Her Day: A Guide for the Maid of Honor.* "This looks great. Thanks," I said to the girl. "I really need to spend more time in bookstores. I could probably solve every life dilemma."

"You really could," she agreed, leading me back toward the counter.

When I finally took my bag full of books out of the Book Tree, I felt my phone buzzing in my pocket. I jogged to my car, tossed my bag onto the passenger seat, and grabbed the phone, swiping it on. "Hello?"

"Hey, Lilo," said the ever-cheerful voice of my brother, Cameron.

"Hey, Cam. What's up?"

"Serafina wants me to ask if you need us to keep you company while your boyfriend is out of town."

This was typical of my new sister-in-law's thoughtfulness, and in fact she and Cam had taken me out twice while Jay was in New York. "Actually, Jay has returned, but it would be fun if you guys came to dinner anyway."

"He's back, huh? And how are things going? He didn't meet some woman in New York, did he?"

"*No*, he did not. You can stop being suspicious of Jay now. We've worked things out and everything's been great since Christmas."

"I know. Just checking. I'm always available to beat him up if he stops treating you right."

"Thanks, Cam. You know, Jay thinks very highly of you. He's impressed by you as a brother. He never had a sister, but he says he would be just like you are, if he had one."

Cam sounded distracted now, and as usual he was eating something into the phone, although he knew it was a pet peeve of mine. "So what day do you want to get together? It has to be soon, because Fina and I are going to Rome over spring break."

"Oh, Rome," I sighed. "That sounds so romantic."

"She misses her family. And I have yet to meet them, despite the fact that I married their daughter and sister."

"You met one brother, right? Carlo."

"Yes. And Carlo has kindly vouched for me to the family. But obviously I need to meet them and prove that I am a worthy husband for the beautiful Serafina."

"She really is beautiful," I admitted. "And very nice. So nice that she made you get off your duff and call your sister."

"Yes." Now he sounded bored.

"Anyway, Jay's social calendar is really filling up. He has dinner on Friday and a gallery opening on Saturday, assuming he can make both of those. So maybe something on Sunday? Brunch or something?"

"Sounds good. We'll pencil you in," joked my brother. I could hear Serafina in the background, saying something in her luxurious Italian.

"Serafina says you guys should come here. She says I'll cook," Cam said dryly. Serafina was a terrible chef, but Cam, when prodded, could produce good food.

I laughed. "Okay. I'll let you know if we can't do it. I'll talk to Parker tonight."

"See you later, then. Say hi to Jay."

Cam rang off and I got in the car and found my favorite oldies radio station, where I was pleased to hear Three Dog Night singing "Shambala." Bouncing to the music,

I drove away from Frazer Street and back to Main, the heart of Pine Haven's downtown district. I was close to Cardelini's, the restaurant where Ross had proposed to Jenny, when I saw Angelo Cardelini himself, sauntering down the sidewalk to his place of business. *Angelo.* Once I had been desperately in love with him. Now he was merely one of my employers, since I had a Friday feature on his television show, *Cooking with Angelo.*

On a sudden whim I pulled up next to a parking meter and jumped out of the car. "Angelo!" I called.

He stopped just short of the entrance to Cardelini's, squinting at me with his lovely brown eyes; his brown-black curls seemed to glint in the sun. "Lilah," he said. "You are beautiful today! Your hair is like—"

"Hey," I said, stopping him before he could launch into one of his flowery metaphors. "I was talking to Jay, and he said that *Cooking with Angelo* is playing in New York."

Angelo put his hands on his hips and treated me to his glamorous smile. "Ah yes, yes. They have been breaking into that market, so. We wait to see how it goes."

"Angelo! You need to tell me these things!"

He moved closer to me while he pulled a phone from his pocket and glanced at it. He tossed it back into his pocket and said, "Lilah *mia*, you become so nervous. Remember the first time on my show? You almost fainted. Why would I complicate the ease you now feel?"

"That's beside the point. I was unaware that my face was appearing in New York."

"Are you wanted by the police in that state?" Angelo

joked. This was rare for Angelo; he normally wasn't sarcastic, and clearly he was delighted with his own comment. He grinned at me.

"Hilarious."

"You have signed a contract, Lilah, and the contract says that the show may eventually appear in cities besides Chicago."

"Well, still. It would be nice to get a heads-up."

He feigned solemnity. "From now on I will mention things of this nature."

A woman stopped next to us. "Oh my gosh! It's Angelo." She poked her companion. "It's Angelo from *Cooking with Angelo*! And you're Lilah!" She pointed at me.

This had probably happened to Angelo before, but it had never happened to me. He shook the woman's hand. "Yes, I am Angelo, and this is my restaurant, Cardelini's. You have eaten here, no?"

The woman gibbered on for a moment about how much she liked the food, and Angelo pointed at me. "And Lilah does a wonderful job, yes?"

"Oh, you do!" the woman said, now facing me with her gushing enthusiasm. I could feel the blush rising on my face, and it grew hotter when she said, "Can I have your autograph?"

She produced a little notebook, and I wrote, "Cook with love," which was Angelo's sign-off phrase, and then my name. It felt surreal to be signing an autograph for a stranger while confronting an ex-lover on the sidewalk about being on television in New York.

Angelo signed for her, too, and then gave her a kiss on

the cheek, which had her howling with joy, and then he signed an autograph for her friend, and posed for a picture with them, and then yanked me against him so that they could photograph us together.

Finally I pulled away and said, "I have to run, Angelo." And I did actually run back to my car and drive away before the starstruck ladies could jot down my license number.

When I finally reached the safety of my own driveway, I found a text from Jay Parker. I'm thinking of you, too. Give me a call.

With a sigh of relief I went into my house, set down my books, and let out Mick, who had been cooped up for far too long and, despite a brief noon escape courtesy of Britt, was still quite eager to go outside.

I let Mick back in and fed him some dinner, then made myself a sandwich and grabbed a little bag of deli chips, which I took to my counter table along with a can of Diet Coke. "Ah," I said.

My phone rang, and I grabbed it from the counter without getting up. "Hello?"

"Hi—Lilah Drake, please."

"This is Lilah."

"Oh, hi. You left a message on my machine about a photo session? This is Wade Glenning."

"Oh, right. Yes. First off, I have to ask—what would you charge for, say, a half-hour session? I'm interested in taking some nice, romantic pictures for my boyfriend."

"You mean boudoir photos?"

My face grew hot. Even over the phone people could

make me blush. "No, not those. Just—you know—tasteful, pretty, romantic shots that he'll enjoy looking at. We both work and we're apart a lot, so—"

"I get you. I can do that, no problem. Do you want this done in your home, or did you want to come to my studio?"

"Uh—in my home."

"That would cost two hundred, but that includes a file with all the retouched digital photos and an eight-by-ten, a five-by-seven, and three sheets of wallets—you choose the shots."

"Um." I hadn't expected it to cost quite so much, but I had some money stowed away, thanks to the two jobs I'd been working since Christmas. "Okay, I'd like to do it. When can we shoot?"

He rustled some paper. "I have openings on Thursday and Friday. Do you have a time in mind?"

"I work weekdays until two," I said.

We went back and forth until we decided on Thursday at four. "Choose at least three different outfits," he said. "And make one of them sexy. Something low-cut."

"Uh—?"

"It will look very tasteful in the photo. You said romantic, but guys find sexy romantic. And if I know guys, which I do, you should wear your hair down. No fancy buns or ponytails."

"Okay," I said, blushing again because I'd been planning to pin my hair up.

"See you then, Lilah."

I thanked him and hung up the phone, only to have my

doorbell ring. I felt nervous every time someone rang my bell, because my house was off the beaten path, so it wasn't visible to every solicitor who wandered by.

I peered around my kitchen wall to see a familiar head of blond curls. To my vast surprise, it was Will, the culinary student from Haven who spent most of the day arguing with Gabby. Will and I were merely work associates, and I had never told him where I lived. I hesitated, tempted to pretend I wasn't home, but a part of me was extremely curious about why Will would come to my house.

Curiosity won out, and I strode through the living room with Mick at my heels to open the door. "Hey, Lilah," Will said, looking a bit nervous. He was holding a large navy blue book.

"Hey."

He must have seen a question in my face, because he said, "I know this is weird, but I looked you up in the online white pages. I figured you should see this, I guess." He held up the book.

"Come on in," I said.

He followed me, looking around. "I should probably show this to Jay, too. Is he here?" He bent to scratch Mick's head, but I could still see the hopeful expression on his face. He had some serious Jay Parker hero worship.

"Not right now. What's this all about?" I pointed to a chair in my living room, and he sat down.

"Remember this morning, you were talking about that

whole new investigation Jay had? And I said I remembered that kid Cash Cantwell from high school?"

"Yes."

"So I guess I was just curious; I went back to my senior yearbook to see what Cash wrote in it. We had a couple classes together, so we were pretty friendly that whole year. You know how it is with high school friendships. They feel so permanent, and then you graduate and never see that person again."

"That's true, mostly."

"Anyway, I found what he wrote. Open the back cover and look on the flyleaf."

I took his book, which was called *The Pine Haven Papyrus*. The theme for the year was "Beyond Our Wildest Dreams," and the front cover bore an etching of a ladder going into the clouds. I flipped to the back page and said, "Oh my."

"Yeah, sorry about all the swearing. Kids who sign it just think *you're* going to read the stuff, not—other people."

I navigated through all the bawdy suggestions and f-words until I spied the name "Cash." His handwriting was surprisingly neat and precise compared with some of the barely legible scrawls on the page. He had written, "Hey, Will. Let's be sure to open that bar in Jamaica just like we planned. You get your mom to donate her awesome car, and I'll poison my dad for my inheritance."

He had signed it with his name and a little picture of a beer bottle with a fancy umbrella in it.

I stared hard at the page. He had been a teenager, and

he was joking around. Right? Except that he had said *poison*. Did that bear further scrutiny? Was it just a co-incidence that Cantwell's son had joked about poisoning him, and two years later Cantwell was dead by poison?

"You're right," I said. "This is a big deal. And we need to tell Jay."

CHAPTER SEVEN

WE CALLED PARKER, WHO SAID HE WAS TOO BUSY to come out but that we could stop by the station with whatever it was we wanted him to see.

I told this to Will, who was clearly tempted by a chance to access Parker's domain. "Aw man. I can't—I have a class in half an hour. But tell him hi for me. I'll leave the book with you, and you can give it back to me tomorrow, unless they end up using it as police evidence or something."

"Okay. Thanks for bringing this by, Will. I'm sure it's nothing, and yet it does seem—odd."

"Yeah, my feelings exactly. But Cash was always a cool kid, so I feel kind of like a traitor bringing this here. Still, man. That's a pretty weird coincidence."

"Yes," I said. I walked him to the door, and he looked around without disguising his curiosity.

"This is a pretty cool place."

"Thank you."

"I almost didn't find it; your number is 2157, but that big place in front of you is 2155, and the one next door is 2159, and I was like—how did it jump from 7 to 9?"

"Yeah, I'm sort of tucked away here."

"It's awesome. I would never even think of looking at a place like this to rent out. It's way better than renting in some big apartment house."

"Yes, it is. I am very lucky."

Will tucked some of his blond hair behind his ear and hovered in my doorway. I was tempted to start inching the door closed in the hope that he would get the hint.

"Hey, one quick thing," he said, attempting a casual look but achieving a young and vulnerable one instead. "What's your take on Gabby? Do you think she's going out with anyone?"

"*Finally*," I said.

"What?"

"I'm glad you're finally admitting that you like her."

"What? I didn't say that!" he said, clearly thunderstruck.

"Will. Don't be a jerk. You have liked her since you started working at Haven, and what's more, she likes you. Although if you confronted her she'd probably be like you and deny it, so do me a favor and just pull her into a corner somewhere and kiss her and be done with it."

"What?" he asked, with a dumb little smile.

I sighed. "Everyone sees it but you two. You are attracted to each other. Ask her on a date, and she will probably say yes, after her initial surprise."

"Wow. Okay, well—okay. I'll think about it."

"Just do it, Will."

"Okay. See you, Lilah."

He moved down the walk, and I saw for the first time that he was driving a little white Smart Car. He climbed into it and backed down the driveway. From a distance, his abundant hair looked like a halo.

THE PINE HAVEN Police Department was housed in an ivy-covered building in the center of town. Today the parking lot was almost full, and I wondered how many vehicles belonged to visitors, and what they all needed from the police on a Monday evening.

Parker had instructed me to go through the lobby, where I should say his name to the security guard and then proceed to the elevator and up to the third floor. I did this, and the doors opened to reveal a spacious room with offices at the outer perimeter and about a dozen desks in the center. Directly in front of the elevator was a large reception desk, at which sat a dark-haired woman wearing a crisp white blouse and a phone headset. She held up a finger to me to indicate that I should wait, then said, "Pine Haven Police, Homicide and Investigations, how may I help you?" She listened with a patient expression, then said, "I'll transfer you to that department. Thank you," and punched some buttons on her phone. Then she hung up and said, "Can I help you?"

"I'm here to see Jay Parker," I said. "He's expec—"

"Are you *Lilah*?" she asked, her face brightening into friendliness.

"Uh—yes."

She stood up and offered her hand. "Oh my gosh, you made that delicious dessert casserole that Jay brought a couple months ago! We're all still remembering it very fondly. I'm Penny."

"Hi," I said. "I can make more anytime."

"That would be awesome." She pointed to a far corner. "Jay's office is back there by the water fountain. He might be in Maria's office, though, or maybe with the chief. Hang on."

She clicked a button on her phone, and in a moment I heard her voice on an intercom. "Jay Parker, please call the front desk. Jay Parker."

She winked at me. "I don't usually do that, but I thought just this once."

It had the desired effect; Parker poked his head out of an office, his brows raised. Then he spied me and waved. "Lilah, come on back," he said.

I had never been in Parker's professional environment. I had stopped by the station once when I was still harboring a big crush on him; he had given me his jacket, and I went to the PD to return it, hoping to get some time with him and see where he worked. Instead, Maria had claimed the jacket and I hadn't gotten farther than the lobby.

Now I studied the large room with its old, dignified chandeliers and surprisingly bright work space, even in the light of the setting sun. I walked past several cubicles where people at desks made no secret of their curiosity, to the point that I was blushing intensely by the time I reached Parker, who looked a bit harried but gave me a peck on the cheek while everyone watched. He grinned, then said, "Let me introduce you to some people. You know Maria, right?"

Maria had come striding out of an office, studying a file, and now she looked up and said, "Hey, Lilah!"

"Hi. Good to see you," I told her, feeling shy. I was distracted as always by Parker's good looks; today he wore a white shirt with the sleeves rolled up. It was tucked neatly into a pair of black pants, and he wore a blue-and-black silk tie that was slightly askew. His tanned forearms made a handsome contrast with the whiteness of his shirt, and my gaze kept traveling to them and the hint of muscle visible when he moved.

"Let me introduce you to our boss," Parker said, clasping my arm and pulling me toward a corner office.

I looked back over my shoulder at Maria and said, "Hang on—you're going to want to see this, too."

She gave me a thumbs-up and moved gracefully over to the drinking fountain.

Parker led me into an office where a white-haired man sat talking on the phone. While Pine Haven PD seemed to have a diverse workforce in its main room, that didn't seem to be the case when one moved up the ladder.

The man ended his call and said, "What's up, Jay?"

"Sir, this is my girlfriend, Lilah Drake. Lilah, this is our captain, Zane Harris."

Parker had never introduced me as his girlfriend before, and my smile was probably stupid as I shook the captain's hand. He said, "It's nice to meet you, Lilah. We've all heard a great deal about you. I guess we can't overwork Jay as much as we did in the past, now that he has a special someone in his life. He might even want to take some of his vacation time."

I laughed, and Parker put an affectionate arm around me.

"What brings you here today, Lilah?" asked Harris.

"Oh—uh—someone came to me with something they thought might be pertinent to Jay's case. That is, the murder of Mr. Cantwell."

Harris's face was shrewd. "I understand you were there when that happened."

"When he collapsed, yes. The drink was delivered before I got there."

The captain's phone rang, and Jay said, "I'll check in later, Zane," and the captain waved as he picked up the receiver.

Jay still had his arm around me, and he steered me to his office, a fairly large room with a desk and a window that overlooked Paris Park. "This is nice, Jay!" Distracted from my task, I darted away from him to study the knick-knacks on his desk and walls. On the wall facing the desk he had a nature calendar and a framed picture of the Chicago skyline. There was a tall bookcase against the wall behind his desk, on which he had some impressive stone lion bookends and a statue of a knight in armor. Grouped around these were lots and lots of books about law and policing. "Have you read all these?" I asked.

"Some were there when I got the office. I've read the ones I brought in, yes."

"That's sexy, Jay. Women love a man who reads."

"Huh," he said, riffling through some mail he found on a table by the door.

I focused on his desk and was confronted by my own image, enlarged to a five-by-seven and framed in faux gold. It was a slightly out-of-focus picture he had taken on his phone. I was glad that soon I'd have a better one to give him—one that would guarantee he was always slightly distracted.

"I guess you should show me what you've got there, Lilah. I hate to say it, but I don't have a lot of time."

"I know, I know. Hey, this paperweight is neat!" It was a glass ball with an autumn leaf preserved inside.

"Thanks. Lilah?"

"Oh yeah. I hate to even bring this up, because I really like Cash Cantwell."

Jay's face grew sharp with interest. "So?"

I pulled Will's yearbook from my capacious purse. "This guy Will who works at Haven mentioned that he went to high school with Cash. I had told him that you were working on a new case. Remember when you met Will and Gabby one time when you came to pick me up?"

"Those kids who act like they're in a romantic comedy?"

"Yup. They've both been fascinated by you since then. They're always asking about what you're doing. Anyway, Cash's name came up, and Will was surprised. Then tonight he showed up at my door with this yearbook that Cash signed when they graduated. Look at the back flyleaf."

Parker sat down at his desk so that he could study the book; I stood behind him and massaged his shoulders.

"That's nice," Parker said. "Wow, these kids swear a lot."

"I know. Did you find Cash?"

His shoulders tensed. "Oh boy," he said.

"Weird, right?"

He stood up and turned to face me, leaning against his desk. "I need to talk to him. I get to indulge in your prettiness for two more minutes, and then I really need to go. I still have a few interviews I have to do tonight."

"I probably won't see you later, then. I have to head to bed early and be at work early to get ready for a weekday birthday party."

He smoothed the hair at my temples. "Sorry about that. Things are very important in the hours right after the crime."

"I know. I get it. Oh, but Jay? All sorts of people have been asking to meet you. My friend Jenny just got engaged. Remember her, from the Christmas party we went to?"

"I remember I kissed you at that party."

The memory had me feeling a little dizzy, as did the look in Parker's eyes. "Well, she wants us to get together for dinner Friday—you, me, and her fiancé, Ross."

"I'll say a tentative yes. Maria can cover for me."

"Great. But then we also have a Saturday and a Sunday invitation."

"Hmm. What are they?"

"Saturday at Britt's gallery. She's showing a painting by Prudence Cantwell."

His brows went up. "That one I definitely want to attend. I assume her family will be there; sometimes it's easier to talk to people in a casual setting than in a formal one. So far the Cantwells have helped not at all. You've actually learned more than I have—this yearbook and Prue's showing. Yeah, we'll be going to that one, and you put your observation goggles on."

"Okay. I like it when we're cop partners," I said.

Parker grinned. "What's Sunday?"

"Cam and Fina want to have us over."

He nodded. "That's fine, but I'll have to work first. Maria can take second shift. So tell them dinnertime."

"Great! I'm so excited that I get to show you off to everyone."

"Like I just did with you?"

"I did feel like I was being scrutinized. Is that because they're all cops?"

"It's because you're lovely, and because they all want to see Parker's girlfriend. They probably didn't believe I had one."

"Seriously? They probably thought you had twelve."

He shrugged. "I've always been a devoted-to-the-job kind of guy."

"Now you're devoted to Lilah." I pulled his head down

toward me and gave him a warm kiss. Then, reluctantly, I moved away. "Do you need that yearbook, or can I give it back to Will?"

"I'll bring it back to Haven tomorrow. Then I can mooch some food like always."

I laughed. "Esther has you figured out, although she seems to love feeding you."

"Just like you." He took my hand and walked me to the door. "Thanks for the tip. I'll talk to you soon."

Maria Grimaldi appeared at the door, holding an apple and looking vaguely like a model in a police station shoot. "Here's dinner," she said cheerfully. "So what's so important, Lilah?"

Jay handed her the book, open to Cash's note, and pointed. She read it and frowned, and suddenly I remembered that Maria's niece had a crush on Cash. Maria exchanged a look with Parker that I did not understand; it was clear that, Parker's girlfriend or not, I would not be privy to cop conversations about suspects.

"I'm sure it's not Cash," I said. "He was very philosophical today about his father's death."

"Today?" Maria and Parker asked in unison.

"Oh—yeah, I forgot to mention. I ran into him and Peach at the bookstore, and he was saying that it was sad his dad died on his birthday, just like Cassius in *Julius Caesar*. The character he's named for. And he told me how his dad chose the name and everything. He clearly misses his father."

Parker and Grimaldi looked unmoved. "Murderers can be sad about what they've done," Grimaldi said. "They often are, in fact." She gave the book back to Jay and sighed. "Let's hope that in this case you're right, Lilah."

When I left they were talking, their heads close together. At one time that would have made me insanely jealous, but now I felt quite content, because I genuinely believed that Parker cared about only one woman.

I DROVE HOME through a Pine Haven fragrant with spring while my CD player regaled me with Leonard Cohen's "Hallelujah" and I tried to sing along. It put me in a reverent mood, and when I reached my little house, I reunited with a joyful Mick, snapped on his leash, and headed down the driveway for our evening walk. As I passed Britt and Terry's place, I noticed that Terry was kneeling under one window, snipping some lilacs from a low bush.

"Hey, Terry."

Terry jumped up and turned to face us. "Hey, guys! Taking the ol' evening constitutional?"

"Yeah. Wow, those flowers smell good. Your yard is an exercise in sensory pleasure."

"Britt is the one who loves the flowers. I had a lot of these trees put in when she and I first got together."

Even in the dusky light I could see a shadow pass over his face. Terry was always cheerful, always positive, so it was odd to see him looking—what? At best his expression was pensive; at worst it might even have signaled sadness. "Is everything okay, Terry?"

He shrugged. "Yeah, I think so. I mean—have you noticed anything weird about Britt lately?"

"Weird? She seemed fine yesterday when we were talking to Prue Cantwell. Although . . ."

"Although what? You noticed something?"

"She just seemed to get bummed out at the end, after Prue left. She looked sort of sad, but she didn't want to talk about it."

"Yeah, exactly! She doesn't want to talk to me, either, but something's clearly bugging her." He sighed and stared at the lilacs in his hands, as though he had forgotten they were there. Then he looked at me with a new gleam in his eyes. "Listen, Lilah. You know I love Britt and we've always been good together, but I'm a guy, and I ran out of ways to try to talk to her about whatever is going on. But I care, you know? I guess I'm just not saying the stuff she wants to hear. Is there any way—can you approach her, woman to woman, and try to find out what's up? She just hasn't been herself. I miss my happy Britta."

"I don't know if you really want me in the middle of things, Terry—"

"I do. I'd really appreciate it, Lilah."

I sighed. It didn't seem like a good idea, but Britt and Terry were my good friends, and they were always ready to help me when I needed their aid. At Christmas, they had offered me a bedroom when my broken window was being replaced. "Okay. I will definitely try to talk with her soon. I'm going to her gallery Saturday, so if I don't catch her before then, I can try some time Saturday night, if things aren't too busy for her. Would that be okay?"

"Yeah, that's great. And afterward, maybe you can spare a minute to fill me in. Whatever you hear, okay?"

I must not have looked enthusiastic, because he said, "You don't know how much I appreciate this, Lilah. I know I always seem happy-go-lucky, and I mostly am. But Britt is my weakness. I really love her, and I—lately I've started to think I'm going to lose her."

I put my free hand on his arm. "I'm sure that's not it, Terry. Don't jump to the worst scenario. She might just be having a sad spell. I'll talk to her."

"You're the best," he said with a big smile. "You want some lilacs?"

I laughed. "No, thanks. Britt already gave me a bunch of cherry blossoms, and my house smells like heaven."

Mick tugged on the leash, impatient, and I began to walk. I waved at Terry and shouted a friendly good night. He waved, looking more vulnerable than I had ever seen him.

As Mick and I turned out of the long driveway onto Dickens Street, I said, "Boy, love sure can mess people up, can't it, Mick?"

Mick, who was leading our expedition, was facing away from me, but I thought I saw his head nodding slightly as he marched down the sidewalk.

CHAPTER EIGHT

AFTER WORK ON THURSDAY I RUSHED HOME, GAVE
Mick an abbreviated walk, and then chose my ward-
robe for the photo session. The first outfit was an apricot-
colored dress with a square neckline; Parker had admired
it once and said that the color looked nice with my hair. The
second choice was a flowery spring romper with a femi-
nine collar that I thought would look romantic in pictures.
The third choice—the one the photographer had said should
be sexy—was a silky chocolate brown blouse with a short
black skirt. I had received the blouse as a gift from Serafina
but had never worn it because it had no buttons or zippers,
just two overlapping front silk panels. The effect was something outrageously low-cut, suitable only for a model on
location in a casino or on a yacht. I would have to wear it

Julia Buckley

without a bra, and I supposed if it were just for a photo it could look quite nice, as long as I didn't have to interact with anyone or try to move my arms or function in a real-life way. As a fantasy, the blouse was perfect.

When Wade Glenning arrived with a young assistant, who looked a bit like a frightened rabbit, he approved of my choices; I was wearing the flowery romper, and he said that it had a Victorian look. "Sort of like a girl in a locket," he said. "I can make something of that." He strolled around the house and then said, "Your kitchen has the best light. Let's work in there."

He took one of the high stools from my counter and set it in the center of the room. The assistant, a college photography major he introduced as Stella, took a little comb and flicked it carefully through my hair. She breathed rather loudly in my ear and made me feel nervous.

Wade positioned himself at the window, with the light at his back, and worked on securing his camera into a tripod. He was more handsome than I remembered from the party, with a head of thick brown hair and an intense expression that some girls might have thought of as soulful. He smiled at me while he worked. "So you were at the Cantwell thing the other day. What did you make of that whole scene?"

I tried to smooth my hair, at which point Stella darted in and started flicking her comb through it again. "Oh, it was terrible. I feel bad for all the kids. They seem like a pretty close-knit group, considering they're stepsiblings."

He nodded. "Yeah, I guess. I only really know Cash—

he's the cool one. And I sort of know Prudence. She hit on me one time, but I shut that down." He smiled a little at the memory. "Stell, can you go out to the car and grab my other lens? I didn't find it in this bag."

Stella darted down the hall and out the front door.

"Prue Cantwell really hit on you? It seems like you could do a lot worse than Prue Cantwell, by the way."

"Oh, no doubt. She's gorgeous. But like I said, Cash is my friend, and I wouldn't want to jeopardize that by getting involved with his family. They seem—complicated."

"Yeah, I guess. But every family has its issues, right?"

"Lift up your chin; let me check the light here. Good. The light is just perfect right now; it's making your hair glow."

"Great. So how long have you known Cash?"

Stella ran in with the new lens and then moved to Glenning's photo bag to root around.

He thought about my question while he snapped a few test shots. "About two years. He was still in school, I know, and I had just graduated. I have this friend Amber and she knew Cash. At one point we were at the same party, and she introduced us, and we hit it off. And we've been friends ever since."

"And Amber? Is she still his friend, too?"

His face grew shuttered. "Absolutely. She'll always be his friend."

I thought that was a weird response, but I didn't have time to think, because his instructions began. *Tilt your head; smile gently; now smile with your teeth; now be seri-*

ous. I realized that I would make a terrible model, because I felt weirdly conscious of my face and was forgetting how to make it do things.

Wade seemed to sense this. "Okay, I want you to pretend that there's something in your backyard, but you can't quite get it in focus. Look out there—it's a mystery! What is that thing? Good. Good." He snapped some more pictures while I stared at the mysterious thing that wasn't there.

"Okay. I've got some great ones in this outfit. You want to change into the dress now?"

"Sure."

"Do you want Stella to help you?"

Stella looked about as eager to help me as I was to have her help. "Oh, no, thanks—I've got it." Stella looked relieved. She pushed her dark hair behind her ears and knelt to pet Mick.

I changed in my room upstairs, swiftly, since I knew my session was short. I came back, and Wade took me all the way outside and had me pose under my budding elm tree. This time I was instructed to look playful. "It's not winter, but pretend you have a snowball, and you're waiting for someone—who would you like to ambush with a snowball?"

"My brother," I said.

"Okay, so your brother is about to come around the corner. You're about to nail him. Imagine how that would make you feel. Great! Very playful. That's a good one, Lilah." *Click, click, click.* "And now, think about his face after he gets hit with the snowball. Well, that's an interesting expression! Do you hate your brother or something?"

"No, not at all. We just enjoy hassling each other. And in fact last winter Cam happened to surprise me with a snowball during the Christmas holidays, and he laughed for *far* too long."

He chuckled and took a few more shots, posing me under the tree, near my little barn of a garage, and against the fence, studying the one tulip I had in my garden. Occasionally he ordered Stella to hold up a weird thing that looked like an umbrella.

I sent him what I hoped was a casual glance. "So not to be nosy, but who's this Amber? I thought Cash liked Lola."

He raised his eyebrows. "You have the inside scoop, huh? Well, it's kind of complicated, but no, he's not involved with Amber. Not that way, at least. I don't know. I mean, it's Cash's business, but—anyway, I like Lola. She's a nice girl."

"She seems to still have feelings for him, but he doesn't realize it. That seems to be going around lately."

He raised his brows again. "What do you mean?"

"Oh, just some people I work with. Same kind of dynamic."

"Huh. Yeah, Cash is the type who will always have the ladies around him. He's got charisma." His face was something between respectful and jealous. "We can go in now."

As we walked back toward the sliding glass door of

my kitchen, I said, "You have charisma, too. You've made me feel very comfortable doing this, and I was afraid it would be worse than awkward."

"Thanks! That was really nice of you to say." We went inside and he leaned against my kitchen island. He held his camera at his waist and pressed some buttons. "Oh yeah—these look great. Okay—you can switch into your evening outfit now."

That sounded strange, but I went inside and ran upstairs to don the brown silk blouse. When I returned to the kitchen, Wade nodded his approval, and even the seemingly emotionless Stella gave me a thumbs-up. "That's great," Glenning said. "The color brings out your hair and your eyes. Okay, I'm not making a pass, but let me just adjust this a little bit." He lifted the material at my shoulders and shifted the blouse around a bit. "There. Great." He was looking at his camera when he said, "So, you're pretty and you know Cash. I'm wondering if you and he were ever an item."

I laughed. "Number one, Cash is about six years younger than I am. Number two, I just met him at his dad's party."

Something fluttered in his eyes. "So you were just there?"

"I went with a friend of mine. She lives next door."

"Ah."

I realized that this moment was the sort of thing Parker would want me to pursue. Trying to sound casual, I said, "I know they're saying someone walked in there to Mr.

Cantwell and handed him a poisoned drink. It's so hard to imagine! Do you remember seeing anything?"

He paused in the adjustment of his camera. "I don't think so—I've been trying to go over it in my head. Do you think the police will ask me that?"

"I don't know. They haven't asked me anything yet."

"It's funny—I never really liked their dad. I mean, I wasn't around when they were growing up, but in all the time I've known Cash, I always thought the dad was kind of a jerk."

I remembered my instinctive discomfort around Cantwell when I stood in his living room; but Ellie had assured me that he was a delightful man, misunderstood by many. "What made you think he was a jerk?"

He shrugged. "Let's get you right in the window here; yeah, that's good. Just leave your arms by your sides, but look at the camera. Pretend there's a little tiny mouse peeking out of the lens. Yeah, good. Amused is good; now pretend it's not a mouse but a lizard. Okay, that one didn't work."

We both laughed; Stella made a sort of snorting sound, and Mick licked her cheek. I said, "It's got to be a challenge, getting people in touch with their own faces."

Wade was fussing with his camera again. "Yeah. It's fun, though. You actually have very mobile features. It makes for interesting photographs. And your eyes have a lot of depth, especially in this light."

"Wow." Then, trying to sound casual: "Anyway, you were saying, about Mr. Cantwell?"

He grinned. "I wasn't saying, but okay, if you want some gossip. I would be over there sometimes, and I'd hear him laying into the two older brothers for one thing or another. Don't get me wrong; those two are idiots, and they probably deserved it. They're like Laurel and Hardy dressed in expensive suits. And that Scott thinks he's the only person who's ever had a law degree. It's kind of pathetic."

His lip twisted as he snapped some more pictures. "But maybe they got it from him—from Marcus. He never had a kind word to say, as far as I could tell."

"Did you ever speak to him?"

"Look out the window now. Pretend you're pining away for someone. Like a woman waiting for her lost sailor."

This one wasn't hard; I recalled too well how it felt to miss Parker.

"That's good! Yeah, I spoke to him now and again. I talked to him on the day he died, too, but only for a minute or so. I said happy birthday and stuff and then got back to work. He did thank me for taking pictures—I'll give him that. But of course he was paying me handsomely. Or maybe the kids were. I'm not sure who was footing the bill. But I did get paid."

I thought about this while Wade Glenning poked at my shoulders. "Don't hunch up; that ruins the effect," he said.

"Do you think Marcus was hard on Cash?"

"Hell yeah. Cash didn't even want to go into finance, which is what his dad had him majoring in. It's funny, because he clearly liked Cash the best—well, everyone does—and yet it was like he kept trying to turn Cash into Scott or Owen. He couldn't just let Cash be Cash, which is a strength, not a weakness. He couldn't let people be what they were, and even Amber—" He looked almost angry when he said this, and he snapped his mouth shut.

"This Amber sounds intriguing. Was she at the party?"

I had lost him again; it was almost physical, the way he receded inside himself. "She was there for a while, yeah. Okay, a couple more and we'll be done. I want you to look away, and then quickly look back at me. Let your hair fly around a little. Don't worry—it will look good."

I did it, feeling stupid. "Good! Yeah, that's good. You'll be surprised. You look mysterious, and definitely sexy, if you'll forgive me for saying it."

"I don't mind anyone calling me sexy," I said. "The question is whether or not I believe them."

He laughed again. "Okay, we're all done. Let me and Stell stow some stuff in my car, and then I'll give you a sneak preview on my camera."

"Great—thanks!"

As soon as he went out to the driveway I grabbed my phone and pressed speed dial number one: Jay Parker. He answered tersely. "Jay! It's Lilah. I only have a second. You need to ask Cash Cantwell about someone named Amber."

"Amber? Amber who?"

"I have no idea; he just said Amber."

"He who? You need to be more specific, Lilah."

"Wade. Oh, shoot. I can't talk now."

I heard Parker saying something in the background, but I was focused on looking innocently at Wade Glenning as he came back into the kitchen. "Okay, you ready to see some great shots?"

"Sure," I said. Into the phone I said, "Thanks so much for calling, but I have to get going. Maybe I'll catch up with you later."

"Lilah, what's going on?"

"Oh, nothing. So will you be stopping by tonight? I can make dinner."

"That sounds good," Parker said, his voice wary.

"Okay. Talk to you later. I love you." I clicked off the phone.

Wade was already seated at the stool on which I had posed, scrolling through photos. "Take a look at these," he said. Stella had apparently not returned.

Curious, I leaned down and looked at his display screen. The woman in the photos seemed to be me, but a much better version of me. "Oh wow," I said. Then, as he kept scrolling: "Oh wow! It's going to be really hard to decide."

"Like I said, you'll get a whole CD full of photos, so you can select quite a few of them. Then I'll touch them up, although it doesn't look like they'll need much work. I can have it to you in about a week."

"That will be great," I said. "Thanks so much, Wade. I know you must have a busy schedule."

He shrugged and flicked off his camera, then started zipping it into a case. "On weekends, yeah. Weekdays are easier, especially with Stell around. So it just worked out."

I went into the next room and wrote him a check, then returned and handed it to him. He thanked me, pulled out his wallet, and tucked the check inside. Something suddenly dawned on me. "Hey—you were taking photos at the party.

Don't you think the police will want to study them, just to see if they can spot any clues?"

He frowned. "They were at my house the next day. They said I could give them my camera or they would subpoena it, so I figured I'd just hand it over. They said they'll have it back to me soon. Meanwhile I'm working with a spare. Good thing I have that, or my business would be in jeopardy, right?"

"Yeah. Still, what if they find the murderer from your photos? That would be pretty great. You might be famous."

He laughed. "Yeah, I doubt that. But sure, glad to help. And that one cop is pretty hot—the tall, dark-haired one?"

"That's Lola's aunt—did you know?"

He stood still. "No, I didn't. So she—is related to Lola? Wow. That's a weird coincidence."

"I guess."

He put his wallet in his back pocket and slung his camera bag over his shoulder. "Nice working with you, Lilah. I'll be in touch next week. Your boyfriend is a lucky man. And it's sweet that you guys say *I love you* over the phone. My family was never big on the *I love you's*, but it's nice when someone's not afraid to say it out loud."

"Uh—yeah." I walked him to the front door, waved as he walked to his car, and shut the door, then locked it. Then I went to my couch and collapsed on it, saying, "Oh no, oh no, oh no." Mick walked up to me, concerned enough to leave his basket, and I shook my head. "I blew it, Mick."

I staggered into the kitchen and dialed speed dial number three: Jenny Braidwell. "Hello," said Jenny's sweet voice.

"Jenn. I have an emergency."

"Lilah? What's going on? Are you okay?"

"I was talking with Parker on the phone. But I was distracted, because I had someone else over, and I was trying to send Parker kind of a secret message, and then this other person walked in—"

"Slow down, Lilah. It's okay."

"No, no! Because I had to go, and I said I'd see him later, and then I said *I love you* just before I hung up the phone. Just automatically, the way I say it to Cam or my parents."

"So?"

"So we aren't at the *I love you* stage, and Parker is the most restrained person on earth, and he certainly won't want to be rushed into love, and I might have blown it. What if he gets all distant now, like he used to be? He's been so sweet and friendly lately, and now I've probably scared him half to death, and he hasn't called back—oh God, he hasn't called back! Isn't that a terrible sign?"

"Lilah." Jenny's voice was decidedly calm and tinged with sarcasm. "Stop for a second and listen to reason."

"Okay."

"First. He is at work. Even if he wanted to talk about this, do you think he can do it in a busy police station in the middle of the day?"

"No, maybe not. I don't know."

"Second. Do you love him?"

"What? I don't know! Yes."

"I'm going to assume your third response was the truth," she said lightly. "So if that's the case, you have every right to say it."

"Jenny, you don't know Jay Parker."

"No, but you do—so well that you fell in love with him. You can't stop that train, and neither can he. Just go with it now."

"What is that supposed to mean?"

"'Que Sera, Sera.' Remember that Doris Day song your mom used to sing with us, back when we were in college and she made us watch old movies?"

"Yes. Oh God. Am I overreacting like a weird teen-ager?"

"Yes. But it's cute. I haven't seen you this moonstruck since the early Angelo days."

"Oh no—*Angelo*! I have to be on the show tomorrow, and I don't have my food prepared. I have to run."

"Everything will be fine. Hey, can you two come for dinner tomorrow night?"

"Yeah. He might have to join me there, but he said yes. Assuming I haven't scared him off."

"Lilah, don't be silly. Go do your job, and later on you can talk to Jay like a mature, sexy woman."

"God, now that you're engaged you sound like a television psychologist."

She giggled. "See you tomorrow. I'll text you with the details."

We said good-bye and hung up; Mick was still watching me with doggy concern. "She's right, Mick. What's done is done." Mick nodded.

I ran back into my kitchen and started assembling ingredients. Not only did I have to make an Irish one-pot stew on Angelo's show, but I had to deliver a Reuben sandwich casserole to one of my private clients, and I hadn't started either one. It had been a long day already. . . .

Two hours later I was almost finished and washing my hands at the sink; such had been my state of flow as I worked that I realized for the first time that I still wore my sexy silk blouse and short black skirt. This made me laugh aloud, and Mick lifted his head in his basket, ready to share the joke. I called him to the door so that he could go out for his evening yard walk.

"I don't normally try to be alluring just to work with food, Mick," I told him. He didn't seem to find it as absurd as I did. He went outside and sniffed around; two minutes later he came back in.

Still smiling, I went into the living room and headed for my little spiral staircase, bound for my bed and some relaxing TV watching. The dinner hour had come and gone; I had no idea when (or if) to expect Parker, and I was suddenly weary. As I pulled off my shoes, I thought about what Wade Glenning had said about Marcus Cantwell. Every single person who had known Cantwell painted him as a different sort of person. Jay had known him as a good, fatherly influence. Most of his children suggested a sort of Jekyll and Hyde type of father, alternately neglectful and indulgent, while Wade Glenning depicted him as critical and mean, a cold father. I sighed and glanced out the front window in time to see police lights on Dickens Street. To my shock, they turned into my driveway and came all the way back in the growing dusk. The lights went off and the car materialized into Jay's. He leaped out and ran to my door.

Fear paralyzed me, and I couldn't even bring myself to open the door right away when Jay pounded on it. What was this? Why was he speeding to my house? What terrible news could he have?

I finally got the door open, and Parker lunged in. He grabbed my arms, about to say something, but then his eyes darted down to my daring outfit. "I— Lilah, what are you wearing?"

"Oh—I—this—ha-ha. It's kind of funny—"

"Was that a man's voice I heard on the phone?"

"Um—yes. That was Wade," I said. "What's going on?"

"What do you mean, *That was Wade*? Who's Wade?"

"Parker, I—it's a secret. I don't want to talk about it." For the life of me I couldn't figure out a good excuse, especially under his intense scrutiny, and I felt a bit angry that he was trying to ruin my surprise. I scowled up at him, and his face, normally shuttered and uncommunicative, flashed several emotions at once: surprise, jealousy . . . and fear. It was the last one that made me relent.

"Lilah—?"

"Okay, fine. You've ruined it." I punched his arm.

"Ow," he said automatically, his face still shocked.

"Wade is a photographer. I was trying to take some sexy pictures. For *you*. They were supposed to be a surprise. I thought maybe if I gave you the pictures, you—"

"I what?"

I looked past him, out the window at his car, and said, "No, *you* answer some questions now. Why did you come racing up my driveway with your police lights on? What the hell is going on? Did someone get murdered again?"

He shook his head. "No. I was in a hurry, so I cheated. I've never done that before."

"What do you mean, you cheated?"

"I used my lights to get through traffic more quickly."

"Why?"

He slid his arms around my waist. "You keep scowling at me."

"Parker, I swear to God, I am about to punch you again if you don't—"

He put his face an inch from mine. "You told me you loved me on the phone, didn't you?"

I felt the telltale blush on my skin. "Accidentally."

"Because you didn't mean it?"

I stuck out my chin. "No, I meant it."

"I couldn't call back because it got so hectic, so for the last few hours I was worrying, wondering what you would think that I didn't call. But I wanted to come in person."

"Okay—?"

"To say that I love you, too."

We stared at each other.

"Jay," I managed. He yanked me against him and kissed me hard, and my hands floated up into his hair while his slid up and down my back, and then those same hands were stroking the silk of my shirt and sliding beneath it to find my extremely hot skin. "Ah," I said, with my eyes closed; then Parker had turned away, but one of his hands grabbed tightly onto mine, and he pulled me after him as he marched the ten feet to the spiral staircase that led up to my loft bedroom.

We didn't say a word. We got to the top, where my bed sat covered with colorful pillows and a lavender duvet. Parker smiled at it for a moment, and then he pulled me against him once more to press his mouth on mine. "Lilah," he whispered. His lips grew softer, more tender, and he paused for breath, his forehead touching mine. "I see you whenever I close my eyes."

With a burst of intensity I shoved him backward onto my bed; he was laughing when I dove on top of him, but moments later neither of us was laughing and he was flinging pillows onto the floor, muttering, "What is the *point* of all of these?"

"They add something special," I said defensively. "They brighten my world."

He smiled and touched my hair. "That describes you exactly," he said, and his hands slid under the chocolate silk and eased it off my shoulders.

CHAPTER NINE

A T SIX O'CLOCK THE NEXT MORNING WE SHARED A makeshift breakfast of toast and jam, smiling contentedly at each other. "I have room in my closet," I said between bites. "If you ever want to leave some stuff here."

"Me, too," he said. "And I can get a dog bed and some food or whatever. So you wouldn't have to leave early to tend to this guy." He pointed at Mick, who had already eaten and retired to his basket.

I smiled at my dog. "He came wandering up late last night; I think he was surprised to see you there."

"He needs to get used to it," Parker said, studying me with his azure eyes.

"Yeah, he does. Do you feel like . . . resting some more?"

He grinned. "That's tempting, especially because your robe is falling open and I can see some things I'd love to explore in more detail"—I gasped and hastily adjusted my clothing—"but I have to get to work. And you have a TV show to tape, glamorous girlfriend. How about tonight?"

"Tonight we're having dinner with Jenny and Ross. And then after that we can come here. Or your place. Whatever."

"Okay." He stood up and put his plate in the sink. "I'll wash that later," he said, looking at his watch. "I've got to run. I have to stop at home and change my clothes, and if I don't get to work before Maria I will face an elaborate grilling and some intense mockery."

"I take it she saw you go racing out yesterday?"

His face was grim. "She did."

"It was romantic, Parker."

"It was nerve-racking, Lilah. But I'm glad that I sped over here like a madman and finally told you what I've wanted to tell you for what seems like years."

"You're poetic," I said.

"And you're sexy."

"Wait until you see my photos. Wade positioned me in a number of alluring ways."

Parker scowled. "I don't like the idea that this guy was posing you like some doll."

"Oh, Parker. It's funny when you get jealous. Wade didn't notice me at all, except as a subject. I think—he might be in love with someone. I'm just not sure if it's

144

with Cash or this mysterious Amber. He seemed protective of both of them. Did you find out about her?"

"No, because I didn't talk to Cash yesterday. That's on the docket for today." He bent down to kiss my ear. "I have to go, and I'm going to try not to think of you, because otherwise I won't be able to do my job."

"I understand," I said solemnly, and Parker grinned, then blew me a kiss before he disappeared out my back door.

I got up and shifted into gear. I showered and dressed in record time; I returned to the kitchen, pulled out the stew I'd made the night before, and measured out a second set of ingredients to use during the taping. I separated them into their various dishes and containers, then stowed all of the samples and the finished Crock-Pot into a large cardboard box.

Kissing Mick on top of his soft brown head, I promised I'd see him soon. He nodded gently, still half asleep. I moved briskly out to my car and drove to the Chicago studio where Angelo's show was taped. I'd become familiar with the drive and the overall routine, so it was quick work to drive into the lot, show my pass to the attendant, and then march my box inside the old brick building and to the elevator. Soon enough I was standing before Angelo, unpacking my box and listening to his chiding about my lateness.

"And you look too tired. This is not good for television. Tabitha! Can you do something with the shadows under the eyes—so?" He pointed at my face, and Tabitha came rushing out with her obligatory clipboard, which she set aside to study my face.

"Oh my. Hmm. Okay, let's go to the makeup room."

Angelo held up a finger. "Wait, though. Look at this, Lilah!" He pushed a newspaper toward me, open to the Metro section, and there was a large picture of Angelo and me—the one that a woman had taken outside the bookstore.

"Newspapers print pictures from their readers now?" I asked.

Angelo shrugged. "Why not? It is a good picture. They make reporters of people on the street. It saves them money. If they paid her at all, it was probably pennies." It was a great picture: Angelo's easy smile, his casual arm around me, my hair looking surprisingly good, and my eyes creased with near-laughter. We looked almost in love. "Look at the caption!" Angelo said.

Beneath the photo it said, Cooking with Angelo *is the most popular food show on Chicago cable, and networks are taking notice. Angelo Cardelini is pictured here in his hometown of Pine Haven, along with Lilah Drake, a popular guest on his show.*

"Oh my," I said.

"This is the best publicity for us. For me and you both," he assured me. "Also I need to speak with you about a promotional opportunity. A chance to meet with people in the food industry and to sell our show and our talents."

"Okay. When is this?"

"It takes place in Las Vegas in May. We should go out

there for the weekend. I'll buy you a lovely dinner, and then it will be all business."

I stared at him. "I can't go *away* with you!"

"Not in that way, no. This would be business."

"Jay would hate it either way! I can't do that, Angelo."

He shrugged. "So we bring Jay. Make this happen, Lilah. You've always wanted a career. Here it is."

"But I never asked to be on TV."

"Still. There will be people of all sorts there. Restaurateurs, caterers, writers, producers. Power people."

I rubbed my eyes. "I can't think about this right now."

He sighed and rolled his eyes at Tabitha. "She's all yours. We'll talk about this later, Lilah."

It was strange to have this new routine with Angelo and Tabitha. When I had dreamed of a career in food preparation, I had not envisioned myself on television, and yet fate had led me here. It was Angelo's show, but I sometimes got letters and e-mails from "fans" who liked me on the show or who tried my recipes and enjoyed them.

Tabitha was sponging away at my face, *tsk*ing at me. "Are you working on any plays right now?" I asked.

She sighed. "I just finished a show in the burbs. A friend of mine is trying to get me a job at the Goodman. That would be amazing. I'm waiting to hear back."

"Good luck with that."

"Thanks. Okay, that looks a little better, but your eyes are kind of red. You have to make sure to get enough sleep before a show, Lilah."

"Right."

She shook her head and pointed me back toward Angelo. I set out my ingredients, and he told me when to join him at the table. Then I went into the wings, and Angelo did his usual movie star turn, greeting the audience and reading letters from viewers. I had trouble concentrating on this because I was experiencing flashbacks from the previous night, some of which had me grinning to myself and some of which made my face grow unexpectedly hot.

I heard Angelo introducing me, and I walked out to the applause of the studio audience.

"Good morning, Lilah! What have you cooked up for us today?"

"Angelo, this is an easy Irish one-pot stew that you can make in a jiffy, but your family will think you slaved all day over a hot stove. It's delessius. Delicious, I mean."

"Wonderful! While you set out your ingredients, we'll hear this word from our sponsor."

The camera light went off. Still grinning at his audience, but with a quick flick to turn off his mike, Angelo said, "You look terrible, and you can barely speak your lines. What kept you from your sleep?"

I turned off my mike, as well. "None of your business," I said, smiling at the crowd, too.

"I can guess, I suppose. The policeman? This new man in your life?"

"Like I said, Angelo. None of your business."

He ignored this and turned toward me. "I have no problem with this. He seems like a good man."

"Gee, thanks."

"Don't be sarcastic, Lilah. It does not become you."

"Angelo, you need to join this century. I don't need to worry about what *becomes* me."

"Is he good to you? This cop?"

"Yes. He is very good."

"All right, then. Will you please try to get some sleep on the night before tapings? This is important, Lilah. The producers will be unhappy if you look like death, and I don't want to lose you from my Friday segment."

He seemed to be in earnest. "I'll do what I can, Angelo."

He sniffed. "There was a time that I was responsible for your sleepless nights."

I opened my mouth to retort, but Tabitha came running up to us, her face horrified and perspiring. "Why are your *mikes* off?" She bent over each of us in turn, fiddling with our equipment and turning the sound back on. She gave us a last suspicious glance before she hurried off and the cameraman pointed at Angelo, then held up five, four, three, two, one.

"We are back with the lovely Lilah Drake, who is prepared to make us some delicious stew. Is there anyone in the audience who would be willing to taste test this delightful concoction?"

A roar came from the audience, which was made up of mostly women but did contain a few men. Angelo waved grandly, then said, "Lilah, how do we begin?"

WHEN I GOT home with my box full of empty containers, my brother's car sat in the driveway. I lugged my box to the door and struggled with the key, then said, "Cam?"

"I'm in here petting your dog."

"Don't you teach today?"

"I had a morning class, and I have another at four. That's actually why I'm here."

"To teach me Italian?" I said lightly, setting my box on the table and turning on the faucet to fill my sink.

"No, to ask what your boyfriend is up to."

I flicked off the faucet and turned to face him. He sat on one of my kitchen stools, and Mick leaned against his leg, enjoying the head massage that Cam was giving him. As always Cam looked effortlessly handsome in his casual white button-down shirt and black jeans. His chestnut hair looked like it needed a trim.

"Jay? What do you mean?"

He lifted Mick's ears into the alert position. "He appeared in the door of my morning class, along with some woman. She looked Italian herself."

"That's Grimaldi."

"Okay. So they showed up in my class—actually interrupted it. I was afraid something had happened to you." He let Mick's ears fall again, and Mick leaned against him a little more.

"I'm sorry they scared you. What did Jay want?"

"He wanted one of my students. Pulled her right out of class, scaring her half to death. She's just a little freshman."

"What's her name?"

"Amber Warfield. Any idea what this might be about?"

"*Amber.* Wow, he moves fast."

"Meaning what?"

"Jay's investigating a murder. I know I told you about it—the guy who lived next door to Ellie?"

"So? This girl couldn't have anything to do with it."

"Well, apparently she's a friend of Cantwell's son. It's all a little bit confusing. . . ."

"You're telling me she's actually a suspect?"

"I'm not privy to police information, but I know that her name came up as a result of some conversations, so naturally they have to talk to her."

"Naturally. And they have to pull a kid out of class in front of her friends—"

"Oh, I get it. You're just looking for a reason to criticize Jay."

Cam's eyes widened, and he opened his mouth to protest, but someone pounded on my door. "Hang on," I said. I followed Mick's wagging tail to my front entrance, where a delivery person stood silhouetted against the glass. I could see the telltale clipboard in his hands.

I opened the door and faced a young man wearing a cap that said *Flower Fields*. They were one of the more upscale florists in Pine Haven. "Hello," I said.

"Lilla Drake?"

"Lilah, yes."

"Sign here, please. Someone likes you a lot." I signed, and he lifted the arrangement from its spot on the porch next to him. Only then did I see how huge it was. My face grew hot with surprise and pleasure.

"Oh—thank you. These look lovely."

He nodded and jogged back to his car. I carried my unwieldy burden to the kitchen, where I plunked it down on the counter and began stripping away the paper with all the enthusiasm of a three-year-old on Christmas.

My brother looked nervous. "What's the occasion? I know it's not your birthday. That's this summer."

"No occasion," I said, ripping away the last of the paper to reveal a sheaf of red and pink roses; their scent was intoxicating. I found the card tucked into the greenery and pulled it out with careful fingers. I read it and avoided eye contact with my brother.

"Why are you blushing? Your face is as red as a tomato! This is something romantic, isn't it? Are those from Jay?"

"You're just full of questions," I murmured. "God, these smell good."

"Wait a minute. A man doesn't send what looks like hundreds of roses unless he's in trouble or—oh God. Are those sex flowers? No, don't tell me. I don't want to know."

"You're one to talk. I am pretty sure that when I visit your apartment you guys you have either just finished or are just about to start. Or both."

Cam grinned briefly. "It's a good life," he said.

"Yeah. So lay off. I happen to love Jay Parker."

His eyebrows shot up. "Really! Does he know that?"

"Yes." I couldn't keep the smugness out of my voice. I found my purse and dug around for my phone. "Ah, there it is!" I started snapping photos of the flowers from different angles.

"What's that all about?" Cam said.

"I need to show them to Jenny. And Mom. And a few more people."

Cam stood up. "Okay. I guess I'm glad that Parker is showing the appropriate appreciation of your charms. This is far preferable to you mooning around for him and singing sad show tunes from the 1950s."

"There are happy show tunes, too," I said brightly. The song in my head, at present, was not a show tune, but "A Groovy Kind of Love"—the Phil Collins version.

Cam strolled over and sniffed a rose. "Can I bring one to Serafina?"

I was tempted to say no, but Serafina was always ridiculously generous to me. I selected a gorgeous red bloom and slid it out of the vase. "Just one. The rest are all mine."

My brother sent me a wry smile, kissed me on the cheek, and made his way to the door, escorted by my footman, Mick. "I'll see you Sunday, lovebird," he called over his shoulder. "Tell Jay to bring some wine."

Moments later Mick came trotting back, and I told him that I would soon be headed back to bed for an indulgent nap.

He nodded; Mick believed in the power of naps.

I scratched his head, looking at my flowers, and confessed that I had never been given anything so beautiful— not the hand-carved Italian wood recipe holder that Angelo had given me early in our relationship, or the sapphire blue hand-fired Le Creuset stoneware baker that my parents had given me for Christmas, or even the lovely earrings Jay had given me before he left for New York—no gift had made me feel the level of joy that this giant vase of flowers brought me.

Perhaps it was because of what he had written on the card.

For Lilah, my love. You are more beautiful than any rose.

CHAPTER TEN

PARKER PICKED ME UP THAT EVENING AT AROUND SIX. I gave Mick a kiss and told him to be good; then I grabbed the caramel apple pie I had made for Jenny's dinner party and ran out through the chilly twilight to the car. I had worn a standard little black dress with some black tights and a delicate yellow scarf. I thought it looked nice, and that Parker might find it alluring.

I practically dove into his car and leaned over to cover his face with kisses. "You are the sweetest man in the world!" I said. At first Parker seemed rather stiff, but I was relentless, and he eventually turned toward me and kissed me back. I pulled away eventually and smoothed his hair, since I had just rumpled it significantly. "Thank you so much for those amazing flowers," I said. "I've never gotten anything so wonderful in my life. You are the most perfect boyfriend—what's wrong?" I asked.

Jay was already backing down the long driveway, his eyes on the rearview mirror. "Nothing. Long day," he said.

I didn't believe this for a second. I knew Jay Parker, and he was stewing about something. "Okay, that's not the reason. You should probably tell me before we get to Jenny's," I said, buckling myself in.

We were on Dickens Street now, but Jay immediately pulled the car up next to a parking meter and slid the gearshift into park. "All right, Lilah."

I watched him, my mouth hanging open, while he leaned into the backseat and dug around in a bag on the floor of the car. Then he pulled out a newspaper, folded down at the Metro section. "Oh," I said. The car's interior was dim, but I knew exactly what he was holding.

"I wonder if you've seen this." He held up the picture of Angelo and me—the same picture Angelo had showed me earlier in the day. In Jay's hands the picture looked ten times worse. I felt almost guilty looking at it, as though Angelo and I were truly having an affair.

"Yes, Angelo showed it to me. He's very excited about it because of publicity. That's all it is, Jay. This was taken right on Dickens, right outside his restaurant."

"And you and he just happened to be strolling there?"

"No! I was in my car, and I saw him, and I jumped out to ask him about New York—what you told me about the show playing there. And then this woman walked up who was a fan of Angelo's, and she asked for a picture. I guess she sent it in to the paper. It all happened in about two minutes—

what's the big deal, Jay? After what we said yesterday, after last night, why is this even an issue? You know Angelo is in my past."

He looked out the windshield, then down at the photograph. My own smiling face seemed to mock me from the folded paper. Jay picked up the paper and flicked it into the backseat. "I know you *told* me that."

My face felt stiff with surprise. "What is going *on*? Is this—are you telling me you don't believe me?" He said nothing. "Oh God. I know what this is. This goes back to the darn chili thing, doesn't it? You said you could move on from the lie I told, but you can't. Because you're Jay, and you're never going to trust me." I scowled at him.

He finally met my gaze with his amazing blue eyes, and his expression was half remorseful and half defiant.

I snapped my mouth shut and turned away from him, toward the window. "Fine. Just drive to Jenny's. Hopefully you can pretend you like me enough at her house. You can go back to hating me afterward."

"I don't hate you." He started the car and began driving again.

"No. You just confronted me the moment I got into the car, even though I greeted you with love and kisses and gratitude."

"Lilah. You always make me sound terrible."

"You make *yourself* sound that way."

"And yet, if you saw a picture of me with some beautiful woman, and we were both smiling and her arm was around me, that wouldn't bother you?"

I thought of my resentment of Maria before I knew

Julia Buckley

that there was nothing between Parker and her. Maria, with her tall, shapely form and her dark hair and pretty face. Yes, my mistrust had been deep and resounding, and I had attributed to her qualities that she really did not possess—bitchy, slithery qualities that had made me dislike her intensely. "No, it wouldn't," I lied.

"Huh," he said. We drove in silence for a while. Finally Parker said, "You look nice."

"Huh," I said to the window.

Then we didn't talk at all.

When he pulled up in front of Jenny's building, I turned to him. "I do not want to be embarrassed in front of my friend, so you are going to have to pretend that I'm a girlfriend that you love and trust, not a woman you suspect of two-timing you with an ex-boyfriend. And I in turn will pretend that I'm not incredibly mad at you, even though I am." I got out of the car and slammed the door, then opened his back door to retrieve my pie. I slammed that door, too, and walked up the pathway without checking to see if Parker was following me. I halfway expected to hear his car driving away, and a part of me felt he would be justified in doing so.

I normally wouldn't have been such a drama queen, but Parker and I had one Achilles' heel in our relationship, and it had to do with honesty. We both valued it, and now it seemed that Parker still didn't think I was honest—not deep down—or he would never have suspected that I had feelings for Angelo. I didn't even know if he suspected that I was cheating, or if he just feared it. Maybe Parker didn't want to lose me, and I could understand that.

But he needed to understand that he had hurt my feelings, and that his mistrust had opened up an old wound.

I rang Jenny's bell, and Parker appeared next to me, tall and handsome. He looked wonderful; he wore a pair of jeans with a forest green shirt and a dark patterned tie. "You look nice, too, Jay. I was going to say that earlier."

"Lilah," he said, reaching out to stroke my hair, but Jenny buzzed us in, and I slipped past him before he could touch me.

JENNY AND ROSS, in a terrible contrast, could not keep their hands off each other and had an annoying new habit of calling each other "honey."

"You want me to check the roast, honey?" Ross asked, massaging Jenny's shoulders.

"Oh, thanks, honey—that would be great." Jenny grinned at us. "We're so glad to have you guys here. It's our first double date, if you don't count that Christmas party we all attended. The first of many double dates, I hope!"

Parker and I forced some toothy smiles, and he walked over to study the things on her mantel. Jenny sent me an uncertain glance, and I waved her away. "This place looks amazing!" I said. "Those flowers on the table are gorgeous. Are those tulips?"

Jenny adjusted a barrette in her reddish hair. "Yes. Oh my gosh! Jay, I saw those flowers you sent Lilah. She texted them to just about everyone she knows. They're pretty spectacular."

"Thanks," Jay said. "So is Lilah."

I knew his blue eyes were on me, but I would not risk their hypnotic spell. Those darn blue eyes . . .

"The roast looks good, hon," Ross said, bounding back in. "Should I turn off the oven?"

"Oh, would you, sweetie? And then we can all wash up and sit down."

Sometimes Jenny sounded like the grade school teacher she was; still, we obediently washed our hands before we went to the kitchen. "You two sit on that side," Jenny said, ushering us to her beautifully made table. The cloth was pale blue, and a vase of purple tulips sat in the center. She had set out blue ceramic plates with purple cloth napkins, each of which was held in place by a clementine.

"This looks lovely, Jenny. Thank you for inviting us."

"Well, I had to celebrate with my maid of honor!" she said, bubbling with enthusiasm. Then she darted to the stove to get the dinner that smelled so amazing.

I smiled at her fiancé. "I'm so excited for you both. And that was a sweet proposal, Ross. Very romantic."

"It was a great night," Ross said, beaming. "I still can't believe Jenny said yes."

Jenny returned with a steaming roast, set it down at the end of the table, and began to slice it with a lethal-looking knife. Ross passed around a salad and then a bowl of potatoes. "So tell us about you two," Jenny said with a smile.

I didn't want to talk about love, but I also didn't want to air our grievances in front of our friends.

"Jay is working on a case, as always," I said.

Ross looked intrigued as he forked up some salad. "That must be so cool, man. Walking around with a gun and catching bad guys. It seems like something on TV. The most dangerous thing I ever do is break up playground fights."

Jay nodded. "Sometimes it seems appealing to get a job like that. Mine can be depressing. And it has never allowed for much of a social life." His blue eyes moved to me. "Luckily Lilah is pretty busy herself most of the time, so she's not as lonely as she could be."

"Aw," Jenny said with great sympathy. "You need to take some time off, Jay! When's the last time you had a vacation?"

"I don't remember," Jay said, looking surprised. He also looked tired, I realized, thinking with some guilt about the nap that had left me feeling refreshed.

Ross wasn't finished talking about crime. "So what's this case you're working on? You handle homicides, right?"

"Yes, when they occur. Pine Haven isn't exactly the murder capital of the world, but I've been pretty busy in this last year. And there was a recent murder."

"Wait—is this about Cantwell?" Ross asked.

Jenny turned to him, surprised.

He shrugged. "It was in the paper. He's a big deal around here."

Jay straightened in his chair. His cop sense was tingling. "Did you know Marcus Cantwell?"

Ross nodded. "I did. He was a member of the board

at JFK. All his kids went there, so he was a staple from way back. Pretty influential, too, as far as I could determine from the few meetings I attended. I only go when they're discussing something that might directly affect the curriculum."

"So when was the last time you saw Cantwell at a meeting?" Jay asked. He seemed to remember, belatedly, that this was supposed to be a casual meeting of friends and not an interrogation, so he pasted on a smile and took a sip of the wine Jenny had just poured him.

Ross thought about this. "Huh. I guess it would have been right around the beginning of the year. The first meeting of the board. Cantwell told us he would be retiring soon, but that he'd stay on the board until they elected a replacement. He was sort of eccentric, but he seemed on the ball mentally. He made some shrewd comments; I could see why they liked having him there—he wasn't just a figurehead."

"Did they discuss anything controversial?" Jay asked.

Ross frowned. "Not that I recall. I'll have to think back."

Jenny was pouting slightly. "Hey, this is supposed to be a social occasion. Let's not talk about murder or our jobs or anything."

The men looked at her blankly for a moment; then Ross nodded. He would be an eternally supportive husband, I realized, because there was that special something in his eyes that said even if he didn't understand why Jenny wanted it, he wanted to give it to her. "Sure, honey.

Hey, we forgot the bread. I'll run and get it." He leaped out of his chair and went to the counter, where he found a long baguette and began slicing it.

Jenny turned back to us, her pretty face flushed with happiness. "I'm so excited that Lilah will be my maid of honor. Ross and I are thinking maybe next November for the wedding."

Parker had been looking into the depths of his wine, which he was swirling moodily. Now he looked up at Jenny and said, "What color will the dresses be?"

I stared at him, shocked, but Jenny didn't notice anything amiss. "I'm not sure; Ross likes the idea of a burgundy color, like this wine, but I was thinking about a winter white. Not the same shade as my dress, which will be ivory, but several shades lighter."

"Lilah would look beautiful in that color. I saw her in a white dress once that she got from Serafina. It was amazing. She looked like some rare flower."

Jenny and I exchanged a glance. "How much wine have you had, Jay?" Jenny joked.

Jay shrugged. "No one should be surprised that I find Lilah beautiful, especially not Lilah." His expression was moody again. I never knew quite what was going on in Parker's head, but I felt a little burst of warmth at his words.

Ross returned with the bread. "I guess this is a good time to ask this. Jenny wants four bridesmaids; her three sisters and Lilah. I only have two brothers and one best friend; I wonder if you'd do me the honor of being the fourth groomsman, Jay."

Jay's eyes widened. "A groomsman—with a tuxedo and all that? Wow. I actually have never done that before. One of my brothers eloped, and the other had a small ceremony in the mountains—just him, his wife, and a minister. I don't actually know how to do it."

Jenny's eyes were bright. "Oh, it's easy. You just rent a tux, and the rest is all laid out—the rehearsal dinner and the wedding. You just have to be there to stand up for us and celebrate us."

Jay smiled, and it transformed his face. "I can do that. Thanks for asking, Ross. I would be honored."

"And then you can see Lilah in her white dress," Jenny gushed.

"That would be a perk," said Parker, and he put an arm around me, pulling me closer.

"You two are perfect together," Jenny said. "I think it's great that Lilah and I both got involved with someone around the same time. Pretty soon I'll be helping Lilah plan her wedding!"

"Let's not rush things," I said, my eyes on my plate.

THE EVENING PASSED pleasantly enough, mostly because Jenny was her usual vivacious self and clearly enjoyed being a hostess. She looked beautiful in love, and I drew great pleasure from simply watching her as she regaled us with stories. She and I had shared the occasional philosophical chat, back in college, about love and what we thought it was and whether we would ever find it. Jenny had said at the time that she knew she wanted to marry and have children, so she hoped she wouldn't settle for the first suitable man, but would shop around for her soul mate.

Ross was certainly not the first man she had dated, but he was definitely the first one she had ever loved. Still, I doubted she would ever regret her choice.

Over dessert I studied Parker while he listened to Ross's animated questions about police work. I had thought I loved a boy in high school, but in retrospect it hadn't been love—just a sort of euphoria at the idea of shared attraction. In college, too, I had dated someone that I felt I loved, but by the end of our relationship I hadn't even liked him.

Then there was Angelo. I had truly been in love with him, and now that time had passed I found I still liked him, but my passion for him had burned out, and all that was left was an admiration for his culinary gifts. Why couldn't Parker understand that? What was it about Angelo, I wondered, that made Parker feel so threatened? Or was he truly convinced that I was untrustworthy?

I narrowed my eyes. The beautiful sentiments Parker had sent with his flowers and the actual sentiments he had expressed in the car, juxtaposed as they were, felt jarring. Deep down, he could only really mean one of those things.

Parker turned to look at me; he seemed to read my thoughts. He opened his mouth to say something, but Ross said, "Jay, if you have a second, I'll show you the tuxedo that Jenny picked out for the groomsmen."

Jay snapped back to attention. "Sure. Lead the way."

They filed out of the room, talking in jovial male tones, and Jenny sat across from me. "Spill it," she said.

"You can tell?"

She curled her lip. "You've been shooting daggers into him with your eyes since you got here. What's going on?"

"Nothing. I had a beautiful night with him last night, and then he sent me beautiful flowers, and then he got all jealous of some picture of me and Angelo in the paper."

"What picture?"

"Nothing. Just some publicity shot in the Metro section."

Her phone, which was never far away, was suddenly in her hands, and her fingers were working. "Googling now. Okay. Oh *my*. Lilah, this looks like a wedding photo."

"It's not my fault! I had been talking to him for about one minute—arguing with him, really—and some woman came up and snapped our photo. I had no idea."

"Obviously Jay is overreacting, but—I mean, this photo looks—romantic."

"But it's not. Which I told him. So at what point do you have to believe someone because you trust and love them?"

Jenny shrugged. "Maybe it will just take him a day or so."

"Fine. He can have all the space he wants."

"Don't make your sad little orphan face."

"I don't have an orphan face."

"Yes, you do. It's kind of hilarious. But it just proves how hung up on Jay you are."

"I love him, Jenny."

"Tell him, then."

"I did—remember the phone call yesterday? I did tell him, and then he said he loved me, too."

"Then just let this blow over. Don't say something you'll regret. Just stay away from him for a while until he misses you. And for God's sake, stay away from Angelo."

"Angelo is my boss."

Jenny gave me a serious look. "Are you willing to quit that job to prove a point to Jay?"

I hadn't thought about that. "I don't know. Maybe. But I kind of like it. Variety is the spice of life, and it adds variety to my week."

"Just think about it. How much would you want Jay to work with an ex-girlfriend?"

I nodded. "I'll think about it."

"Good. Your pie was amazing, by the way. Ross told me to get the recipe."

"It's easy. I'll e-mail it to you."

"Hey, that was pretty funny when Jay asked about the dresses."

I smiled in spite of myself. "Yeah. Parker has a little romantic streak, but he hides it really well."

The men were coming back in now, and they were talking about Marcus Cantwell. "He was a pretty cool guy as far as I could tell," Ross was saying.

"Did you ever speak to him one-on-one?"

"Not usually, but at that last meeting, he and I happened to walk to the parking lot together, so we had a little bit of conversation. He said something about his money—how everyone assumed that he was rich—and that he actually had a lot of expenses. He was paying alimony to three wives, and he said his kids had always been expensive. Even more so now that they were older—that's what he said. And of course he had six kids, so that's a lot of kids to support."

"Five kids," I corrected. In one day I had become a Cantwell expert.

"Oh yeah—five," said Ross. "That's still a lot of kids, though."

Jay was making his thoughtful face. "Did you ever hear him talk about—opposition of some kind? Did he have any enemies on the board, for example?"

Ross scratched his head. "Not that I know of. I mean, some people found him a little pompous, but that's just the kind of snarky talk you hear after a school board meeting. It wasn't anything significant."

Jenny was looking aggravated again. "Who wants some more pie?" she said. "You know when Lilah makes it you can't have just one piece."

"I do," said Jay Parker. He took my hand and dragged me back toward the kitchen.

AFTER WE SAID our good-byes at Jenny's, Parker's car was very quiet once again. I stared out my window, considering several ways of beginning a conversation and then rejecting them all. Jenny had made me realize that Parker's complaint had at least a shred of validity, but I didn't want to apologize, because I had done nothing wrong.

Parker stopped at a red light. "Lilah," he said.

"Yes?"

"I meant everything I said to you last night. I just—to see his face with yours this morning—it was like an invasion of our happiness and our privacy."

I chose my words with care. "I understand why you might feel jealous, but you need to know that I am not interested in Angelo, I am not involved with him, and I never will be. I told you that at Christmas. Sometimes people will take photographs of us, I suppose, but it's not like I'm clipping them out and putting them in a scrapbook. Angelo is my job."

"I know." His voice was grudging.

"It's a brand-new job, Jay. Do you want me to quit?"

The light turned green, and he accelerated down the dark street. "What do you mean?"

"Do you want me to quit the TV show? Is that what it would take to prove that I don't care about Angelo and I do care about you?"

Parker's face was unreadable. "Don't be silly."

"That's not an answer.".

"Would I be glad if he was totally out of your life? Yes, okay? But would I ask you to sacrifice a part of your burgeoning career? No. I would never want that. Believe it or not, Lilah, I care about your happiness."

"Is it a bad sign that we always end up arguing? After last night, I thought we'd never argue again."

Parker said nothing. This infuriated me. I glared out my window until Parker pulled into the long driveway that led to my house.

"I still have some work to do," Parker said coolly. "So I probably shouldn't come in."

"Fine." I gathered my purse and my empty pie pan. "I'll see you around."

"We're going to the gallery tomorrow, right?" he asked.

"Yeah. But I think I'll go with Britt, so I'll meet you there. That way if your job interferes, you don't have to show up at all." I was already on the driveway and about to close the door when he held up a hand.

"Lilah, come on. Let's talk for a minute."

"I think I'd rather go in, Parker. I can look at my flowers and read your card and pretend it's yesterday." I shut the door and stalked to my house. Parker waited until I had unlocked the door and had turned some lights on. He always did this, and I felt a pang that I had been so obnoxious and yet he didn't go tearing down the driveway in a huff, but waited to make sure I was safe.

It was actually a couple more minutes before I saw the car slowly reverse down the drive. I wondered what he had been thinking, or if he had considered coming in for a reconciliation.

I wondered, too, if I was disappointed that he had not.

Mick nuzzled my leg, so I let him out the back door. While I waited for him to do his business, I picked up one of the Miss Moxie books I had purchased at the bookstore. They still sat in a little pile on my counter, near the beautiful and fragrant roses. The book I selected was called *Miss Moxie Says Sorry*.

I paged through the little book with its sweet illustrations and read the story of Miss Moxie and her friend Miss Dixie, who always sat in the porch swing and ate tapioca pudding together at the end of each day. One day Miss Moxie made fun of Miss Dixie's hat, and the next night she sat on the porch alone, eating tapioca pudding that didn't taste the same.

Mick came to the door, and I let him in, then returned to the book. Miss Moxie had to think of the many reasons why she owed Miss Dixie an apology: she had failed to consider Miss Dixie's feelings; she had taken a risk with their friendship; and, to be honest, it was a very nice hat.

Miss Moxie walked to Miss Dixie's house in the end, holding a sign that said, "I love your hat!!" When Miss Dixie answered the door, she smiled. Then Miss Moxie made a beautiful apology.

That night they ate pudding together again, wearing their hats. Miss Moxie reflected on apologies and said, "Saying I'm sorry is the best thing you can do when you've done wrong to a friend. Sometimes *I'm sorry* can be beautiful music."

I set down the book and went to my phone. I dialed a familiar number and let it ring until, predictably, it went to voice mail. Then I said, "Angelo, it's Lilah. I am so grateful for all that you've done for my career—I can't tell you how much I appreciate it. But for reasons I can't go into now, I need to stop doing the show. I'm sorry to give you only a week's notice, but I know you can find someone else. So—just to be clear—I quit. Sorry again, and thank you."

Julia Buckley

I hung up and looked at Mick, who nodded. It was done. I think Mick recognized my relief, and he seemed to feel it, too.

"Mick, I have a sudden craving for tapioca pudding. Do you?"

He nodded, and we made some from scratch.

CHAPTER ELEVEN

IN THE MORNING I HAD NO TIME TO CONTEMPLATE MY love life; I had to get some ingredients for a dish I'd be delivering soon, and I had to work at Haven, so I walked Mick at seven thirty and was in the grocery store by eight o'clock. I raced up and down the aisles with my basket, then lugged it to the cashier and waited behind a man who was buying a six-pack of beer. He looked vaguely familiar from the side, and when he turned his head briefly I recognized him as Owen Cantwell. There was still a faint bruise on his face from where Prue's Damen had punched him.

He must have felt my stare, because he turned and offered me a smile. "Hey," he said while the cashier bagged his beer. Then he looked more closely. "Do I know you? You look familiar."

I nodded. "You're Owen, aren't you? I was at your dad's birthday party. I'm very sorry for your loss."

"Oh yeah." He nodded at the memory. "You were standing there with that cop. Grimaldi." His jaw tightened slightly. Clearly Grimaldi had not yet been forgiven, despite the fact that she had wanted justice for the family. "Thanks, anyway. I appreciate it."

"How are you doing?"

He took his bag and moved aside so that the cashier, whose name tag said *Martin*, could ring me up. "We're hanging in there. At first I thought this whole thing would cause a permanent rift between us kids, but now—I think it might ultimately bring us together. We're all adults now, and we need to bury the hatchet for some old grievances. You know how it is in families."

"Sort of. Mine isn't as big as yours—I just have one brother."

"Huh." He scratched at his blond head. "Well, we're doing as well as can be expected. You know."

I didn't know exactly, but I was curious about what some of the "grievances" might have been. "Are you planning a funeral?" I asked.

He shrugged. "My dad was a private guy. He has some notes in his will about not wanting a big public affair. We are currently in talks about how to potentially honor him without going against his wishes."

I handed the cashier my money and took my receipt. To my surprise, Owen Cantwell picked up a couple of my bags. "Let me walk this out for you," he said in a rather gallant manner.

"Thank you! I appreciate that." We walked out to the parking lot in a companionable silence, but Cantwell seemed to have something on his mind.

"Listen," he said halfway to the car. "You were there at the party. And you're not familiar with the whole family dynamic, so I'm curious to get an objective view. Did you notice anything strange? Anything that seemed weird?"

I must have looked surprised, because he was quick to add, "I mean, these are the questions the police are asking us, but we don't have a good answer. Off the top of your head, did anything strike you as strange?"

Just your father, I thought. "Not really. It seemed like a standard birthday party—it was clear how much you all cared for your dad, with the live music, the great food, the photographer, the lovely gifts. I was impressed."

"Huh," he said.

We reached my car, and Cantwell helped me tuck things into the back. I thanked him and said, "I understand you were making some cool drinks for everyone that day."

He grew slightly pale. "Where did you hear that?"

Maria had told me, so I lied. "Oh, someone at the party mentioned it."

"Yeah. Uh—I don't know if I should say this, but—the drink is what someone used to poison my dad. The drink I made him. It's hard to believe." He stared at his bag of beer with a bemused expression.

I feigned surprise. "Oh, that's terrible. I'm so sorry. He was actually drinking it when I talked with him."

"You talked to my dad? Like, alone?"

"Yes, for a few minutes."

He got a strange look on his face then, something between envy and amusement. "So what did you talk about? Did he say anything about his kids?"

"We mostly talked about dogs."

Cantwell's smile disappeared. "Huh," he said for the third time.

"He seemed really devoted to you guys, though. He did seem glad to have the party, and grateful that you were all acknowledging him."

Cantwell nodded, thinking about this. I remembered that Cash said he was a philosophy major, and he did have the look of a philosopher about him, with his fair hair and wise eyes. "Yeah, I guess when it came right down to it, he was grateful to us. Just as we were to him."

"You have a nice family," I said, thinking of Cash and Prue.

"Thanks. I appreciate it. I'm sorry. What was your name again?"

"Lilah Drake," I said.

"Thanks, Lilah."

I gave him a little wave and started to walk toward the driver's door. "Thanks so much for your help with the groceries."

He looked a bit lonely when he said, "Hey, would you ever want to get a drink sometime?"

Had this been the previous spring, I probably would

have been excited about the invitation. I smiled at him. "That is so sweet! But I'm actually in a relationship with your former next-door neighbor, Jay Parker."

"With Jay?" He looked truly surprised, his mouth open. Then: "He's a cop now."

"Yes." I paused, then plunged in. "He's actually investigating your dad's murder."

"Yeah—I mean, Scott told me. I guess Jay has already questioned him, and he said he's going to talk to all the siblings. He hasn't gotten to me yet. I wonder if that means I am a suspect, or I'm not."

"Neither, I'm sure. Jay talks to everyone. He likes to be thorough."

He looked thoughtful now, and a bit concerned. "Well, tell Jay I said hi. It was nice seeing you, Lilah."

He waved and moved farther down the store lot until he reached a blue Dodge. I got into my car, and when I turned around to see if the way was clear to reverse into traffic, I saw that Owen Cantwell was standing next to his own car, seemingly lost in thought, his eyes fixed on me.

I DROVE HOME and hurried inside to make my dish before it was time to go to Haven. I was making a taco fiesta casserole for a friend of Ellie's (someone, Ellie assured me, who would "be discreet"), and I needed to deliver it on my way to work. As I put the final layer of meat in the dish, I wondered what Cantwell had meant when he asked if his father had said anything. He had specifically said,

Did he say anything about his kids? or something to that effect. What exactly had that meant?

I sighed. I was tired of people and their many layers. I was especially tired of trying to figure out Jay Parker, but at the same time I enjoyed trying to figure out Jay Parker. He was an enigma, and I loved him. "I love him, Mick," I said to my canine friend as I slid the casserole into the oven. "I love Jacob Ellison Parker. Did you know that was his middle name? But I'm so mad at him. And yet . . ." I looked at the giant vase of roses from Parker, and something twisted in my stomach. Two nights ago he had said many sweet things to me, and I had been convinced that we were perfect, solid, wonderful, forever.

Mick was staring at me. "I know, buddy. I need to let you out and stop obsessing like a sixteen-year-old. Come on. You go do your business, and then I have to change."

Mick nodded and strolled to the door with me. Unlike Jay Parker, Mick did not pick fights. He was a peaceful companion, and our disputes didn't exist, unless I forgot to feed Mick at mealtime. He took exception to that.

I gave Mick a few minutes to wander the fragrant yard with his dreamy expression, and to sniff the air currents with his complicated nose. Then I called him in and gave him a dog biscuit, and I ran upstairs. I could still smell roses on my way up the staircase.

I CALLED BRITT that evening and asked if I could go to the gallery with her. "Parker might have to work late, so I figured I'd just tag along with you."

"That's fine, of course, but I'll be going in a bit earlier than everyone else to get things ready."

"No problem. I can help you."

"Okay—come down the driveway around six, then."

I did so, wearing a slinky black pantsuit and black high heels, along with the diamond earrings from Parker and a long, sparkly necklace made up of silver beads and intermittent Austrian crystals. I had swept my hair into a casual twist that looked elegant enough for an art gallery, and I felt ready to face the ever-stylish Britt.

She came out, holding her keys, and she did look great, but also a bit tired. She wore a midnight blue dress with matching shoes and what looked like real sapphires in her ears. "Ready? Let's get going, then. I'm so glad you're coming tonight! Prue's latest painting is amazing," Britt said, steering toward the street where her car was parked. "It's called *Disillusionment*, and it's a compelling visual depiction of a person changing before your eyes."

"I can't wait to see it."

"She's a real talent. It won't be long before she's a household name, I'm sure; I can never hold on to her paintings. I have buyers contacting me from all over the world."

"That's amazing. What it must feel like, to have a talent like that!"

Britt looked at me. "You do, Lilah. I've tasted your cooking. And you barely even need to use recipes. It's almost magical, the way you can make ingredients come together. Climb in; it's unlocked."

We got into her gorgeous sea glass blue Passat, a gift

from Terry, and I marveled anew at the way Britt lived life. She was like a woman from a movie—with great looks and expensive toys and an elegant job. I wanted to be Britt when I grew up. In my mind's ear Nat King Cole was singing "Unforgettable," because big band–era romance ballads, for me, somehow equaled sophistication.

"Your car smells nice inside," I said.

"That sounds accusing," she said with a laugh as she started the car.

"It is. My car smells like chili and Mick. Yours smells like some expensive perfume."

Britt giggled and shifted into drive. We merged into traffic on Dickens. "You always crack me up, Lilah. I needed that laugh."

I studied her more closely and saw that she looked pale. "Okay, tell me what's going on! Are you sick?"

"No, I'm not sick. Neither is Terry. Everything is fine, Lilah."

"Except that it's not."

She sighed. We stopped at a red light on Bristol Road, and Britt turned left. "You would laugh. My problem isn't even a problem, and yet it's making me so unhappy."

"Spill it, Britt. You've helped me through all kinds of problems. Now it's time to let me reciprocate."

She pursed her lips for a moment, then stopped at another light and faced me. "I will. Absolutely. But right now I have to focus on gallery things. Maybe if there's time afterward we can sit down and talk."

"Fine. I will not let you leave the gallery until you've told me what's going on."

"Fair enough." She shot me a little smile, then drove to Canfield Street and made a right and another right into the parking lot of the Blackwood Gallery. Blackwood was Britt's last name, and Terry had insisted that she name the gallery after herself, although she had been tempted to name it something more philosophical like the Artist's Dream. I had to agree with Terry—it was a great name for the gallery. It sounded professional and sophisticated, and in fact had established a stellar reputation in the five years since Britt had opened it.

We got out of the car, and Britt opened a little black bag to hunt for her key. It was a chilly night, but the breeze held the scent of spring flowers that made the twilight romantic. I had a sudden yearning for Parker. I wanted to wrap my arms around him and tell him he was the only man for me, which was the truth.

"How are things in the love department?" Britt asked with a canny expression.

"I'll talk when you do," I said.

She laughed and opened the door, and we moved into the wide, airy room that was her gallery. The building was gorgeous: a high-ceilinged space with a clear red oak wood floor. There were four different rooms for displays, but the walls were only eight feet high so that the large ceiling was visible overall. Against one wall, outside of the divided "rooms," was a dais with a microphone where visiting artists could speak and take questions. This was flanked by floor-to-ceiling windows through which the evening light filtered softly in.

At the back of the gallery was a small employee office

where Britt had a freezer and refrigerator so that she could keep food on hand for her evening soirees. I went with her now to unpack some bottles of wine and champagne and to set them out on a marble-topped gallery table, along with a giant tray of French cheeses and fancy crackers.

Britt arranged things deftly and lit a few little candles to add some ambience to her beautiful table.

"Perfect," I said. "Do you mind if I look at the art?"

"Of course not. Prue's painting is in room one, which is a local artists' display. Room two is all Jerome Merault, a recent discovery of mine. I am in love with his use of color. Room three is all sculpture, and room four is being reimagined, so it's not open this evening."

I nodded and went to room one, a large, beautiful space filled with framed works. Somehow I knew immediately which painting was Prudence Cantwell's. It dominated the area, not only in size, but in dramatic power. It was a giant portrait of a man's face against a backdrop of clouds, and yet the face was somehow melting, transforming, turning into someone—or something—else. She had used color to great effect, starting with vibrant hues that eventually melted into jejune paleness. It was brilliant; I had been disillusioned before, and the title *Disillusionment* was perfect for the painting. People could in fact transform before your eyes when you realized they weren't who you thought they were.

"Amazing, isn't it?" Britt said, appearing beside me with a glass of wine in her hand.

"It is. What a talented woman. Is this a watercolor?"

"No—oil. She mostly works in oil, although I've seen some of her watercolors. They're lovely. She did a whole series about Lake Michigan that I'm trying to get her to show here. Can I get you some wine?"

"Sure. White, please."

"Of course."

She slipped away, and I continued to study the paintings, amazed by the diversity of the talent in the room and overwhelmed by the intensity of it all. So much feeling, so much passion had gone into these artistic messages. How lucky for them that they all had an outlet for their deepest feelings. I didn't need my brain to give me musical accompaniment, because Britt had music playing, soft and in the background, but enough to worm its way into my head. Right now it was something that I recognized as one of Vivaldi's *Four Seasons*, but I couldn't remember which one it was.

I left room one and moved into room two to see Britt's new discovery, Jerome someone. Even from the doorway I understood what Britt meant about color. The images on the canvas seemed at first to be one color, but upon closer examination I could see a whole spectrum in every brushstroke. I couldn't even imagine how he had done it.

He liked cityscapes, and there were images of Paris, London, New York, Budapest—all with recognizable icons in beautiful washes of color that indicated a time of day: Paris in a blue evening mist; London in a red sunrise; New York in a pink and shimmery midday.

I stopped in front of a painting called *Summer Walk,* immediately entranced. Two people were strolling with a dog down a street lined with overarching trees in purple evening light. The woman had long blond hair, and the man's hair was dark. His hand was wrapped around her waist, and she held the dog on a dainty leash. The dog, brown and bulky, could have been Mick, and the couple could have been Parker and I. It wasn't just the strange resemblance that I loved, but the amazing kaleidoscope of color that permeated the canvas, although the dominant colors were blues and purples, because this was clearly an evening walk—the last one before bed.

Could I afford it? My eyes darted to the price tag: $2,500.

Britt appeared and handed me my wine. "Isn't it lovely? That woman could be you, Lilah. I just love his magical use of light. Look at the way it shines off of the park bench there. And how luminous the trees are as they bend lovingly over the couple."

"And the path that they're walking seems to have a special light, as well."

"Good eye! If you didn't already have two jobs, I'd try to get you to work here."

I smiled and sipped my wine. "So who is this artist? How did you find him?" I studied the corner where a scrawled blue signature said *Merault.*

Britt's eyes lit up with enthusiasm. "That's a funny story— oh, hang on. People are starting to arrive."

People were indeed at the door, and Britt didn't make it back to me because of her hosting duties. I saw some faces I recognized from around town, and eventually Prue Cantwell herself came in, accompanied by Damen. He had a possessive hand clamped around her shoulders, and she seemed happy, so I assumed they had made up. She was greeting people she knew as she headed for room one, and she spied me lingering in the main aisle. "Hello!" she called, waving at me. She and Damen moved forward, to my surprise, until they were in front of me. "It's Lilah, right? I won't forget it now."

"Yes. Nice to see you, Prue."

"Lilah, this is Damen. I don't think you two met—the other day."

I shook his hand, and he said, "Nice to meet you." He really was handsome, and his eyes were friendly. Perhaps he looked more natural to me now that he had ditched the black leather. He was wearing blue jeans and a white button-down shirt with a skinny black tie. Now he was studying me more closely. "Did I meet you? You look familiar."

Prue saw someone she knew and said, "I'll be right back."

I said, "You met me at Mr. Cantwell's birthday party. Or saw me. As Prue said, we weren't introduced."

He blushed slightly. "I wasn't at my best that day. I apologize."

I shrugged. "Sometimes our families can push us to our limits. Or our spouse's families."

"Prudence isn't my spouse," he said with a slightly yearning expression.

"Significant others, then. Her painting is amazing. I

would love to see more of her work, and I know Britt would like to display more of it. Wow, the people just keep flowing in. Are they all for Prudence?"

Damen glanced at the door. "A lot of them are, because Britt sent out notices that she had a special new painting. Some people are here for other artists, or just here because it's a special event. Prue's painting will sell before the evening is over. It always does." He said this with the easy confidence that the partner of a talented person often develops. He probably didn't fully understand Prue's art, but he understood its popularity.

I heard a familiar voice talking with Britt near the doorway. I looked up to see Parker, still in his work clothes of a white shirt, red tie, and gray jacket with black pants, chatting with Britt as he scanned the room. Then his eyes found me, and we exchanged a long look.

"Will you excuse me?" I said. "My date just arrived."

"Sure. Maybe we'll talk later."

"I'd like that. Thanks, Damen."

I started to move toward Parker, but Britt was ushering everyone toward the back wall, where the dais was. I followed, assuming Parker would find me. The long windows were now blue-black with night. "Thank you, everyone, for coming to the Blackwood Gallery. We're featuring local artists in room one, and we're excited to have a new painting by Pine Haven's own Prudence Cantwell, whose last show was dubbed 'a masterpiece' by the *Chicago Tribune* and by the *Art Review*. We are lucky to have Prudence in our midst! I'm going to put her on the spot and ask her to say a few words about her painting *Disillusionment*."

Prudence waved and took the microphone, shaking her head at Britt as if to say, "I'm too modest to speak." Then she scanned the crowd and said, "Thank you all for being here tonight. Britt always has impressive art in this gallery, and my painting is just one of many pieces for you to enjoy. I do hope you'll connect with my work; Britt and I are in talks to stage a larger showing sometime around the New Year."

The crowd applauded politely at this, and Prue's face grew serious. "I am here without my family tonight because we recently lost my father; I considered not coming, either, but then I realized that this is like another family—the world of art—and I take great comfort from being here. Thanks so much to all of you."

There was more applause after this, and Prue's eyes were moist as she handed back the microphone. It was true that no one in her family was present; I hadn't noticed that until she mentioned it. I wondered if her father's death was the only reason her siblings hadn't come out to support her.

My focus was on Parker, and I wanted to move toward him where he stood near one window, but it seemed Britt was still in presenting mode. "Thank you, Prudence. I appreciate your willingness to come out tonight, and I toast your talent." She handed a glass to Prue Cantwell, and life went into slow motion.

The glass in Prue's hand shattered, and champagne

sprayed outward into the air. Britt and Prudence screamed in unison, and Jay Parker loomed forward, his gun in his hand. "Get down, everyone!" he shouted. "Get down! I'm a police officer, and that was gunfire. Get down and away from the window!"

CHAPTER TWELVE

THE CROWD, PANICKED AND MAKING SOUNDS BE-tween whimpers and shouts, did as he ordered, crouching down and moving toward the middle hallway, where there were no windows. Parker lifted his gun, ran toward the entrance, and disappeared. He was chasing a murderer, and my skin went cold at the thought.

Prudence was crying in earnest now, and Damen was tending to her hand, which was bleeding. I edged forward, still in a crouch. "Did he shoot your hand?" I asked. My lips felt numb.

"It's glass," said Damen in a soothing voice. "I think I got it all. Now we'll just wrap this up and fix it at home." Admiration for him surged through me; he was just what

Prudence needed: a large, calming presence in a frightening atmosphere.

Prudence held out her hand, allowing him to minister to her, her face almost childlike. In that instant she looked like Peach. I turned my attention to Britt, who was wiping at some champagne on her dress with trembling hands.

"Britt," I said. "Are you okay? Did any glass get into your skin?"

"I don't think so," she said. Then she looked at me; her eyes were wide and her pupils were dilated. "What just happened? What just happened in my gallery?"

"Jay will find out. He'll get to the bottom of this," I said. I looked out the windows and saw blue and red lights. "And he's already called for backup. Look, the police are here."

Soon there were official people swarming all over the gallery, inside and out, and we guests were ordered into room one until the police could process the scene and ask some questions. Britt told some officers where they could find folding chairs, and the men and women in blue set these up hastily so that we could sit while we waited. I slumped into a chair next to Britt, feeling empty. I was facing Prue's painting, and I suddenly understood it far better. *Disillusionment*. The face wasn't melting; it wasn't the face of the person who had proved to be something different. The face on the canvas captured the expression, the feeling of the disillusioned person—the falling away of the scales that kept him from seeing the truth. I knew this viscerally, as my own skin felt as though it was sliding off of my bones and I realized that the gallery would never be the same, could never feel the same, because someone's evil act had intruded. Britt or Prudence could have been killed.

This brought me to another thought. Prudence's father *had* just been killed. Was someone trying to kill her, as well? Or was it Britt the gunman had been aiming for? I reached out to Britt and took her hand. "Are you okay?"

She shrugged. "I am having trouble believing this is happening. I wish Terry were here."

"Where is he?"

"He's with a client. He said he would come by later."

I squeezed her hand. "Do you know of anyone who—might have a grudge?"

She shook her head. "No. My clients are pleased with what they purchase, and they are all wealthy enough not to quibble over price. What other reason would there be?"

A good question. Why had this happened?

"What about Prue? Does she have any enemies?"

Britt's eyes still looked disturbingly wide. "No—just family stuff, you know. Like we were talking about at my house. She was just telling me that she had an argument with Cash today—oh, I shouldn't be airing her family things. Look at her over there; she's crushed."

Prudence was closer to the door of room one with Damen, who looked very pleased to have an opportunity to protect her. I wondered why Damen didn't seem more traumatized.

"Damen's ex-military," Britt said, reading my mind. "He seems to be in his element, doesn't he?"

I was still curious about Prue's argument. "Why was Prue in a fight with Cash? Maybe it's important."

She shook her head. "I doubt it. Prue just happened to remember that right before their dad died, like a couple of days before, Cash brought over some girl named Amber, and they met privately with him. Prue only knew about it because she had been there to make arrangements about the birthday party, and she was leaving when Cash got there with this girl."

"Amber again," I said under my breath.

"What?"

"Nothing. Just—I heard her name once before. Go on."

"Apparently the meeting really upset Marcus. Later on he told Prue indignantly that he didn't want 'that Amber' to come over anymore."

This was indeed strange. I wanted Parker to hear it, but he was busy with his crime scene. "Does Prue have any idea what was happening?"

"No. And I guess she raised it with Cash today and got nowhere. He said she should mind her own business, which shocked her, because Cash is always so sweet."

I looked back at the painting. *Disillusionment*. Family could cause it, too.

I realized that the people in the room had all calmed down with the presence of the police; they had rehashed the event itself by telling the story to one another, and now they had slipped back into gallery talk while they waited to be questioned. I heard words like *flowing, bold, dramatic,* and *light.*

Britt's hand still lay limp in mine. I shook it a little.

"Hey. We're stuck here for a while. Tell me what's been bothering you."

Her eyes filled with tears, and she wiped at them angrily. "This is silly. It's the stress of this shooting, not—the other thing."

"What other thing?"

She smiled at me. Her eyes were shining with tears, and she looked very pretty. "You know how long I've been with Terry? Five years. And I still love him as much as I did on the very first day."

"Of course you do. I can see that."

"And what I love best about him is that he's such a free spirit. He doesn't go by the book, you know? Terry lives life on his terms. And that's worked for us. We work together."

"I agree."

She slipped her hand out of mine and clasped hers together. "But I'm getting older, and I find that I've changed. I was always so antitraditional, and now—" She smiled at me and shook her head. "Suddenly I find myself wanting the things my parents had. The things my mother had. And I always said I was nothing like my mother."

"You're Britt. You are your own person," I assured her.

She nodded, looking at her lap. "Terry and I always said we didn't need all the trappings that other people craved—marriage, children, cozy house and two-car garage. We were an adventure couple, and we would seize life by the horns."

"You have!"

"Yes. And Terry wants to do it forever. But, Lilah—I've done a lot of soul-searching in the last few months, and I have to be honest with myself. I wish that Terry wanted to marry me, because suddenly that's what I want."

"There's nothing wrong with that!"

"But there is. Because it's a betrayal to Terry, and to this agreement that we had. And the thing is—the whole reason I love Terry so much is that he's the sort of guy who doesn't marry. You see the problem? If he married me it would force him into domesticity, and I would never want that for him. I love him the way he is!"

"But you also want him to propose to you and give you a ring."

She laughed. It was a bitter little sound. "Yes. And a married life together. And I can't bring those two images together. I can't tell Terry about this at all. It's ridiculous, but there you have it."

I thought about this for a moment. Would Terry want to settle down, go through a wedding ceremony, wear a ring on his hand? I had to agree with Britt—this didn't sound like something that the wildly independent Terry would want. And yet I knew he loved Britt very much. Wasn't love about meeting in the middle? "Marriage isn't death, Britt."

"No. But it's a box of sorts. That's how Terry would see it, and I agree. You commit to marriage, and you're shaping your own future."

"That's very grim. My father told me once that it was a relief to marry my mother. He had wandered around looking for someone like her, and once he found her he said he was happy to live on his own little island with her. She is his oasis."

"How sweet," Britt said. Her face remained sad, though.

Suddenly a uniformed officer was standing before us. "Miss Blackwood? Detective Parker would like to speak with you."

She nodded and walked away with her police escort. I found it both impressive and obnoxious that Jay could summon people to himself, a king amidst the detritus of crime. I wondered fleetingly if Jay Parker would ever want to marry me. It seemed doubtful, considering that our rekindled relationship had already encountered roadblocks.

After about half an hour, a junior officer came to question me, and then I was released. I looked for Britt, who seemed exhausted. "Oh, Lilah—listen, I'm just going to stay a bit longer. I need to get the window patched, and the police might have more questions for me. I've asked Prue and Damen to take you home. Do you mind?"

"No, of course not. Call me, okay?"

Britt promised that she would. I never even had a chance to say good-bye to Parker, who was immersed in questioning people. I followed Prudence and Damen out to his car, which was a surprisingly sedate Chrysler minivan. I climbed in the back and thanked them, and Prue turned to me from the front passenger seat. "No problem. Thanks for coming out tonight."

"Your painting is amazing. I understood it better after the shooting."

She studied my face and nodded slowly. "That makes sense. Thanks."

We drove the reverse of the route that Britt had taken hours before, mainly in silence. Damen attempted a few more things in his soothing voice, but Prue and I were lost in our own thoughts. When they pulled up in my driveway, I reached for the door handle.

Prue turned around, suddenly urgent. "Lilah, I know Jay Parker was there tonight. Do you know why? I mean, he's been working on my dad's case. . . ."

"He was there for me," I said. "On a date. But lately that's how a lot of our dates end: with Jay working. You don't have to worry—he'll get to the bottom of both things."

"Right! You said you were dating him."

"Yes. Since December."

"That makes sense, then." But she looked concerned.

"Thanks again, Prue. Damen," I added, nodding at him. "I appreciate the ride."

"No problem at all, Lilah. Good night," Prue said.

Just before I shut the door, in the glare of the car's interior light, I saw Prudence send a worried look to her boyfriend. I was suddenly too tired to worry what it might be about.

I slammed the door, and the car backed out of the driveway.

Nat King Cole's voice was back in my ear, but this time he was singing "Mona Lisa," a song my Grandpa Drake had once sung to me whenever he found me coloring. I had a sudden longing for childhood and Grandpa

Drake and a Pine Haven I had known before people started getting killed.

But if you hadn't seen murder, a little voice in my other ear said, *you would never have met Jay Parker.*

And a third voice wondered if it would have been better that way.

CHAPTER THIRTEEN

O N SUNDAY MORNING I DELIVERED A BREAKFAST
casserole to a new client. I had prepared a lovely egg
dish flavored with dill, and the smell of it had made me
hungry. I was trying to decide what to make for my own
breakfast when I pulled up the long driveway and saw
Terry in his garden, doing some more weeding. In the
past Terry had paid landscapers to do this sort of thing;
I wondered if he was using it as a sort of therapy. My
parish priest, Father Schmidt, had once said that nothing
was healthier than getting one's hands in the ground.

I parked the car and climbed out, walking back to
Terry's place so that I could greet him. He stood up ea-
gerly, wiping the dirt off his hands with a rag. "Hey,
Lilah! You're up early today."

"You, too. I never noticed you gardening before."

He shrugged. "Britt says I need more fresh air. I tend to seal myself up in my office."

"I would, too, if I had an office as cool as yours." Every part of Terry's house was awesome. His office, located on the top floor, was bright and masculine, with one wall dominated by a giant window, and another made entirely of brick. Against this wall was his massive desk, and above it hung all sorts of Terry-like things: guitars, vintage travel posters from all over the world, license plates from cars that had belonged to his grandfather, a framed portrait of a much-loved and long-deceased dog. His computer equipment was state-of-the-art, and when my clunky little printer died, I often went over to Terry's and begged to use his stuff.

We stood there for a moment, smiling at each other with a certain degree of discomfort. There was a slight spring wind blowing; it smelled like Terry's flowers and freshly turned earth. Terry finally tossed his rag aside and said, "Pretty crazy last night."

"Yeah. I'm still feeling weird about it."

His face was grave; this was an expression unusual to Terry. "I'm going to ask your friend Parker to give me some protection for Britt—maybe that woman who guarded you at Christmas. For all I know, some stalker is after her."

"Did Parker talk to you yet? Ask you any questions?"

He looked surprised. "No. Do you think he will? I'm staying close to home today, anyway. In case Britt needs anything. She's still upset—I made her stay in bed with some tea and a book."

"You're a good boyfriend."

His expression went from grave to miserable. "Lilah, before things went crazy last night—did you have a chance to talk to Britt?"

I cleared my throat. "Um—yeah, we talked a bit. It was pretty chaotic—you know. With what happened." I felt reluctant to reveal any of what Britt had said. It was for her to share with Terry, not for me.

"I know. I wish I had been there for her." He looked down at his boots, then up at me. A loud car passed on Dickens Street, and he waited until it was gone. Then he said, "Does she want to leave me?"

His face was so sad that I broke my own rule. "Oh no, Terry! God, no. Just the opposite."

He moved closer, his face eager. "What do you mean? What did she say?"

"She said she loves you."

Now he was frustrated. "Then what is the *problem*? I can't get her to say one word to me—"

"Terry, listen." I was stuck in the middle, and it didn't feel good. "The fact is, Britt is worried about you leaving her."

"What?" His face was a picture of surprise.

"She—the thing is, she—her feelings have changed. No, not about you, but about what she wants. And she loves what a free spirit you are, you know? So it's hard for her. You need to just ask her directly."

"About what she wants?" he asked, his eyes wide. "You mean—from me? Do you mean, like, marriage and babies?"

"I think so, yes."

"*Britt* wants that?"

"Yes."

He shook his head. "That's never been her style, man. I have trouble believing—although that would explain a few things. Oh man." He ran a hand through his messy blond hair.

"This is none of my business. You need to talk to Britt."

He smiled at me, but he was clearly still processing the information. "Yeah, thanks, Lilah. I will do that."

I waved to him and walked back up the driveway, feeling nervous. What if Britt was angry that I had breached her confidence? What if she and Terry broke up? I couldn't imagine living in my house without knowing that the two of them were happy in theirs. They were Britt and Terry— I truly couldn't picture one without the other.

I let myself in to my place and greeted Mick, who looked as though I had woken him up. He had a new textured pillow, and half of his face bore the imprint of the material. "Hey, groggy. Were you fast asleep? Sorry to wake you." I patted his big head, and he closed his eyes. Then we walked down the little hall to the kitchen, where Mick got back in his basket and put his head back on his pillow. I laughed.

My cell phone throbbed in my pocket. I took it out, hoping for a text from Parker, but it was from Serafina, saying she hoped we were still coming today for dinner. I texted back that I was planning on it but didn't know if Jay could come because of a shooting the night before.

The fact that Parker hadn't texted or called made me angry, even though I knew he was working. Since our one beautiful night together, we had been at odds, and I wondered if we were drifting away from couplehood, as we had once before. Surely it couldn't have just been a picture of Angelo that had made Parker not trust me? Was there something about me that was essentially untrustworthy?

Moodily I went to my computer and turned it on. I flicked through my e-mail, read the important ones, and responded to them. I suddenly thought of what Britt said Prudence had told her the night before about Cash Cantwell and the mysterious Amber. On a whim, I went to Google. What had Cam said her last name was? Warfield. I searched "Amber Warfield, Loyola University." Three things popped up, two of which had nothing to do with my search terms. The third was a Loyola Language Department web page, expounding on all of its student activities. Under one photo, the caption read, *Freshman Amber Warfield asks questions about the study-abroad program.*

So this was Amber Warfield. She was what my grandfather might call "a slip of a girl," small and thin with chestnut brown hair and a dusting of freckles on her nose. She was pretty in a girl-next-door sort of way. With a start, I realized that I had seen her before, at Marcus Cantwell's birthday party. I must have just gotten a glimpse of her as a face in the crowd, but I recognized her freckles and her large eyes.

I sat back and thought about this. What had Amber

Warfield been doing at the party? Had she been visiting
Cash? Helping out Wade Glenning, who said he was also
her friend? But hadn't Prudence told Britt that Cantwell
didn't want Amber around? So why would she have been
at his birthday party? Did Jay know when he interviewed
her that she had been at the party on the day Cantwell
died? Should I call to tell him?

My baser instincts took over, and I shook my head. If
Parker wanted to talk to me, Parker could call me. Then
I would tell him the information.

I walked over to my counter, where Parker's roses,
while still beautiful, had lost some of their perfect firm-
ness. Soon the petals would start to fall. In that moment
I understood Terry's fear that Britt would leave him. One
could sense, after all, when a relationship was starting to
wilt and die.

PARKER TEXTED ME at four o'clock to say that he hadn't
forgotten dinner and would pick me up at five. I wrote
back tersely and went to get ready. As usual, I dressed in
a way to make Parker eat his heart out. That was an expression from Grandma Drake, from an oft-told story
about how she had won the heart of my grandfather. I
decided that I needed to call them, since they had been
continually in my thoughts.

While I donned a lavender knit dress and the same
necklace and earrings from the night before, I thought
about my grandparents. When they retired (she from teaching, he from architecture), they had decided to pursue a

lifelong dream to visit Alaska. They had loved it so much they'd relocated there. They came home once a year to visit everyone, and Cam had been there to visit them, but I had not. I imagined myself bringing Jay Parker to Alaska to meet my ever-youthful grandparents. I knew what Grandma Drake would say, when she pulled me aside: "Oh, honey, he is *luscious*." That was her word for attractiveness, which she had picked up on a soap opera or something. This made me laugh, and I was in good spirits when I went downstairs to feed Mick and let him out.

Parker arrived at five on the dot and escorted me to the car. We were both as stiff as people on a blind date, and I couldn't think of one thing to say to him. He looked a bit tired, and I realized with a twinge of guilt that he had made time for me despite his ever-pressing job.

Once we were on the road I said, "I looked up Amber Warfield. I realized that I saw her at Cantwell's party. Did you know she was there?"

Parker looked surprised. "How did you know I talked to Amber Warfield?"

"Cam told me that you pulled her out of his class."

"Huh. Yeah, she told me she was at the party. She claims she was only there for a few minutes to see her friends Cash and Wade, and that she never went inside."

"Prudence Cantwell told Britt Blackwood that she had argued with Cash about Amber; apparently Cantwell was angry after a meeting he had with Amber and Cash, just a couple of days before he died."

Parker's jaw tightened. "She did *not* mention that in our interview."

"Well, now you know."

I looked out the window and watched the scenery flash by. Soon enough I was looking at the beautiful tossing waves of Lake Michigan. Cam had a wonderful view of the lake from his apartment.

Finally Parker let out a loud, exasperated sigh. "How long are you going to freeze me out, Lilah?"

I turned to him. "Freeze you out? I'm just following your lead, Jay! Remember how you saw a photograph and overreacted and things have been weird between us ever since? That's on *you*, not me. I was happy and in love."

"And what are you now?" he asked quietly.

"I don't know," I said, turning back to the window.

He found parking—amazingly—near Cam's building, and we walked to the door together. Parker hadn't even bothered to say that I looked nice, although I'd caught him studying me with some admiration when we had first left my house.

We went through the lobby, passing Rosalie's Salon, where I had once gotten my hair done and met a mobster, and walked onto the elevator. We rode it to the fourth floor and made our way to Cam's apartment. I dreaded the whole visit now, when once I had been looking forward to it.

Parker seemed to feel the same way, because he hesitated before he knocked. A moment later the door was flung open and there was Serafina, looking glorious as always with her tumbling brown curls and her red silk blouse and black silky pants. "Oh, for God's sake," I snapped. "Do you always have to look so amazing?"

That bit of rudeness barely put a dent in her enthusiasm. She hugged both of us and then put her hands on her hips. "What's wrong?" she said.

"Let them in, Fina," Cam called from inside the apartment, his voice dry.

Serafina let us walk past her, then took us both by the hand and led us into her pretty kitchen. "What's wrong?" she asked again. "You have had a lovers' quarrel?"

There was no escaping her scrutiny—we both knew that. Serafina loved love, and she had worked hard to push Parker and me together. It was she who had provided the white dress that Parker remembered so fondly to Jenny Braidwell.

I sighed and rolled my eyes at Cam, who came to join us. He flopped onto a stool and said, "Yeah, what's going on?"

I pointed at Parker. "Jay saw a picture of Angelo and me in the paper. Some woman took it on the sidewalk, where I was asking Angelo a *question* about the TV show. Parker saw it and assumed that I'm sleeping with Angelo, and now we hate each other."

Parker snorted. "We don't hate each other. And you would have to see the picture."

"Where was this picture?" Serafina said.

I bowed to the inevitable. "In Friday's paper, in the Metro section. Go ahead and Google it the way Jenny did."

Serafina and Cam both did so, and Cam whistled.

Parker looked triumphant. "You see?" he said.

"It is nothing," Serafina said, snapping her fingers. "She works for this man. She is posing for a picture with him. So what? I pose with men I work with, for holiday photos and things. Cameron does not become jealous."

Cam held up a finger. "I'm always a little jealous, Fina. But I wouldn't ever leave you over it." He looked at Parker, his eyes narrowed.

Parker made an exasperated sound. "I don't want to *leave* Lilah. I am *in love* with Lilah!"

I stared at him, and Serafina clapped her hands. "Then what is the problem?" she asked.

I felt myself weakening slightly at the look in Parker's eyes, but I held out. "The problem is that Jay doesn't trust me. He thinks that I might go sneaking off with Angelo when he's not looking. Even though I told him I had no feelings for Angelo, and haven't for a year."

Parker slumped onto one of the stools. "I have a problem with jealousy, okay? I admit it. I never did before, but I do now. There's something about that guy—I don't know. I've felt it from the beginning, before we were even going out. I can't explain it." He was at a loss, and Serafina lunged forward and wrapped her arms around him.

"Of course you are jealous! All passionate men are jealous, and you are passionate about Lilah! This is a good thing! It means your love is strong!"

I started to say something sarcastic, but Serafina, her arms still around Parker, pushed me away with her toe and continued. "But, Jay, there is something you must know. Lilah's face never lights up unless she is saying one name: Jay Parker."

Parker's blue eyes met mine; there was a spark of something in them—amusement at Serafina, perhaps, who was still going on. "She comes alive for you alone," Serafina said. "There is no other man for her, and we can all see this. I think that you see it, too."

Cam said, "Okay, Fina, let up on them now."

"No!" Serafina said, her voice magisterial. "Prove that you are passionate about Lilah, Jay. You kiss her right now."

Jay hated being put on the spot, but to my surprise he said, "All right." He stood up and pulled me against him. I tried to resist at first, but then I tried less convincingly, and then I wasn't trying at all. I lost track of all time while Jay and I kissed each other; I was vaguely aware of my brother saying, "Oh, for God's sake," and Serafina laughing and clapping and saying, "Look how much he loves her!"

Eventually it was I who broke away; Jay looked ready to keep going. "Wow," I said.

"I'm sorry," Parker told me. "For what I said that day I saw the picture. I trust you; you know I do."

My eyes darted to Cam, who was watching with something between fascination and disgust. "We'll talk later," I said. "We're grossing out my brother."

Serafina actually smacked Cam's head. "He does not mind. Sometimes lovers need counseling, just like crazy people."

"Lovers *are* crazy people," Cam said, rubbing his temple.

Then Serafina was climbing all over him, apologizing for smacking him, kissing him on the sore spots he kept pointing to.

I grinned at Parker, who was smiling, too. He put his

mouth by my ear and said, "I love you," so that only I could hear it, and my bones essentially melted inside my body.

Through numb lips I said, "We could go to their bedroom."

Parker laughed. "Maybe we can wait until we get home."

Serafina stopped kissing Cam. She had messed up his hair to a comical extent, and he sat there like a big, sloppy baby. "You are going home? But we have a lovely dinner!"

"No, I just said we could *talk* more when we got home," Parker improvised.

"Yes—you can talk all night long," Serafina said with a surprising innocence. "But first we will drink wine and eat this lovely pasta that Cameron has made, and we will discuss love and marriage and babies."

"Oh my," I said, and Parker squeezed me against him.

DINNER WAS A hilarious affair; Parker and I were both so relieved to be back to normal that we fully encouraged all of Serafina's antics, and she was in great humor because she had played matchmaker. She told us of the one fight she and Cam had gotten into, back before I had met her and they were just dating. Cam had promised to pick Serafina up after her class, but he got a flat tire and hadn't remembered to bring his phone. She waited outside the science building for two hours, thinking that Cam had rejected her.

By the time he got there, she was beyond fuming and

unwilling to hear any excuses or apologies. I could only imagine what an angry Serafina would look like.

"So how did he win you over?" Jay asked.

Serafina smiled. "He decided to think like me and be very dramatic. He got out and lay down in front of the car. He told me to run him over."

I looked at my brother, shocked. "That was a stupid thing to do," I said.

Cam's lip twisted, and he pointed at his wife. "She loved it."

"I did!" Serafina said, clapping her hands. "He was making a statement. A very bold statement. And so I forgave him."

"Did you do this in front of *people*?" I asked in disbelief.

Cam started laughing. "We were in the city. On Michigan Avenue."

Then we were all laughing, and Parker was pouring me more wine, and things were good.

I sighed and broke off a corner of my bread. "All I know is, love is exhausting."

Cam's phone buzzed on the table, and Serafina pursed her lips at him. "Cameron always gets work mail," she said. Cam picked up the phone, swiped on the screen, and read something, then put it down.

"Sorry. Just a colleague asking about a presentation we're doing."

"They always bother him," Serafina said.

"I asked him to check in with me," Cam corrected.

"And now he did, so we're all good." Then he turned to Jay. "Hey, what was that about the other day when you pulled Amber out of class?"

Jay smiled down at his plate. "You know I can't talk about that. Her name has come up—several times—in relation to a case I'm investigating. She wasn't particularly helpful."

Cam nodded. "Well, I hope she's not involved in anything. I happened to learn, through a colleague, that Amber has had a tough life. She grew up in the foster care system and then was finally adopted as an older child—twelve or thirteen, I guess. Those parents were good ones, I'm told. They're the ones putting her through college."

Serafina's large eyes were compassionate. "I cannot imagine being a child without a parent. Every day I recall lessons I learned from Mama and Papa."

It was true; good parents were the gift we all took for granted. I sighed and thought, for some reason, of Marcus Cantwell and his mixed brood. Five children from three mothers; had that made things more difficult for them, growing up? Certainly Cash and Prue seemed well-grounded. Why had Marcus Cantwell disliked Amber so much? She was just a child.

A thought dropped into my head, and I sat bolt upright.

Ross had said, when we dined at his house, that Cantwell had six children. *Six children.*

I grabbed my phone and texted Parker: Meet me in the hallway.

CHAPTER FOURTEEN

I WAITED FOR HIM TO HEAR THE BUZZ. HE CHECKED his phone and raised his eyebrows, then looked at me with a silly smile.

"Hey, I just remembered something," I said to the table in general. "I'll be right back." I didn't bother making a better excuse; I just went into the hall and waited for Parker, who appeared one minute later, still smiling.

"Lilah, I think we have to wait," he said, looking both ways down the hall.

"I'm not demanding sex, Parker," I said. Then I touched his face and said, "Not yet. But I just realized something. Ross said Friday night that Cantwell had six children. I corrected him and said five. But what if Cantwell had said six? If he told Ross that he was supporting *six* children?"

Parker picked up on my thinking immediately. "You're thinking Amber is his, and he resents her. Maybe she made demands."

"It's worth looking into, right? But if she was his child, why not acknowledge her? He acknowledged all the others." I stared into Parker's eyes, for once not distracted by their beauty.

"But he was married to their mothers. Amber was never officially his daughter—if she's his daughter at all."

I touched his arm. "But, Jay—if she is, and he treated her badly—that gives her a motive for murder. And she was at the party; I saw her there."

"Interesting," he said.

"And another thing. Let's say, for instance, that she is Cantwell's child. That would mean at least Cash knew about it, right? And maybe Wade Glenning, too. He acted all weird when I asked if Cash and Amber were friends. The three of them seem to have a secret, and this would explain it. But then why would Cash keep it from his other siblings?"

"Have you *met* his other siblings?"

I laughed. "Yeah, they might have a problem with it. Mostly the two brothers, I think. I don't know about Emma. Prudence seems cool. I've met her a couple of times now— once at the gallery, as you know. She seems—normal."

Jay looked thoughtful. "I always got along with her. She was quiet back then—always wandering off to sketch something or to do some painting for her school portfolio. She always seemed close to her dad." He leaned against the wall and said, "The funeral is tomorrow."

"Yeah. Your mom asked me to go with her. Will you be there?"

"I will. For work reasons, mainly. Maria will be outside in her car."

"Why? Are you afraid someone is going to bomb the church?"

He touched my hair. "No, but funerals are emotional; you never know what you might see. So we're both going to be watching carefully."

"Okay. Meanwhile what about Amber?"

He nodded. "Let me make a call. I'll have Maria bring her in."

He stayed in the hallway while I went back in to the warm, happy apartment, fragrant with pasta and Serafina's flower arrangement. Serafina was smirking at me. "Now you can't keep your hands off each other," she said.

"That's mostly true," I said. "But we were talking about murder out there. Jay might have to leave soon."

She wilted at this. "But there is still tiramisu. Stay for dessert."

"Um," I said, but then Parker came in.

"It's fine," he said. "I can stay." Serafina and Cam went into the kitchenette to prepare the dessert and coffee, and Parker leaned toward me and kissed my ear. Then he said, "I talked with Maria, and we agreed to bring Amber in tomorrow morning sometime after the funeral. We don't believe she's going anywhere. She's actually spending the evening with Maria's niece Lola."

"Did you say Amber?" Cameron said, shocked. He always did have supersonic hearing. "You're bringing her in?"

Parker shrugged. "We have more questions."

Cameron shook his head. "She's really not the type. I'm telling you. She's not some kind of criminal."

"Let's hope that's true," Parker said. "Let me help you clear these dishes."

Serafina held up her hand. "No! You sit there and I will bring you coffee. Cameron, take away their plates." My brother did it; I was torn between admiration and disgust. "Now you must eat lots of dessert. There is plenty," she said.

PARKER AND I got back to my place at around midnight. We sat in the car for a moment in a companionable silence. Then Parker said, "Can I hang around?"

I turned in my seat. "Do you mean in general, or to-night?"

"Both."

I studied his blue eyes for a while. "I'm counting on the idea of you staying around, Jacob Ellison Parker."

"In general, or tonight?"

"Both," I said.

He grinned. "I can't stay until morning like last time, though. I have to be at work super early. I'm going to have to creep out of here eventually."

I knelt on my seat so I could lean over to kiss him. "I have to be up early, too. Why don't we quit our jobs so we can be together all the time?"

With a mighty heave he pulled me onto his lap and

kissed me properly on the lips, lingering over his work. "Lilah, you have no idea how good that sounds."

"Mmm. Come inside. I have to let Mick out, and then I have to run upstairs to make sure my bed is made."

Parker laughed. "It doesn't matter. We're going to un-make it, anyway."

"It does matter. It's an honor thing."

We went inside, hand in hand, and greeted Mick, who was, as always, super glad to see us. I fed Mick a snack and let him outside and back in, and then I raced Parker up the stairs. I had remembered to make my bed, after all, but Parker was right: we unmade it in record time.

WHEN HE LEFT it was two in the morning, but I couldn't sleep. I floated around for a while with not even Mick for company; he had climbed to my room and gone to sleep in his nighttime basket, and now I was on my own. I went back downstairs and smiled at everything I saw. My eyes lighted on the Miss Moxie books, and I realized I hadn't even told Parker that I had quit the Angelo job. It wouldn't have been smart, probably, to bring up Angelo's name in any context. I would tell him soon.

My maid of honor book was also lying on the counter. I picked it up and scanned the table of contents, which included sections about the tradition of the bride's right hand, the philosophy of support during special and ritual occasions, and the specifics of what I needed to do for the bride.

I paged through this, which had twenty-five sections. "Oh my," I said. Among other things I needed to be in charge of the other bridesmaids and their dresses, of a shower and bachelorette party for Jenny, of keeping track of her gifts. Those were the ones at the top of the list. I would also need to pay for my own gown and shoes and, apparently, for whatever venue in which we held the shower and the party.

Catering wouldn't be a problem, obviously—my Haven friends would give me a discount. But paying for a hall was something I hadn't thought about, and also something I couldn't afford. I sat at my counter, trying to think of places in Pine Haven that were pretty and elegant, yet inexpensive. There were, of course, none of those. I looked out the window at the moonlight shining on the driveway that led to Terry and Britt's place. *Their gorgeous stone mansion* with a large main room that would easily hold many tables and lots of decorations. *Why not*? I thought. I could at least ask Terry and Britt, and if not their house, why not the gallery? That, too, was beautiful, and would give a touch of sophistication to Jenny's shower.

Warming to this idea, I grabbed a notebook and started jotting down ideas for decorations, along with a note to speak to Terry or Britt about borrowing their space. I would need to call the bridesmaids soon and start organizing some things with them. Now that I had a plan, I felt less intimidated about being a maid of honor.

With a sigh I pushed the notebook aside and picked up a Miss Moxie book. This one was called *Miss Moxie the Spy*. In the beginning of the book, Miss Moxie is explaining to her friend what makes a good spy. She clarifies that a spy is merely a watcher, but a watcher who knows what to look for. "A spy sees things that other people don't see," Miss Moxie says as she peers across a field with a pair of binoculars. Her friend, a giraffe, asks Miss Moxie why she is studying the family of leopards who live across the field; to her, the leopards have always looked and acted completely normal.

Miss Moxie shakes her head at her giraffe friend and says, "When something looks too black-and-white, you can be sure it isn't right."

In the end, Miss Moxie is vindicated. The leopards are smugglers, and the police force, which is composed of bears, comes to take them away.

I closed the book and found some wrapping paper in my drawer, then wrapped three Miss Moxie books for Henry and saved one for myself. The artwork was so lovely I wanted to be able to look at it once in a while.

I tied a piece of ribbon around the package, knowing that Henry would be scornful of this frippery, but still wanting the present to look nice. I was excited to see what Henry thought of Miss Moxie, and I couldn't wait to give him the gift.

Meanwhile I thought about Miss Moxie's advice to the giraffe. What was there in this case that was "too black-and-white"? Was there someone out there wearing an inauthentic face? And if so, how did one separate him or her from the innocent people?

If only we had Miss Moxie and her spy binoculars.

CHAPTER FIFTEEN

ON MONDAY MORNING I MADE A DEEP-DISH LASA-gna and delivered it to Alberto Palladini, a friend of Serafina's who wanted to join his colleagues' progressive dinner party. He thanked me elaborately, hugging me and kissing both of my cheeks. I laughed and ran back to my car, where I grabbed my phone, called Haven, and left a message for Esther, reminding her that I was going to the funeral and would be late. Then I drove to Weston, and the home of Jim and Marietta Becker. They were the parents of my dear little Henry.

I pulled up to their house, which was small but sweet like a storybook home, a two-story brick affair with a red door. I hopped out with my gift and knocked; Marietta came to the door, holding a spatula. "Hi, Lilah! You're up early. I was just making some breakfast—do you want to join us?" Her dark hair was tied back with a bow, and she wore no makeup, but she still looked vibrant and very much like Henry.

"I can't—I'm actually going to a funeral, but I just wanted to drop this off for my little friend."

She smiled. "You spoil him. Hang on—he's in the next room. Henry! Your aunt Lilah is out here with a present for you!"

I'm sure it was the word *present* and not the word *Lilah* that brought Henry to us at such impressive speed. He was still wearing his little pajamas—a matching top and shorts covered with army men—and he was clutching a Batmobile toy.

"What kind of present?" he asked. He also had a severe case of bed head.

"You mean, *Hello, Lilah. How are you*?" chided his mother.

"Hello. How are you?" Henry repeated, his eyes on the wrapped gift.

I pulled him into a hug and ruffled his messy hair. His Batmobile jabbed me in the abdomen. "I'm fine, dude. I just thought you'd enjoy this—it was recommended by a really cute little girl who's your same age."

Henry's lip curled. "I don't like girl toys."

"Who said it was a toy?" I said, trying to sound mysterious.

He stood on his little bare toes. "I'm going to be in Aunt Jenny's wedding as one of the men in tuxedos. I'm wearing the Batman kind."

I handed him the present. "That's awesome," I said. "I'll be in the wedding, too. Will you dance with me at the reception?"

Henry's eyes widened. "No! The guys don't dance."

"Some of them do, Sir Henry."

"Not the cool ones." He had ripped open the books and was staring at them. "What are dese?"

"They're books! Really awesome books with great stories and illustrations. I think you'll like them."

"Henry loves reading," his mother assured me. Henry was looking dubiously inside the first book, where he found a picture of Miss Moxie's friend, a giraffe, entering her house by bending in half at the waist. This made Henry laugh. "Look at this graffe," he said, pointing. "He's got a tummy ache."

"Look them over, and then give me your review," I told him. "I have to run to an appointment."

"Say *Thank you*, Henry." His mother poked him in the back.

Henry made a goofy face that made the cartilage in his neck stand out. "Thank youuuuu!" he said in a weird voice. Henry had trouble being polite, but he had the excuse of being six.

"You're welcommmmmme!" I answered in my own weird voice, and Henry giggled. I patted his messy hair, waved to his mother, and jogged back to my car.

I would let Miss Moxie work her magic, and see if Henry of Weston could resist it.

* * *

THE FUNERAL WAS well attended. The sun wasn't in full attendance for Marcus Cantwell, but there was an appropriate solemnity about the gray clouds that gathered over the Congregational church where Cantwell's family would say their final farewells.

I sat with Ellie, occasionally patting her hand. Jay had joined us briefly to give his mother a kiss and me a slightly longer kiss, but then he floated to the back of the church, where he could keep an eye on the people walking in. Ellie's grief seemed to abate considerably when she observed the two of us together. "So perfect," she whispered to me with a little grin. The Cantwell family members, all in black, presented a united front, all sitting in one pew and occasionally slinging arms around one another. Cash looked handsome in a suit—almost like a different person—and his half brothers, Scott and Owen, sat on either side of him, offering what seemed to be genuine love and support. Prudence and Emma sat together on Scott's right, and Emma's husband and the three children sat in the pew behind them. Prudence seemed to have recovered from Saturday night's events, although she looked pale. I wondered if Parker and Grimaldi were here partly as protection for Prudence Cantwell. I scanned the pews for Damen and saw that he was at the end of the same row that Timothy Britton was in, but the men didn't seem to be interested in acknowledging each other.

A quick glance around the room showed me some other faces I recognized: the much-discussed Amber was sitting toward the back, along with Grimaldi's niece Lola and Wade Glenning, the photographer. Some other people I had seen at Cantwell's party were there at his funeral, as were some of Ellie's neighbors, who had also been Cantwell's neighbors.

Cantwell's ex-wives were there—all three of them—and they sat together in one of those strange little realities of fate. They seemed to like one another, and they spoke in low tones in their pew. I noticed that all of them had the same shade of hair, either through nature or art: a deep chocolate brown.

One woman sat all alone in a side pew; I wondered who she was. She wore a trench coat and a lavender scarf; she looked to be somewhere between fifty and sixty.

Jenny Braidwell, the third grade teacher of Carrie Britton and the former teacher of Tim Britton, appeared suddenly next to our pew and said, "Can I sit with you?" Moments later Carrie turned around and saw her teacher; her eyes widened, and she poked her brother, who also turned and looked a bit starstruck.

I whispered, "You are awesome," and Jenny shrugged.

"Poor kids," she said. "Such a nice family."

The service itself was relatively short, and the minister had clearly been told not to give a long sermon. He said a few brief words about life and the legacies we leave behind and some of those "footprints in the sand" type of comments. His words were comforting without being preachy, and the family seemed to appreciate them.

Soon enough some solemn men lifted the coffin with gloved hands and marched it down the aisle, and Cantwell's children followed with noble expressions. Prudence and Emma cried softly, and the young men looked sad.

We all followed them out, where the coffin was placed into a hearse. Parker and Grimaldi talked in an unobtrusive corner at the top of the stone steps leading to the church door, leaning against a cement wall. People were holding quiet, grave conversations in small groups scattered over the large graduated steps rather than rushing right to their cars. Even the Cantwell children lingered, approaching people and thanking them for coming. Little Peach wandered past, and I called to her. "Hello! Do you remember me?"

Peach waved. "I saw you at the bookstore, and at Grampa's party."

"Yes." I waited until she moved closer, and I shook her little hand. "I wanted to thank you for introducing me to the Miss Moxie books. I've read two of them, and they were great."

"You should read all of them," she said. "We could have a tea party and talk about them. I do that with my mom. We call it book club."

"I would love to be in that book club," I said enthusiastically.

Emma Cantwell's voice said, "We'll have to invite her next time, won't we, Peach?"

Peach hugged her mother's leg, and I stood up. "Hello, Emma. How are you holding up today?"

She shrugged. "It was a nice service. We're happy that so many people came out for Dad. So I'm doing okay." Her eyes were dry now, but her smudged makeup told the tale of her grief.

"You have made quite an impression on all of my children," she said. "They are smitten with you."

I smiled at her. "They are great kids. But I think today they only have eyes for Miss Braidwell."

Emma glanced over at Jenny, who was talking with Ellie, and nodded. "So sweet of her to come."

"She's a great person."

"Oh? You know Miss Braidwell?"

"We were college roommates."

Emma's smile was big and genuine. "What a small world! That is neat."

Tim Britton appeared and put his arm around his wife. She leaned back ever so slightly, into him, and his grip tightened. It made me feel good to see not only that he was there for his wife, but that she was willing to accept his support, to let him be strong for her. "Hello," he said. "Lilah, right? Good to see you again."

Emma stayed tucked into him as she said, "Lilah was college roommates with Carrie's Miss Braidwell."

Now it was Tim's turn to smile. "Is that so? We heard a little rumor that Miss Braidwell is engaged."

"She is. I'm to be maid of honor."

"That's exciting," Emma said.

"She's marrying another teacher at the school—Ross Peterson."

Tim and Emma both started laughing, and I stared. "Is that funny?"

"Sorry," Tim said. "It's just funny, because when we were at parent-teacher conferences last month, Em went on and on about how surprised she was that Miss Braid-well was single, and that she couldn't believe someone as cute as Mr. Peterson was around and not asking her out."

"Well, you were right on the money, because I think Ross has had eyes only for Jenny for quite some time. They started going out around Christmastime."

"That's sweet," Emma said. "The kids are going to make such a big deal of it. Even Tim will be excited when he hears, and he's normally too cool to get enthused about things with the girls." She and her husband exchanged a fond glance.

Tim Senior said, "Speaking of our kids, I'd better go round up the older ones and take them to the car. It was good seeing you, Lilah."

"You, too." I waved as he moved away, and then Emma was pushing Peach toward me.

"Say your good-byes, Peachie. We're going to pray for Grandpa and then have some lunch."

"Bye," Peach said. "See you at book club."

I waved, and they moved down the steps and toward their car.

I turned to see that Cash Cantwell was near me, in a close and serious conversation with Amber. He saw me and lifted a hand. "Hey, Lilah! I don't know if you've ever met Amber Warfield. She's a friend of mine." They exchanged a mysterious glance that they assumed I couldn't see. What did it mean? That she was his half sister, but they assumed no one knew that?

"Hello," I said.

"Hi," Amber offered with a little smile. She wasn't as tiny as she had looked in the photo, but she was petite and pretty in a freckled way.

I could feel Parker's blue gaze on us from his unobtrusive post. Soon he would be swooping in and telling her he needed to ask a few questions. "So how do you two know each other?" I asked.

Cash scratched his arm and scanned the people on the steps around us. "I started hanging out with Amber around the time I graduated high school. I think we met at a party or something. She just came up to me and said hi. And we found out we had a lot in common."

"Wade said he was a part of your group, too."

Cash nodded. "Wade and I started hanging out after I graduated, and I introduced him to Amber. And the three of us—I guess we've been kind of a trio for a while now. The three of us started doing some stuff together and going to the same parties and stuff." He looked at Amber, who nodded with a pixielike grin.

I could actually feel someone staring at us, and I turned, expecting to see Parker, but instead got the full effect of the glare from Lola, Grimaldi's niece. I looked back at the two in front of me and realized how it must have looked to Lola—handsome Cash wearing a rare suit and standing next to a pretty girl.

Amber had spied someone she knew. "I'm going to say hi to Jonah," she told Cash.

He nodded. "See you later."

"Nice meeting you," I said, and then Amber was gone.

Cash had spied Lola and called out to her, but Lola flounced away in the other direction. Even at a funeral she could play the role of the jilted woman.

Cash looked dejected, and I touched his arm. If one more guy failed to see the giant cues a woman was sending, I would despair for the species. "Cash, do you know why she's always walking away from you?"

His eyes were wide. "You noticed that, too?"

I sighed. "*Cash*. Everyone sees it, because she's really obvious, hoping you'll pick up on her message."

He looked at me, his face a blank.

"She likes you. She obviously still likes you, and she is *jealous* because you were talking to Amber, who is pretty."

"But—why did she walk away, then?"

"*Because*, Cash—she is angry and feels rejected by you. Your role in this elaborate dance is to chase her down and say you still like her, too. You might have to do this more than once. Then she will admit she likes you, and then you can kiss her and all will be well."

"Who says I still like her, too?" he said weakly, his eyes on Lola. I rolled my eyes at him, and he laughed. "Okay. I get it. I'm not that stupid. I'll take your advice."

"Not this instant, because that would be weird timing. We're standing in front of a hearse, which Lola should be acknowledging. But soon. You can resolve it soon."

To my surprise, Cash pulled me into a sudden crushing hug and said, "I like you, Lilah. I knew I liked you on the first day when you were at my dad's party with your dog."

"I like you, too, Cash. And I'm sorry for your loss."

He let me go and smiled. "I was talking with my brothers and sisters today, and it was good to talk—to just kind of air everything. I think we're all going to be okay."

Just as he said this I saw Scott Cantwell standing near the hearse and glaring at someone nearby. I craned my neck to follow his line of vision and saw Prudence and Damen talking to some people on the sidewalk. Scott's venom seemed to be aimed at his sister. This gave me a bad feeling. What had Prudence said about Scott and money? That he had always been "a greedy little boy." What would make Scott angry with Prudence?

I felt a sudden chill, and it wasn't just the spring breeze. Could Scott feel angry enough to have shot a bullet through Britt's gallery? None of the siblings had been there with Prudence.

A moment later Scott moved away, and I wondered if I had overreacted. Perhaps too much people-watching was having an effect on me. I was ready to leave this place and get back to work. I joined Ellie and Jenny and told them as much.

"I have to get to work, too," Jenny said, looking at her watch. "My sub was only for the morning."

Ellie nodded. "Will you drop me off at home, Lilah? I think Jay is busy."

"Of course. Then we can chat."

Parker and Grimaldi were still in scanning mode, but they had homed in on Amber and were moving down the steps, slow and careful as predators. I jogged up toward Jay. "I know you're working—I'm just saying good-bye. Maybe I'll see you later. See you, Maria."

"See you, Lilah," she said, moving past me.

Parker held my arm. "What were you talking about with our friend Amber?"

"Hmm? Oh, nothing. Cash just introduced me, and I asked how they knew each other. They're all in the same group of friends—Cash, Amber, Wade. Somehow they all know Lola, too, I think, or maybe that's just Cash. I'm not sure. He met Amber at a party, right around the time Cash graduated. About two years ago."

"Good to know," Parker said. His phone buzzed with a text message, and he glanced at it automatically, then looked more closely. "What the hell?" he said, mostly to himself.

"What is it?"

He looked up at me with a slightly distant expression. "Oh—nothing. It's not related to work, I don't think." His eyes flicked away; Maria had caught up with Amber and was talking to her.

He looked back at me. "I have to leave now. I'll try to keep in contact."

"You do that," I said. I edged a little closer and said, "I took a mildly incriminating photo of you last night, so you'll want to stay in touch and make sure I can be trusted with it."

He grinned. "Don't leave town." He moved past me and followed Maria, who was leading Amber down the stairs and toward her waiting car. Amber seemed confused, and her body language suggested that she was posing numerous questions to Grimaldi. Maria's nonverbal communication suggested a reluctance to answer those questions until they got to the station. Finally Amber shrugged. Jay joined them and said something to Amber, and they all got into the police vehicle.

I felt a burst of sympathy for Amber. I would not have wanted to be interrogated by Jay Parker, especially if he felt I had held out on him. Upon reflection I realized that I had in fact been in just that position with Parker, and it was not a pleasant experience.

My bet was that if Amber had any secrets, Jay and Maria would get them this time.

CHAPTER SIXTEEN

At Haven it soon became clear that something had changed between Gabby and Will. We all stood at our morning stations, preparing food for a brunch at the women's club, and Will couldn't seem to tear his eyes from Gabby's face. She in turn seemed hyperaware of his gaze and blushed about every thirty seconds.

Esther rolled her eyes at me. We had both thought things would be better if they stopped fighting, but this was potentially more annoying. Was it something about the warmer weather? I wondered. Cash was in love with Lola, Will was in love with Gabby, Ross was in love with Jenny, Damen was in love with Prue, Terry was in love with Britt . . .

And I was in love with Jay Parker.

Esther seemed to read my mind. "Spring is in the air today, isn't it? What's that quote about young lovers and spring?" She smiled down at her phyllo dough.

Gabby blushed again and lifted her head. "What do you mean?"

"Oh, just noticing the lovely scent of spring," Esther said.

Will was barely paying attention. He was focused on his pastry, which was going to be the star of the dessert table. Occasionally his eyes darted to Gabby, whose hair looked more glossy than usual. He didn't seem to remember that Esther and I were there.

Jim came in and opened the large wall fridge, gathering ingredients. "Lilah," he said, "I was thinking, after your conversation with Will the other day, that Cantwell was a familiar name to me, too."

I looked up from my mini quiche cups. "You knew Cantwell?"

"No, not at all. Just the name stood out in my head, and I knew it was connected to a news story—a kind of old one."

"Jim never forgets a name," Esther said almost accusingly.

Jim shrugged. "I really don't. I just have that kind of brain. Anyway, I went on Google and searched for the headline. I knew it had been an act of violence. And I found it—I printed it out for you to give to Jay."

"Well, now I'm dying of curiosity. Can you sum it up?"

Jim had everyone's attention now. "This was fifteen years ago. The headline was 'Local Businessman Stabbed.'"

"What?" I said. "Do you mean Cantwell?"

Jim nodded. "He was well-known even then—a pillar of the Pine Haven business community. He showed up at the emergency room with a stab wound to the arm. He claimed that he had harmed himself doing what he called 'a household project,' but the doctors didn't buy it. They called in the police."

"Oh my gosh!" I said. Then a new thought occurred to me. "I saw a scar on Cantwell's arm on the day I met him. I asked if it was from surgery, and he wouldn't respond."

"He wouldn't then, either. The police tried to investigate but got nowhere because Cantwell wouldn't cooperate."

I thought about this as I poured batter into dough cups. Fifteen years earlier, someone had potentially disliked Cantwell so much that they had stabbed him—perhaps in a fight? Cantwell, for whatever reason, had not wanted to expose that person. But if he had had an enemy then, might he not have the same enemy now? And if he was willing to protect the one who stabbed him—could it have been one of his children?

Jim was shaking his head as he arranged some greens around a tray that would hold canapes. "I felt bad for Cantwell at the time. I can still remember thinking, when I saw the news coverage of Cantwell as he left the police station, that he looked like a lost man."

"What do you mean?" I asked.

"I'm not sure how to say it," Jim said. "I guess I felt at the time that he looked very sorry more than anything."

His kind brown eyes met mine. "He looked full of re-morse."

I ESCAPED TO the washroom, where I called Parker, whose sexy voice briefly distracted me.

"Parker," I said.

"Hey! What's happening? Didn't we just say good-bye?"

"Yeah, but I just heard something. Did you know that someone stabbed Marcus Cantwell fifteen years ago? It's got to be in your police computer somewhere."

"What? Let me call you back later, babe."

"Okay." I hung up but stayed in the bathroom for a while, because I couldn't get the stupid grin off of my face. *Babe*. God, I was as bad as Gabby.

I went back out to the worktable, where everyone had now become absorbed in his or her task. Jim's face was still grave, and I realized that Cantwell's story must have been truly striking to have stayed with Jim for fifteen years.

What, I wondered, would fill a man with *remorse* when he was the one who had been stabbed?

CHAPTER SEVENTEEN

ON THE WAY HOME I STOPPED AT THE GROCERY STORE
for my weekly shopping. I moved quickly through
the aisles, tossing things in my cart and looking at my
watch. Mick was really going to need some outside time
soon.

I dialed Parker again and waited on hold while the
receptionist tried to find him. What had her name been?
Patty? No, Penny. I got in a checkout line and starting
unpacking my cart. The hold music at the police station
was conflicting with the grocery store music. The police
line was playing "Killing Me Softly"—did they not find
that ironic?—and the store was playing a Coldplay tune.
They would both stick in my head, I was sure.

"Jay Parker."

"Hi. I know you're super busy, but I just want to know if I'll be seeing you tonight."

"No, probably not. And I'm very sorry to say that."

"I know." My voice sounded smug.

"But look on your porch. A little elf delivered something for me."

"How exciting! I can't wait."

"I'll call you when I can. Probably tomorrow. But you can text me tonight. I'll read them."

"Okay, sweetie."

"That's nice."

"Are you free for lunch tomorrow, maybe? I could drive out and steal you away for half an hour."

There was a pause; it was slightly longer than it should have been. "Uh—no. I think I'll be busy tomorrow at lunch. We'll work something out."

"Okay," I said. "I am confident that when you do have free time, you will come home to me."

"You're right about that. I've got to go."

"Love you," I said.

"I love you, too," said Jay Parker.

I GOT HOME and lugged some groceries up the steps. A little white bag sat in front of my door, with a card jutting out of it. Excited, I unlocked the house, ran to the kitchen to unload the groceries and let out my dog, and then came back to retrieve the little bag. I opened the package to find a beautiful glass paperweight with a perfect red rose preserved inside.

The card was still tucked into the bag. I pulled it out and opened it to find Jay's familiar scrawl. "The other roses will die," he said. "But this one never will."

I stared at the sentiment for a while, then put both the card and the glass ball on my windowsill, where the beautiful crystal would catch the changing light.

I let Mick back in and put some food and water in his bowls. Then I grabbed my cell phone and hit speed dial number two: my parents. The phone rang three times before my mother picked it up. "Hello?"

"Hi, Mom. Are you going out? You sound distracted."

"Oh no. We're actually just walking in the door. Is everything okay?"

"Yes. Wonderful. I just wanted to tell you—I'm in love."

My mother laughed. "Honey, we knew that back in October. But I'm glad you're willing to talk about it now."

I sighed. "Jay is so wonderful. I have to show you the beautiful gift he got me."

"Oh goodie. Maybe Dad and I will come over some night and bring dinner."

"That would be great. As soon as this Marcus Cantwell thing is over, maybe Jay can join us. Right now he's busy, and getting busier."

"So he's getting close to solving this?"

"I don't know. I found out a couple of things lately, just in conversation, and I passed them on to him. Hopefully they helped."

"Marcus Cantwell," my mother said with a sigh. "Life is strange."

"Wait—do *you* know Cantwell?"

"Well, we weren't friends. But Dad showed Marcus a house years ago. A long time ago now. He was about to make an offer, but then the whole deal fell through. Dad said he got the idea that maybe a relationship fell through, too."

"Years ago? It didn't happen to be fifteen years ago, did it?"

"I'm not really sure. I'll ask Dad." She covered her phone and murmured something in the background, then came back. "Yes, Dad says it was fifteen years ago, because he remembers he and Cantwell talked about the Cubs, and the guys they talked about haven't been on the team since then."

A relationship had fallen through. Might this have been the woman with whom Cantwell conceived Amber, if in fact Amber were his daughter? If that were the case, Amber would have been about three years old when the relationship ended. I had forgotten to ask Jay what they had learned from Amber when they questioned her. Surely they must know by now?

"What was going on fifteen years ago? Aside from the fact that all his kids were little?"

"I don't know. Cantwell was rich even then, and rather eccentric. Dad liked him, but he said he didn't seem the type to make friends."

My father said something in the background.

"What did he say?" I asked her.

"He said that Cantwell seemed to have a real charisma with women, but that men were immune to it."

"What, like some kind of spell he put on them?"

My mother giggled. "Certainly not. Because I met the man back then, and I didn't find him charismatic at all."

My father murmured again.

"What did he say this time?"

I could almost hear my mother blushing. "Nothing. He is insinuating that I could resist Marcus because I was too deeply in love with Daniel Drake."

I grinned. "Isn't that true?"

"Your father is an egotist."

"Mom. Ask Dad if Cantwell got stabbed in the time he knew him."

"What? Hang on." More murmuring. Then it was my father's voice on the phone.

"Hey, sweetheart. What makes you ask about that?"

"Something I heard today. That Cantwell was in the news about fifteen years ago for being attacked, although he claimed it was an accident."

"That's what he said to me, too," my father said. "We would drive around on Saturdays, looking at houses. He showed up one weekend with a huge bandage on. He told me it was an accident and not to believe what I heard on television."

"Did you have any ideas about it at the time?"

"Not really. I just wanted to sell the guy a house. And in the end, I didn't. Which was a real shame, because he was a 'money is no object' kind of guy."

"Huh. And it was never clear why he didn't buy the house?"

"Not really. He was divorced at the time, but he was

looking at big places, in North Pine Haven, where the price tags are big."

"Did he say it was for his children?"

A pause. "I don't remember him mentioning the children once," my father said.

LATER THAT NIGHT I took Mick out for a spring walk; the evening was chilly, but not freezing, and I wore a snug coat. We moved down our long driveway, headed for Dickens Street, when Britt came out of her house. "Hey, Lilah," she said.

"Britt! How are you doing? How's the gallery? Is everything repaired and locked up?"

She nodded, looking distracted. "Oh yes. The police are finished for the time being, but the gallery is going to be closed for the next couple of days. Your Jay suggested that. He wants to find out if it was a random shooting or if someone inside may have been a target. I told him it is not likely that it's me."

"I certainly hope not," I said, indignant.

She nodded again. "Hey, have you seen Terry?"

I felt suddenly cold. *Terry has left her and it's all your fault*, my brain said. "Terry? No, not tonight. Why?"

She forced a smile. "He's been gone all day. No calls or texts. I don't think I've ever been in this position—not with Terry. I—it just makes me nervous. I don't know whether I should start calling hospitals or—you know—preparing myself for something."

"What do you mean?"

"You know what I told you the other night. I don't think I've exactly been myself lately. I think I've been—moping, if you want to know the truth. Maybe Terry got tired of it."

"Britt, he wouldn't just walk out on you without a word."

"I hope not."

Her face was so distressed that I realized it was time to confess my part in their relationship. "Britt, listen—"

We were suddenly illuminated by the glow of headlights. Mick barked once, and a car stopped about six feet away from us. Terry jumped out and stood behind the open driver's door. "Hey, Lilah. Hey, Britt," he said.

"Where have you been?" Britt asked. I knew she was trying to sound lighthearted, as though Terry's absence hadn't bothered her, but her voice sounded brittle and fragile.

"I've been running some crazy errands. I'm sorry I didn't call—I had a chance to see something I wanted, and I had to drive to Michigan."

"You drove to Michigan and back?" Britt said, her eyes wide.

"Yeah. Hey, can you come for a quick drive with me?"

"I—now? Where are you going?"

"I'll tell you on the way. Were you going out?"

"No. Let me grab a coat," she said. She whisked back up the stairs and through the giant door to their house.

I studied Terry. He seemed the same as always, except that a certain nervous energy seemed to be emanating from him. "Everything okay, Terry?"

"Sure. It's a pretty night. Did you see that there's a full moon?"

I looked up at the bright and golden moon, then back at Terry. "Cool. Are you sure you're okay?"

"Fine. Oh, here she comes. I'll see you later, Lilah." He ducked into his car, and Britt climbed in on the other side. Then the car pulled away, and Mick, finally showing his impatience, tugged at his leash.

"Okay, boy, okay. Do you have any idea what's up with those two? Now they've got me feeling nervous."

Mick did not seem to know. We took our usual walk up one side of Dickens and back down the other. Mick liked to look in the brightly lit windows when he wasn't checking the sidewalks for interesting scents. As we walked I tried to fight a growing feeling of unease. Terry had seemed nervous. What if he was in fact going to break up with Britt? It would be horrible and unfair.

My brain told me I was wrong. Who would comment on a beautiful full moon and then break up with his girl-friend? Certainly not Terry, who lived for Britt's smiles.

And yet I realized that I didn't understand other people, not really. Certainly not Marcus Cantwell, or any of his children, or even my own family sometimes.

Mick and I returned home and locked ourselves in our little house. We ascended the spiral staircase and got into our respective beds. I had brought Jay's glass ball upstairs with me, and I studied it after I turned off the light.

Even in darkness the beautiful bloom was visible.

CHAPTER EIGHTEEN

I WORKED A HALF DAY AT HAVEN ON TUESDAY BECAUSE
we had only one engagement. I was thrilled to think
about having lunch in my own house and getting a few
things done. In the meantime I could spend some time
with Mick, who had been a bit neglected lately.

I had just finished a sandwich in my kitchen when my
phone rang. I touched the screen and slid over the call
button. "Hello?"

"Lilah, it's Britt. I'm so glad I caught you at home. Are
you busy? Were you on your way out?"

"No—I actually just got home from work."

"Might you have a moment to come over?"

I felt the same chill I had felt the night before. Britt's

voice was curiously toneless, and I couldn't gauge her mood. "Sure—did you need help with something?"

"I could just use a little company. I'll leave the door open for you."

"Okay."

With some trepidation I handed Mick a little rawhide square and then left my house, locking Mick safely inside. I moved down the driveway and up the flagstone path to Terry's stone steps, which I ascended slowly. What if they really were breaking up? Would Britt blame me for telling Terry what I knew?

I opened the large door and stepped into the hallway. I saw Terry's jukebox sitting in its usual spot, emitting its multicolored light. I felt like going to it and playing "Who's Sorry Now?"

"Britt?" I called.

"In the kitchen," Britt's voice said.

I went down the hall and turned into Terry's giant kitchen, where Britt stood at the stove, lifting a steaming kettle. "I was in the mood for tea; it's a bit drafty in here. Do you feel the chill?"

"Sort of," I said.

"I'll make you a cup, too."

She took out two lovely gold mugs, put tea bags in them, and poured in the steaming water. That's when I saw her jewelry. "What is that?" I said, pointing at her left hand.

She held up her hand so that I could see the ring, which was remarkable. It was a blue circle, which seemed to be a large sapphire, but in this were inlaid little diamond circles in the shape of a flower. It was amazing.

"It's from 1915—a beautiful art deco piece, isn't it?"

"It's like it was made for you."

"No—but it's definitely my style." She smiled at her hand.

"So—how did that ring happen to get on your finger?"

She handed me my mug. "That's what I wanted to tell you. Let's sit down."

We sat at their counter rather than at their formal dining table, and Britt pushed sugar and cream toward me. While I made my tea, she told me the story.

"Last night Terry drove me to a gallery. Not mine, since it's surrounded by police tape, but the gallery of a friend in Chicago."

"I wondered where the heck you guys were going."

She nodded. "I asked him what he needed there, and he said he had brought a new piece in that he wanted to show me."

I stirred my tea, but my eyes were on her. "Does Terry usually—?"

She held up a hand. "When we went into the main room, I saw that the gallery was filled with candles, which were all alight."

"What? That must have taken him—"

"Hours," she said, nodding her head. "And he really did drive to Michigan. For this." She held up the ring, which winked and glimmered.

"So—?"

"He led me to the center of the floor, where there was a painting on an easel, covered with a cloth. It was very strange. I asked him what was going on—he was being so weird, and kept acting restless, and he was kind of . . . sweaty."

I laughed.

"Then he went to the painting. He said he needed my advice about it. He said he'd had it commissioned months earlier, and that he'd just gotten the completed piece. He lifted away the cloth, and it was a painting of me."

"What?"

"By Jacob Ressler, an artist I admire. It was an utterly romanticized vision, with flowing hair and silky clothing. I'll show it to you in a minute."

"What was this all about?" I said. But I thought I knew.

"That's what I asked him. He said that he had fallen in love with the painting, and that he wanted it in his collection forever." Her eyes filled with tears.

"Oh, Britt."

"Then he got down on his knee. Can you imagine? Terry did! And he took out this ring."

She held up her hand again, and I admired its beauty anew. I couldn't begin to imagine what a hundred-year-old diamond-and-sapphire ring would cost.

"He told me that he wanted me in his life forever, and that marrying me was the best way to assure that would happen. He said he couldn't imagine anything better than being married to me."

"Wow," I said.

She turned her lovely wet eyes to me. "I know that you must have said something to Terry," she said. "Because he had no idea what was going on with me."

"Britt—"

"But I'm glad you did, because I just didn't know how to say it, and whatever you said—well, it brought out the sweetest, most romantic Terry I have ever seen."

"Did you say yes?"

She grinned and held up her ring hand next to her face. "Oh yes, I said yes."

I jumped up and hugged her. "Let me see the painting!"

She was out of her chair in an instant and holding my hand, pulling me toward their large, cavernous living room. There, on a wall above the fireplace, hung a picture of Britt in a silky blue dress, her dark hair blowing as though she were walking in a breezy night. Behind her was a dark sky full of stars. It made her look ethereal and beautiful.

"Terry said that he told the artist how he sees me, and that's what Jacob painted."

"Oh, Britt. If you don't marry him, I will."

She giggled. "I'm going to marry him, Lilah."

"Good." I gave her a quick hug, and then her doorbell rang.

"Oh my. I have no idea who that might be," Britt said breathlessly. We walked back toward the kitchen hallway.

"Where's Terry?" I asked.

"He had some stuff to do for a buyer. He'll be back soon."

We went to the door, where Britt peered out and said, "It's Prue." She let in her friend, who greeted me warmly and then pointed at Britt's hand.

"What's that?" she said.

Britt and I laughed, and then Britt told the story all over again, and then we took Prudence to see the painting.

Finally we all ended up back in the kitchen, where Britt made a third cup of tea. "How are you, Prue?"

"I'm okay. I'm glad the funeral is over. We all have to start life over now—a life without Dad in it."

I took a sip of my tea and said, "Prue, this might sound weird, but I wonder if it might be important."

She raised her eyebrows and sipped her tea. "Yes?"

"I—did your Dad ever suggest that he might have another child? One that might have been—not from any of his marriages?"

Britt looked shocked, and Prudence said, "Why would you ask that?" in a sharp tone.

"It just—it dawned on me when I heard something about your dad. Someone from the school where your dad was on the board said that Marcus had six children. I corrected him and said five, but then later I wondered if somehow he had been told the number six."

Prudence looked disapproving, and for a minute she reminded me of Emma. "Our dad was not the type to just go swanning off with some woman."

Britt and I must have looked surprised, because she slumped in her seat and said, "Well, not normally. And you would think that if we had another sibling he'd have bothered to mention it to us." She looked angry then, and she stirred her tea with some ferocity.

"What's going on?" Britt said, touching Prue's shoulder.

Prue shook her head, refusing to look at us, her face still fierce.

"I'm sorry if I brought up a sensitive topic," I said. "I

just wanted to help figure out—I mean, I know they're still looking for the—uh—perpetrator," I stammered.

Britt was watching Prudence. "Prue—you're obviously upset about something. Did you know something about your dad?"

Prudence looked frailer in an instant. She set down her tea and let out a long sigh. "Okay, I'm going to tell you something, but it can't leave this room."

"Of course," Britt said. I said nothing, because if it was good information, Parker was going to get it.

Prudence Cantwell sighed. "Cash told me he had found out we had a relative. A sibling. And that for whatever reason, Dad was not going to accept this person into the family. Cash told me, a few days ago, that he intended to share his inheritance with the outcast child, because he felt it was only fair."

"Wow," Britt said.

She shook her head. "I didn't like it. Cash is too trusting, and sometimes too gullible. I didn't know where he got his information, but obviously he could have been wrong. Anyone with some knowledge of our family could scam him and separate him from his inheritance."

She set down her spoon and sipped her tea. "I told him I did not want him giving half his money away to a stranger. I said if need be, I would have Scott find a way to shut the whole idea down."

Britt murmured something about it being a difficult situation, and they both managed to miss my expression, which probably included wide eyes and an open mouth.

"Prudence, did you have this conversation with Cash before the gallery night?"

"Hmm? Yes. Earlier that day we were chatting about—"

"Don't you realize that this gives someone a motive to shoot at you? Which someone actually did that same night?"

"A motive? What do you mean? Cash doesn't mind me talking to him that way. He knows that I'm his protective older sister."

I shook my head. "Not Cash, Prue. Not Cash, but his newfound sibling. The one he feels so protective of that he didn't mention her to anyone else. You told us your father didn't want to see her. She has a motive for murder, both of Cantwell and you. Cantwell because he didn't like her and apparently wanted to keep her out of the family. And you because you wanted to stop Cash from giving her money. With you out of the picture, she might have more pull with Cash."

Prue's face paled. "You think—you're saying it could be this Amber? I can't believe I didn't—I thought she had just said something rude to Dad, the way kids do to adults sometimes. I didn't even picture that kid as being— Oh wow. So my potential sibling is—"

"Amber Warfield. The sister you didn't know you had," I said. "And the one who might think you tried to cheat her out of an inheritance."

CHAPTER NINETEEN

W HEN I GOT BACK HOME I CALLED JAY PARKER,
who was not in the office. I waited for his message
tone, then said, "Jay, I just spoke with Prudence Cantwell.
She said Cash admitted to her that Amber was their sister
and that he intended to give Amber half his inheritance.
This gives Amber the best motive of all, so I hope you
still have her in custody. Okay—bye."

I hung up, feeling at loose ends. Mick was looking at
me with his "I'm bored" expression, so I popped a leash
on him and we headed down the driveway. It was getting
close to two o'clock, and I realized that despite my lunch
I was still hungry. "Do you feel like a snack, Mick?
Maybe we can stop in at the bakery?" We started our
walk and I concentrated on Mick's happy tail. My head

was swimming with thoughts that made it hard to concentrate on just one thing.

When Mick and I turned on Dickens Street, I was thinking of Britt's amazing new ring, and the fact that she and Terry were going to get married. I smiled at this idea, but then my brain switched back to Prudence Cantwell and her shock at hearing about Amber. She had excused herself almost immediately, saying she needed to talk with her brother.

What was it about the Cantwells, anyway? They were a regular family, in one respect, but in other ways they seemed so . . . odd. Even beautiful Prudence seemed different from the average person, but I couldn't entirely put my finger on why.

Crowding into my thoughts was my song of the day, the Carpenters' "Top of the World," which I had heard that morning at Haven. Esther liked to make playlists for her iPod and then use them as background music while we worked. Now Karen Carpenter's beautiful contralto was in my head, reminding me of the way that love can lift a person to a high and wonderful place.

Mick and I had reached the end of the block, so we crossed the street and started heading back in the other direction. I paused at the window of the local Laundromat, where people hung community notices and flyers. I liked to see the news of upcoming concerts and book signings, along with advertisements for babysitting and items for sale. I glanced to my left, where a laughing, chattering group of people was entering Cardelini's, Angelo's restaurant. He did a good lunchtime business. I felt a quick little twinge of regret at the thought that I would no longer do his show, which had been enjoyable. And, I realized, I was going to miss Angelo himself, who had proved to be much more fun as a friend than he had been as a lover.

The group moved in, and someone else came out, pulling on a jacket. It took me a moment to realize that it was Jay Parker. He didn't have the look of a detective on a mission; instead he had the satisfied expression of someone who had just eaten at Cardelini's.

Mick and I were on top of him in seconds. "Jay."

He turned, saw us, and smiled, but not before something flickered in his eyes. He had a secret. "Hey, babe." He pulled me against him and kissed me. "Hey, Mick."

"What's going on? You told me you weren't free for lunch today."

"I wasn't. I already had an appointment. Here."

Jealousy flared up in me, inappropriate and inevitable. "Oh? And who is it that dined with you here at Cardelini's?"

He paused, and I could see that he really didn't want to tell me.

"Jay? I think we recently agreed that we wouldn't keep secrets from each other." We had made this pact at Christmas, when we decided to commit to each other.

"Lilah." He blew out some air and looked around in his Jay Parker "I'm thinking" way. "Yes. We promised that. But I am worried that you'll overreact."

"That I'll *overreact*?" I yelled, proving his point.

"I was invited here for lunch. I had a nice meal, and now I have to go back to work."

"Great. You left out the part about who invited you."

As if in response to this question, the door of Cardelini's opened, jingling its little entry bell, and Angelo himself appeared with a green doggie bag. "Jay, I'm glad I caught you. This was left at our table, and I know you will want the leftovers. Chicken parmesan tastes even better with the warming."

He finally bothered to take note of Jay's companion, and his face creased into a smile. "Lilah! So here we all are, eh?"

I ignored him and turned back to Jay. "You had lunch with *Angelo*?"

Parker looked ready to run away from us, back to his orderly cop life. "Angelo invited me, yes."

Angelo was still smiling, and I glared at him. "Why are you contacting Jay behind my back?"

Unlike Jay, Angelo thrived in situations of confrontation—and we had experienced plenty. He seemed to find it exciting. He nodded now. "Yes, it was behind your back. I got his number from your cell phone and texted him, asking him to meet me."

My mouth dropped open.

Angelo held up a hand. "Why, you will ask? Because you left the show. You are very good on the show, Lilah, and I thought perhaps you left to prove something to your Jay, so I invited him for a meal. So we talk, man-to-man." He hit his chest, no less primal than a gorilla. "Do not be upset about it."

My mouth snapped shut, and I intensified my glare.

"My boyfriend has a secret lunch with my former boy-friend to talk about me, and I shouldn't get upset?"

"No, you should not, because your boyfriend is a good man. He told me he didn't want to come because he didn't like me, eh? But he comes anyway, for your sake, to try to be my friend. And we have a nice lunch. So. This is why you should be happy. Both of us agree—we wish your happiness, and that is why you should come back, do the show, have a nice life with Jay."

Parker nodded. "I didn't want you to quit the show, Lilah. I just—I felt jealous. I told you that. I would never stand between you and your career."

Angelo ran a hand through his curls. His red shirt was half unbuttoned; he looked like a male stripper wearing a white apron at his waist. "And I have told Jay an assurance. Assured him. That I will not be romantic toward you. I was a fool to lose you, because you are a good woman, and that is what I now advise my friend Jay. Not to let you go."

Parker's blue eyes held a little spark of humor now. "And I don't intend to, even though you look ready to push both of us off a cliff."

I shook my head. "This stupid little meeting wouldn't have been necessary if you had just decided to trust me, Jay."

His expression hardened. "Or if you had chosen to mention that you quit your job because of me."

"I quit my job because I was willing to do anything to save our relationship."

"And that is why I met with Angelo."

Angelo did not find this insulting. He nodded in agreement and clapped a hand on Jay's shoulder. "Jay is my friend now, and I am loyal to my friends. He is going to eat here often because he enjoyed my food, yes?"

Parker's face grew slightly lustful as he remembered his lunch. "I did."

"And I have given him my word that you and I, we are only professional colleagues. I have even told him about the conference in Las Vegas, and invited him to go as well. It would be good for you, so."

"Well, that's nice that you two have just worked out every little detail of my life. Because if there's anything I like better than being manipulated by one man, it's being managed by two!"

Angelo nodded his agreement, as though I had just said something positive, and Parker narrowed his eyes. "I have to get back to work. I really didn't have time for this, but thank you again, Angelo. I enjoyed the food." He turned and started walking away, then stalked back and took the doggie bag from Angelo before marching away again, clearly indignant.

"Everyone enjoys the food," Angelo said, his voice contented, as though we had all just shared a happy party together.

"You are priceless," I said. "And *he* has no right to be angry. I'm the one who gets to be angry!"

Angelo chuckled. "Lilah, this I know about you. Anger is how you protect yourself from other feelings. Perhaps you should think about what those are."

I punched him in the arm. "Shut up, Angelo. Just shut up for once."

He was still smiling. The man was impenetrable. "So you will come back to the show, no?"

"I—you—this—you—unbelievable, Angelo!"

He shrugged. "We will talk later. Hello, Mick, my old friend." He bent to scratch Mick on the head, then straightened and kissed my cheek. "Lilah mia, you have a good man there. Do not blame him. Blame me. I insisted that we meet."

"I *do* blame you, Angelo."

His laughter echoed down the street. "This is why you must stay on the show. You are sweet and funny. Please stay. I will check in with you later, when you are not glaring at me like some indignant and lovely bird." He turned and went back into his restaurant.

"Mick," I said to my patient dog, "that was insulting on so many levels I don't know where to begin."

Mick nodded, although not with as much enthusiasm as I would have wanted.

When we resumed our walk, I realized that, in my anger, I had not thought to ask Parker if he'd gotten my message.

I RETURNED HOME and stewed for a while. Then I shook my head and began to make a list for the week's cooking and deliveries. I was free today, but I had four casseroles to deliver in the next three days. I started jotting down ingredients that I needed and rooting through my cabinets and my fridge. I had all the ingredients for a lovely Greek casserole with feta and olives, so I began to prepare that, working quietly in the kitchen and allowing my anger to seep away as I became one with my task.

When the phone rang I jumped, surprised out of my food reverie. I assumed it would be either Parker or Angelo, calling to apologize, or possibly to tell me why I was wrong, but it was just Wade Glenning, telling me my proofs were ready.

"If you pick some out today, I can touch them up and have your prints and your CD ready by the weekend," he said.

I thought about this. I was not in the mood to give Parker anything, but I was also really eager to see the photos. In addition, this was the only afternoon that I really had free. "Sure," I said. "That sounds good. Give me half an hour to finish something I'm working on, and then I would love to see them."

WADE SHOWED UP on time, although without his little intern. "Where's your friend? Stella, was it?"

"Yeah," he said, busy with his computer. "She had a class. But I don't really need her for stuff like this—just for the photo sessions."

"Ah. Well, lay them on me."

He grinned. "One more second. Okay. Here we go." He spun the computer around, and I studied the digital proof sheet.

"Wow," I said. "You really are good." And he was; the pictures managed to bring out things about me that even I had never noticed before, like the largeness of my eyes and a particular white-gold tint to my hair. Then I grew suspicious. "Did you touch these up? I mean, did you change me?"

"You didn't need changing. Some people do, but you are photogenic."

I laughed. "And you are a good salesman. Hmm, let me see which ones I like best. In this one I'm glancing off to the side, which looks weird. And in this one I was clearly talking. I have a problem with that."

"I noticed," said Wade Glenning with a wry expression.

"But this one is nice. I just look happy, and sort of pretty."

"Don't undersell yourself. You look great in all of them. And that is the last compliment I'm giving you today. I hate giving compliments as a general rule."

"Okay, okay. I appreciate the one I just got, then." I returned to the proof sheet. I realized that I felt comfortable with Wade, in the same way that I did with Cam. I could understand why he and Cash Cantwell were friends. His low-key personality would be a good counterpoint to Cash's outgoing, puppylike charm.

"How many am I supposed to choose?"

"A top five would be good. Then I'll polish those up and get you some prints. But you can keep all of these proofs, as I said."

"I think I almost have them. Definitely number four

and number seven. Also—yes, number ten. And then . . . fifteen. And I can't decide between nineteen and twenty."

Wade turned the computer to look and said, "Twenty."

"Okay. Twenty it is. Did you get all those down?"

He held up a little notebook. "Jotted them in here, but I'm also going to verify with you right now. Come around here to my side for a minute."

I leaned over his shoulder as he clicked through my choices. As I approved them one by one, he highlighted them. "Yes—oh, that one looks even nicer when you open up the screen like that. You're so good at this, Wade! You should be famous or something."

He made a wry face and said, "I *should* be a lot of things."

"I guess that could be the mantra for us all," I said. He nodded and made some notations on his computer. I stood up and stretched my arms. "Can I offer you anything to eat or drink? I've got some cake here that I brought home from Haven."

"I wouldn't say no to a piece of cake."

"Great." I went to my counter, comfortable in my role of food server, and dug out a chunk of Dobos torte that Esther had made as an experiment. She had not liked the results, but the rest of us thought it was delicious, and she had divvied it up among us.

I cut a piece and fussed over the presentation, trying to choose the right color of plate. Behind me Wade was packing up his things. "Ouch," he said.

"Are you okay?"

"Yeah. I just bonked my hand on the edge of the table.

No big deal. Oh, shoot." He stared at his pointer finger. "Do you have some ice, Lilah? I need to pack this before it swells up. Sometimes this happens when I hit it the wrong way. I busted a blood vessel."

"Oh, sure! Wow, that really is turning red. Hang on." I ran to the freezer and dug into the ice bag, then found a plastic bag to seal it in. "Here you go. Press that right against there."

"Great, thanks." He sat down and concentrated on his rapidly swelling finger, which had turned a weird shade of purple. It seemed familiar.

I went back to the counter and chose a green plate for his torte. Then I recalled where I had seen the swollen finger before—Marcus Cantwell had suffered the same malady, and I had commented on it when the traitor Ellie left me alone in the room with him. What had I said to him? I was embarrassed to think of the way I had blathered on, nervous and babbling. I had told him it looked like Achenbach's syndrome, which my mother had inherited. Which I myself might be prone to one day, as might Cam.

The knife in my hand clattered to the counter.

"You okay?" Wade said.

"Oh yeah. Just butterfingers." I made a show of repairing the frosting on the cake so that Glenning wouldn't see my shaking hands. Achenbach's syndrome, as far as my mother and I had been able to determine, was relatively rare, and seemingly hereditary. Was it merely coincidence that Cantwell and Glenning had it?

No, my brain told me. It wasn't Amber who was Cantwell's child—*it was Wade*. In an instant it all made sense. Cash and Amber had met with Cantwell, but what if they had asked him to consider accepting Wade as his son? And of course Wade had had access to Cantwell on the day of his death—he was the photographer! No one would have looked twice at Glenning, not even when he went into the house, because it would have seemed natural for him to go there. He was like the invisible man.

I brought him his piece of cake and smiled. "Here you go. It's delicious. Made by Esther, the owner of Haven."

"Sounds awesome."

"Is your hand okay?"

"Yeah, it's fine." Was it my imagination, or was he scrutinizing my face? "Are *you* okay?"

"Oh yeah. I just made a little mess over here." I went back to the counter and started rewrapping the torte. My phone lay nearby; I grabbed it, turned it on, then clicked messages and found Jay Parker's face icon. I picked it up with the intention of writing a quick, terse message. I typed, Wade is with me and he killed Cantwell and clicked send, but a moment later Wade was looming over me.

"What are you doing?" he said.

I spun around. "Oh, nothing. Just sent a little love note to my boyfriend. Go enjoy your cake."

"Lilah, I've studied faces for a long time. You're lying to me."

"What?" I said. It was perhaps the stupidest possible response, but in my sudden fear I didn't even know what I was saying.

"Give me the phone," Wade said.

That made me angry. "No! Stop being weird, Wade."

"Give it to me! I want to know what you just did."

"Cut it out! I need you to leave my house."

"Lilah, give it to me," he said, grabbing my wrist and prying the phone from my hand.

"Ouch!" I screamed.

He took the phone and turned away from me. I scoured the room, wishing I were close enough to a frying pan or something heavy. I began to edge away from him, but then he swung back. "How did you know?"

"What?"

He held up the message that I sent to Parker. "How did you know?"

I pointed to his finger. "Your father had it, too. It's hereditary."

He looked at his weird purple finger and sniffed. "My *only* damn inheritance."

"Oh, Wade," I said. I don't know if I felt fear or pity or revulsion or some odd mixture of them. Then, because it popped into my head, I said, "You stabbed him! You're the one who stabbed him, fifteen years ago!"

Wade's mouth dropped open. "How did you know that?"

"I didn't—I just thought it. But now I do."

He shook his head. "I was ten. I was angry. He had rejected my mother and me, or that's the way I saw it. They got me therapy after that. But he never forgave me, even though I was just a child. Wouldn't have anything more to do with me, even though he knew I was his son."

I needed to keep him talking. Jay would be on his way. "He should have understood," I said, going for a soothing tone.

"Right. That's what Cash and Amber tried to tell him. Amber was a fellow bastard, so we bonded pretty quickly when we met. She understood what I was going through, and she and Cash sat down with Cantwell. Tried to persuade him to give me another chance. After that he wouldn't talk to Amber, either. Of course he wouldn't reject Cash. Cash is everyone's favorite—even mine."

"So you killed him? Your father?"

Suddenly I saw the ten-year-old boy Glenning had been, along with the anger he had felt then; now, though, it was the mighty, vengeful fury of a man. "Yeah, I killed him. He didn't even know who I was—isn't that hilarious? He let me walk around at his party because he thought I was just the hired help. So I walked in that room and said I needed to take his picture—that his kids wanted it. I offered him a drink. He wasn't supposed to drink, but I knew he had once liked alcohol, so I figured, why not?

"He took it from me." Glenning's mouth twisted into a weird smile. "You know what he said? He said, 'Just this once.' I almost laughed in his face. But instead I took his picture. The last picture of him alive."

"Oh my God." I couldn't hide my repulsion, and that was a mistake. Wade Glenning was tired of feeling rejected. "And you shot up the art gallery! Why?"

His eyes narrowed. "Because Cash was trying to get me what I deserved, and his sister was going to talk him out of it. I guess I was mad. I wasn't shooting to kill."

"You came awfully close."

His face changed then, and I knew that he was going to kill me. Mick was stirring nearby, and I realized that he sensed something was amiss. "If you try anything, my dog will attack you," I said. I didn't believe this of my gentle Mick.

Wade laughed. "That dog wouldn't harm the devil."

"He would if the devil was threatening me," I said. I grabbed the vase with Parker's flowers in it and bashed it against Wade's temple. The vase, a heavy cut-glass affair, did not break, nor did Glenning collapse. He merely touched his temple and swore.

"That was supposed to knock you out," I babbled. In retrospect I think I was in shock.

"Yeah, in a cartoon," he said, and then he lunged at me. I darted to the side and he fell against my counter. I used his miscalculation to sprint out of the room, and I did hear some growling and barking from Mick, who seemed to be pulling at Glenning's pant leg. I tore down my hallway and to the front door, almost screaming with fear, and my clammy hands struggled with the doorknob.

Glenning was chasing me now, lumbering out of the kitchen with desperate strides. "Come back, Lilah!" he yelled.

I wrenched the door open and dove out onto my walkway, where I began to run. "No!" I screamed.

Glenning was pounding after me, saying, "Lilah, stop! I just want to talk to you!"

I ventured a glance over my shoulder, then looked back and ran straight into Angelo Cardelini, who looked not at me, but at the man behind me, his handsome face furious and dangerous.

Glenning barreled toward us, and Angelo's fist flew

out, catching Glenning full in the jaw and knocking him off balance. Glenning fell backward onto the walkway like a giant tree, and Mick ran out, growling, to stand on his chest. Angelo put a foot on Glenning's stomach and said, "Lilah belongs to another man—my friend Jay Parker. I will not allow this to go on!"

I stood trembling, realizing in that surreal moment that Angelo hadn't been saving me from a murderer. He thought I was being chased by an angry lover.

"Angelo, you idiot!" I said, and then I burst into tears, probably from delayed shock.

A second later Jay Parker's car pulled up the driveway, and he got out, his face white. He ran over, trying to gauge exactly what was happening.

I was still blubbering, and Wade Glenning was struggling on the ground, trying to extricate himself from Mick's paws and Angelo's boot. His head was bleeding where I had hit him with the vase. As Parker drew near, Angelo gave him a thumbs-up. "I will not let anyone else try to take your woman, Jay! I have knocked him down for you."

Parker stared at him, then looked at me. I was wiping at my eyes and holding my breath in a furious attempt to stop crying. "Wade was chasing me," I managed.

In one of the weirdest and most memorable moments of my life, Parker lunged at Angelo and gave him a fierce hug. "Thank God you were here! Thank you, Angelo!"

My former boyfriend, still stepping on Glenning with one foot, seemed to finally understand that I had been in danger. "Oh—Lilah, he is not your lover?"

"*No*, Angelo. He was trying to kill me."

"I was not. I just wanted to talk," Glenning protested. Mick put a giant paw on his face.

Parker grew even paler. Now he came to me and folded me into his arms. "Once again I arrive too late."

"But you always come for me, Jay. That's what matters. I know that if I call, you will always come running. Because you love me."

"I really do," Parker said, kissing my eyebrow. "Should we stop your dog from mauling this guy to death?"

"He's not mauling. Just showing that he means business. Mick is more of a warrior than I knew."

Angelo was clearly making a great effort to restrain himself, so I turned to offer him some gratitude. "And so are you, Angelo. That was some punch."

Now he gave us a smug smile. "I trained in the boxing, back in Milan. I have not a chance to use it very often, so I am glad of this." He pointed to Glenning, who glared at us from the ground.

"Get the dog off of me," he growled.

"In due time," Parker said, playing with my hair.

CHAPTER TWENTY

P ARKER WAS BUSY THAT DAY AND THE NEXT, BUT I got a lot of information from the television news. Glenning had been Cantwell's child by a woman named Patricia Glenning, with whom he'd had a brief affair between his first and second wives. She had become pregnant with Wade but did not tell Cantwell because their relationship had ended rather stormily.

Ten years later Cantwell had divorced a third wife, and he briefly reconciled with Patricia, but young Wade didn't know that the two of them were dating again when Cantwell visited his house. His mother, perhaps as a way of keeping away questions, had spun a ten-year narrative about Wade's neglectful father, and the little boy felt abandoned and angry. Unaware that his mother had never told Cantwell about his existence, he assumed that Cantwell had merely rejected him. Cantwell was considering buying a new house to start a life with Patricia and his growing brood of children, but on that fateful night that he came to meet his son, Wade stabbed him. The fallout from that incident made the relationship with Patricia fail once again, although Cantwell paid for a therapist for the child. Cantwell, though, had been traumatized, and he said he never wanted to see Wade again; he resented Patricia for not telling him about the child in the first place.

The Channel Five broadcast put a picture of Patricia Glenning on the screen, and I realized that she was the woman I'd seen at Cantwell's funeral—the one who sat alone. Poor Patricia—she had lost her lover twice, and now she would lose her only son.

The news then cut to a press conference in which Maria Grimaldi and Jay Parker were taking questions. They were doing it outside for some reason, on the sunny lawn in front of the police station.

Grimaldi was at the podium; a reporter asked if it was not true that she had been present on the day that Cantwell died. Grimaldi looked surprised. "I was picking up a family member from Mr. Cantwell's house when he collapsed. A family member attempted to revive the victim. It was at that point that I realized the victim's ailment seemed suspicious."

"Has it been determined that Mr. Cantwell was in fact poisoned to death by Wade Glenning?"

Maria's face closed off. "I am not prepared to comment

PUDDING UP WITH MURDER

on that. I'll pass the microphone now to my partner in this investigation, Detective Jacob Parker."

Parker moved to the podium with his serious cop face on. He looked incredibly handsome, and his dark hair blew slightly in the wind. "We are still in the process of investigation; however, we did arrest Wade Glenning today, and we do not have any other persons of interest in this case."

"Is it true that Glenning was Cantwell's illegitimate son?" asked one persistent reporter.

Parker homed in on the man with his amazing eyes. "We have determined that Marcus Cantwell and Patricia Glenning had an affair. The dates are detailed in your packet. Wade Glenning was a product of that affair, but Mr. Cantwell was not made aware of his son's existence until ten years later."

A young woman who seemed far too interested in Parker edged closer to the podium. "How did the police happen to find out the connection between Glenning and Cantwell?"

Parker's eyes crinkled slightly, but his face remained serious. "We received a tip from a very observant citizen. She happened to notice a hereditary trait that Cantwell and Glenning shared. She promptly reported this to the police."

"Can we know this citizen's name?" persisted the young woman.

Parker's brow furrowed. "That is not necessary to your story, and this citizen has indicated that she wishes to remain anonymous."

I turned to Mick. "That's my boyfriend up there. He looks amazingly handsome."

Mick nodded.

I pressed a button on my cable box to record the rest of the conference. I turned off the television and looked at Mick, who was waiting patiently. I had a casserole sitting on the counter, ready to be delivered, and Mick was smart enough to know that a car ride was imminent.

I put a leash on Mick and grabbed my pan. "Okay, bud. Time to do our job."

AFTER I DELIVERED a casserole to a very appreciative new client, I figured Mick had earned some park time. It was a beautiful spring day, filled with the contradictions of the season: the breeze was cold, but if I stood in the sun I was almost hot.

We drove to Bailey Park, one of Mick's favorite places. We could walk all over it with Mick on the leash, and there was a fenced-off dog run in which I could let him be free and meet canine friends. Mick's tail was wagging before I even parked the car; he knew where we were going.

We crossed the street and entered the tree-filled park; Mick dragged me toward the first interesting smell, which was at the base of a forsythia bush bright with yellow blooms. Not far away were two lilac bushes, and it wasn't only Mick who was in scent paradise.

I heard a familiar voice and looked down the main

paved path, where park benches were placed every twenty feet or so. Two people sat on one of these benches, watching children play on a nearby swing set. I recognized Lola first, Grimaldi's niece. She looked very pretty in a tan trench coat, blue jeans, and fashionable boots. Next to her was Cash Cantwell, who had a casual arm slung around her shoulder and was telling some jovial story into her ear.

"Good for you, Cash," I murmured.

When Mick finished sniffing, we rapid-walked down the path until we were in front of the young lovers. "Hello, Cash. Hello, Lola."

Cash stood up. "Hey! What a surprise to see you."

Lest he think I was stalking him around town, I pointed at my dog. "Mick loves it here—we come here a lot."

Cash nodded. "Same for those guys." He pointed to the swing set, where I spotted Peach and Carrie Britton.

"No Tim Junior?" I said.

"He was too cool to come this time."

Lola laughed. "He just wanted to have some alone time with his dad. He doesn't get that very often."

I looked at Cash. "I'm sorry about your friend."

Cash looked at his feet. "He was my brother, as you know. As everyone knows now."

"Why didn't you tell the others, Cash?"

"They wouldn't have understood. At least that's what I thought. Prue seemed to prove it, when I finally told her we had a sibling. She thought someone was out to scam me. I thought they would all feel that way. I wanted to do what was right for Wade. It wasn't just that I felt sorry for him—I liked him, and he deserved everything we got. He was my dad's son. But dad never liked him. He treated him like some animal that you have second thoughts about, and you send them back to the pound."

"Except he wouldn't have done that to an animal," Lola said sharply.

"Have you talked to Wade?"

"Yeah. I went to see him with Scott. Scott and Owen—and Prue and Emma, too—they've all been really cool about it. They're angry at Wade, but they feel sorry for him. Scott said he's going to help hook him up with a good lawyer—someone he trusts. We're going to foot the bill."

"That's nice of you. I'm glad."

"Yeah—Scott ended up being really cool about it. He said that Wade didn't have all the advantages we had, growing up. Which is exactly how I felt. I know Wade did a terrible thing, but he did it out of pain, you know? Out of rejection. He's not a terrible guy."

I had no comment about that one. I wondered what Glenning would have done if he had caught me when he chased me out of my cottage. Would he have killed me? Or had he just intended to try to reason with me, as he later claimed to the police?

"Well, it was good to run into you. Maybe I'll see you around sometime."

Cash nodded. "You will. Those little monsters practically live at this park, and besides, they love the kids' menu at Cardelini's. You work with that guy, right? I've seen you on TV."

I sighed. "I guess I do work with him, yes."

Peach and Carrie ran over, yelling, "Mick!" They knelt to pet my amiable dog, and I said hello to them.

Peach pointed a little finger at me. "Did you finish your Miss Moxie books?"

"Yes. She even helped me solve a problem. She said, 'When something looks too black-and-white, you can be sure it isn't right.' I realized that was true."

I looked back at Cash. "Because I thought Amber was your father's love child. It all seemed to fit. But it was wrong, and Wade was right in front of my face all along."

Lola bristled slightly at Amber's name, and Cash laughed. "Amber and Lo are friends, but Lola thought I had something going on with her. I never did—we're just friends. Poor Amber—everyone was assuming things about her that aren't true."

"Parker found out it wasn't true, but I didn't ask him, and he didn't tell me, and so the revelation of Wade was quite a surprise."

I looked at Peach and Carrie. "Hey, you two. I'm going to let Mick run around behind that dog fence for a while. While he plays, would you like to hear some things I'm planning for Miss Braidwell's wedding?"

Carrie looked on the verge of fainting, and Peach jumped up and down like a human pogo stick. "Yes, yes!" Peach cried, and Carrie nodded vigorously. I handed Carrie Mick's leash and said, "Go ahead and open that fence, and I'll be right behind you." They scampered forward with my happy dog, who slowed his pace for them slightly.

I smiled at Cash and Lola. "You two can go a discreet distance and make out for a while."

Cash gave me a thumbs-up. "We might just do that," he said.

WHEN MICK AND I got home, he was clearly ready for a nap. I let him in, gave him some water, and laughed as he went straight to his bed by the stove. He was snoring moments later.

The doorbell rang, and I ran to the front to see Britt smiling at me through the window. I opened the door and said, "Hey, neighbor."

"Hey, Lilah. Do you have a moment? I have something for you."

"Sure." I stepped away from the door, and Britt grabbed something that she had leaned against my house. It was a large, flat parcel covered in brown paper.

We went into my living room, and Britt leaned her parcel against a chair. The two of us sat down on the couch. "Lilah, Terry and I have been talking, and we know that it must have been uncomfortable, being put in the middle of our love life."

I shrugged.

Britt tinkled out a laugh, carefree as it had once been. "Anyway, we're both so grateful to you for counseling us and being our friend. We couldn't have done it without you." She glanced at the crazy, beautiful diamond-and-sapphire extravagance on her finger. "So we wanted to give you a gift."

"Britt, that's not necessary."

"No resisting. This is a gift of love, and you cannot refuse it."

I sighed. Britt and Terry and their wild generosity could sometimes be burdensome.

She stood up to retrieve the thin package and brought it over to me. "I noticed that you admired this, Lilah, so Terry and I would like you to have it."

I stripped away the paper and saw that she was giving me a painting from the gallery. It was the Jerome Merault painting I had loved so much, the one called *Summer Walk*. In it the man and woman were walking a dog who looked like Mick, and at a glance the couple could have been Parker and I. I already knew that the multitude of colors he had used in this brilliant work would perfectly complement the tones of the room in which we were sitting.

"Oh, Britt," I said. "This is—beautiful." And as I recalled, it was also incredibly expensive.

She pulled me into a sudden hug. "So are you, Lilah." She held me at arm's length and smiled widely. "And clearly you had to have this—it could be you and Jay and Mick, your hero dog."

"It really could. Well—thank you so much. I'm going to hang it right there above the fireplace, and I will enjoy it every single day."

"I will pass that on to Jerome. Someday you have to meet him. He's brilliant."

"That sounds great," I said, my eyes drawn back to the people in the painting, and the beautiful world that one man had created with his talented hands.

* * *

JENNY BRAIDWELL WAS thrilled with my plans for her wedding shower. Britt had agreed enthusiastically to let us use her lovely home, and she even volunteered to help with decorating. Jenny did indeed choose winter white for the bridesmaids' dresses, but we were all allowed to choose our own style. Jenny thought this would make it look elegant and layered, rather than pursuing what she called "a cookie-cutter wedding party."

I spent some time looking at dresses online while Jay and I were visiting Ellie. Jay was watching football with his brother Eric, so Ellie and I escaped to her office to consider various elegant styles.

"This off-the-shoulder number would look lovely on you," Ellie said. "And not too terribly expensive. But you would have to wear your hair up, or we wouldn't see your shoulders."

"Jay doesn't like it up," I said.

She shrugged. "Men don't, do they? And yet it would look quite elegant—perhaps a French braid or something?"

"Put that one in the maybe pile," I said. "Then keep scrolling."

We heard a bang outside and I jumped. Ellie looked up vaguely and said, "Oh, that's just Cash Cantwell. He will always slam that door, as if he couldn't just close it quietly. He's probably walking the dogs."

"That's nice—that he's taking care of them."

"They're nice little dogs. Well trained. Cash is good with them—his father would be proud."

"So have you talked to all the children? Are they all doing okay?"

"I have talked to them all, yes. They come to see Cash frequently, although Prudence and her boyfriend have gone off to the islands somewhere—doesn't that sound glamorous? Just packing up and going to some exotic locale to get away from it all. I guess you can do that when you're an artist, and whatever he is."

"How about Emma and Tim? Will they go to the islands?"

"No, but Emma tells me that they just celebrated their fifteenth wedding anniversary, and that Tim bought her a lovely ring and read her a poem that made her cry. He's quite romantic."

"Who is?" Jay said, entering the room with a beer in his hand. "Do I have competition again?"

"You've never had competition and never will," I offered placidly as he reached my side and put his arm around me. "You are in a class by yourself."

Ellie smiled at us. "So sweet together."

"We owe it all to you, Ellie," I joked. "Now finish telling me about the Cantwells."

"Hmm? Oh. Well, Emma told me that Owen got a job teaching philosophy in Arizona. He's very excited about it. And Scott will remain at his law firm; he's being considered for a partnership."

"What about Wade?"

Ellie shrugged. "The children have surprised everyone—and perhaps themselves—and come out en masse to support him. Their lawyer says that he will do jail time, but that he will certainly make parole with good behavior and the backing of the Cantwell children. Such an odd thing, but sweet, as well. They feel bad for him. Emma says that for all Marcus's faults, they still know that they were privileged, and that poor Wade was not."

"Parents and children," I said. "A mystery from beginning to end."

Jay looked impatient. "I'm tired of hearing the name Cantwell. Mom, can I steal Lilah for a while? I want to make out with her on the couch."

Ellie beamed, and I giggled.

"Of course, Jay. You go kiss your pretty Lilah, and Eric will help me dish up dessert. I have made—once again—a rice pudding casserole." She said this for the sake of the son who didn't know our secret and sat one room away. "We have to clear away the unhappy associations with that dish, because it was delicious, and I for one will want to serve it often. Eric has been going after it for an hour now, and even though he tried to cover his tracks, I see the telltale signs of scooping."

Eric appeared in the doorway. "It's awesome, Mom. You should make it all the time."

Ellie's face glowed with pleasure at the compliment, and Jay squeezed my hand.

MUCH TO MY surprise, Wade Glenning's assistant, Stella, showed up at my door about a week after his arrest. She handed me a package that contained a CD of all the pictures Wade had taken, along with the photos of the ones

I had selected. I expressed my surprise at their arrival, and Stella lifted her chin. "Wade said to tell you he's a man of his word. And that he's sorry about what happened. He's not really that kind of guy."

I didn't open the package, but I handed the whole thing to Parker when I saw him next, and he was thrilled with it.

"Won't they give us a bad feeling every time we see them?" I asked.

Jay shook his head. "I'll only think of you when I look at these. Look how beautiful you are! The guy has a gift."

"Well . . . I did pay for them. And they were supposed to be your present, so if you like them—"

"I do. Thank you," he said.

I put my arms around him and tucked my chin on his shoulder. "Do you ever have daydreams of just pulling up stakes and flying out to some tropical island?"

"Since I met you I have daydreams like that all the time."

"Prue Cantwell just did it, with her boyfriend. Maybe we should do it sometime, too."

"No maybe about it," Parker said.

THAT NIGHT JAY Parker stood on a step stool in front of my fireplace, holding up my new painting. "To the right a little. Now up. Yes! Perfect right there. I love it."

Parker made a mark with a little pencil he had tucked above his ear. Then he brought the painting down and pounded in a nail. Mick and I watched him as he worked, and I admired the way that he looked in jeans.

Soon he was lifting the painting again, and he balanced it carefully on the large nail.

Then he stepped down, and we looked at his handiwork.

"It works well in this room. The colors are perfect."

"And the people could be us, couldn't they, Jay?"

He slid an arm around me, and we admired the couple in the purpled twilight, walking their dog to an unknown destination. "They could. So it's art imitating life."

"Or we could imitate our painting, and take Mick for a walk."

Parker smiled and looked at our canine companion, who studied us with a wise expression. "Mick, does that sound good to you? A nice little spring walk in the evening light? And maybe a guy who wants to be painted into the picture permanently?"

Mick didn't have to think twice.

He looked at Jay Parker and nodded.

Lilah's Rice Pudding Casserole

Rice pudding warms the hearts and pleases the taste buds of young and old alike. Try this version on your family and friends.

INGREDIENTS

2½ cups rice (uncooked)
1 teaspoon salt
4 cups water
12 eggs
7 cups milk
1 teaspoon cinnamon
1 teaspoon nutmeg
¾ cup granulated sugar
¼ cup light brown sugar
1 cup raisins (optional)

Preheat oven to 350 degrees. Heat rice, salt, and water in a large pot until they are close to boiling. Without draining rice, add the remaining ingredients and stir well. Pour into a greased 13 x 9 casserole dish. Bake for 45 minutes to 1 hour or until a fork inserted into the center comes out clean.

This dish can be served warm or cold.

Some suggested toppings are whipped cream, cinnamon sugar, or maraschino cherries.

Lilah's Raspberry-Almond Deep-Dish Coffee Cake

I first made this dish for my friend Britt, but it was so popular that I've made it several times since. Few people can resist the lure of a good coffee cake.

INGREDIENTS

1 cup raspberry jam (and some fresh raspberries kept for
*   serving)*
½ cup light brown sugar
⅛ stick of butter, solid
1 cup flour
½ cup sugar
1 teaspoon baking soda
½ teaspoon salt
½ stick butter, melted
2 eggs

    1 teaspoon vanilla extract
    ¼ cup sliced almonds

GLAZE

    ½ cup powdered sugar
    1–2 teaspoons milk
    ½ teaspoon vanilla extract
    ½ teaspoon raspberry extract
    2 softened pats of butter

First, grease and flour a square glass casserole dish (or use a larger one, but double ingredients; I use a Pyrex 10 x 15 dish that my mother gave me, but then I double the recipe to feed more people).

Preheat oven to 350 degrees.

Mix raspberry jam, brown sugar, ⅛ stick of butter, and a teaspoon of flour along with some of the raspberries in a bowl. Keep this handy for later in the recipe.

Next, find a larger bowl to combine all of the dry ingredients. Mix your melted butter with the eggs and add the teaspoon of vanilla.

Put half of the batter in your pan. Take your raspberry mixture and carefully spoon it, as evenly as possible, onto the batter. Then put the rest of the batter on top.

Find your sliced almonds and sprinkle these in a pleasing arrangement across the top of the batter.

Set your timer for somewhere between 35–40 minutes, but only remove from the oven when a fork inserted into the center of your cake comes out clean.

Combine glaze ingredients; if they become stiff, add tiny amounts of water or milk until the frosting is the desired consistency.

Drizzle the glaze over a warm (but not hot) cake.

Serve with fresh raspberries, whipped cream, a pot of tea or coffee, or all of the above. My brother, Cameron, chooses all of the above. ☺

Lilah's Egg and Dill Delight

This breakfast casserole can serve well as a dip, too! It's cheesy, delicious, and quite nutritious, especially if you go the low-fat route. My mother always said that spinach was good for the digestion. I don't know if this is just one of those motherly sayings, but I do know spinach is healthy for a lot of other reasons, and this casserole is filled with the leafy greens. It's also easy enough to make even when you're away from home, and even if you're in a hurry.

This was featured on one of my Friday segments of *Cooking with Angelo*, and it got many positive reviews on Angelo's website. Enjoy!

INGREDIENTS

10 eggs

1 cup cottage cheese (can substitute low-fat, if desired)

4 ounces cream cheese (low-fat, if desired)

4 ounces shredded Swiss or Monterey Jack

1 10-ounce package chopped spinach (buy frozen, then thaw
    and wring dry)
2 tablespoons fresh dill weed
dash black pepper
¼ teaspoon salt

Preheat oven to 350 degrees.

In a large bowl, beat eggs, then add cheeses, spinach, dill weed, pepper, and salt; stir gently into the egg mixture.

Pour into a greased 9 x 13 baking dish.

Set a timer for 45–50 minutes; check the dish when it rings, but don't stop baking until a fork inserted into the center of the egg mixture comes out clean.

Serve with a side of toast, bacon, tomatoes, or all of the above! Your diners will ask you for an encore.

Cameron Drake's
Mushroom Collezione

My brother, Cameron, gave me this recipe; he said that it is easy enough that bachelors can make it to impress their girlfriends. This is sexist of Cam, since he is suggesting that no men can cook, and that they might use food merely as a lure to get women to eventually cook for them. He should know better, since his own wife, Serafina, cannot cook at all.

In any case, I ate this at Cam's house and found it

delicious, so I plan to work it into one of my covered-dish recipes soon.

INGREDIENTS

1 teaspoon salt
1 small onion
2 tablespoons Angelo's Gourmet olive oil
1 package presliced mushrooms, fresh
1 cup chopped prosciutto
1½ cups heavy cream
dash pepper
1 large package uncooked Collezione
⅓ cup Parmigiano cheese, fresh, grated
½ tablespoon fresh parsley

Fill a pot to ¾ full of tap water. Add salt; bring to a boil.

In a separate pan, sauté the chopped onions in olive oil until slightly browned.

Add the chopped mushrooms to this mixture, and brown lightly. (Note from Cameron: At this point, your wife might appear at your shoulder and try to pour in some Sangiovese. Do not let her. However, if she overpowers you, this can also taste surprisingly good.)

Add chopped prosciutto and stir in. Add cream to mixture.

By now your kitchen smells amazing; add salt and pepper to desired taste.

Your water should now be boiling; add the Collezione.

When the noodles are al dente, drain them and pour into

a large mixing bowl. Add the mixture from your pan and toss together.

Before serving, add in the cheese and parsley.

Serves about four people with good appetites.

Enjoy with a fresh green salad and crusty homemade bread.